HIGHWAY

An Apocalyptic Thriller

M.L. Banner

Toes in the Water Publishing, LLC

A Quick Note About Highway

This novel is set in a contemporary America of the very near future. As I've mentioned on the disclaimer page, this is a work of fiction. However, the particular set of circumstances covered in this book is absolutely possible. Yes, it's fiction, but the threats covered in this book are as real as they can be.

In other words, consider this a warning to prepare yourself and your family, because this fiction could become reality.

Phase One

Chapter 1

Lexi and Travis

July 4th

A flash of light changed all American life in an instant.

Their father overcorrected and they swerved so hard, Lexi rolled over on top of her brother in the back seat. Then they veered the other way and she was planted back in her place, face pushed against the door by their car's inertia, Travis now on top of her.

Shattering glass and sparkles of light filled her senses.

The stop was sudden and—for a moment—completely silent, as if the air had been sucked out of the car's interior.

Travis came to rest on her lap, face upturned, eyes fluttering, lips slowly moving as if they were trying to form random words. He looked like a dazed turtle, with legs limply hanging out of its shell, covered in a blanket of pea-gravel-sized fragments of glass that glittered like diamonds.

Crickets called to her out the window's ragged opening.

Her brother's weight squeezed down and something else was pressing against her right side, painfully pinning her in place. That something glistened in a crimson morning hue.

As she lifted her free hand to touch the post pushing against her, tiny sparkles of glass fell off her arm, more additions to the many already covering the bench seat.

It was metal and looked to her as if it came from inside her back seat and ran to the inside of the front seat, like some poorly constructed strut that had been there all along but she had just never noticed before. Her mind couldn't decipher its meaning, only that it was because of the accident.

She shuddered, just realizing this strut had pierced her seat right where she was sleeping just before they crashed. She could have been like this seat, a Lexi shish kebab skewered by this post.

Her hand slid forward across the smooth metal, coated with splotches of liquid and glass, following it to its end, inside the flaps of the broken canvas.

Studying the red smears covering her fingers, the wheels of her mind were locked in place. It was a jigsaw puzzle where someone purposely mixed in pieces from another box.

Rubbing her fingers together, smudging the redness further; a crucial piece of the puzzle finally clicked in.

Blood!

She jerked her head back toward the front seat. "Daddy!" she yelled.

A fire hydrant of knowledge burst open; the most important pieces of this jigsaw connected all at once, and with that knowledge came a flood of terror, revulsion, and panic.

Lexi reached over with her bloodied hand, her other pinned underneath her, and pulled open the door.

They both tumbled out hard onto the ground, the impact taking her breath away.

"Dad," Travis croaked right next to her.

She pushed herself up from the dirt and gravel and stood somewhat wobbly, like she had just come out of some possessed carnival fun-ride.

They were on the side of the highway, no one else around. Her gaze followed their car's tracks along the side of the road, where a jagged point stuck out of the ground several car lengths away, then back onto the road, where their black tread marks showed where they had swerved violently.

But from what? She wondered. There were no other cars and they hadn't smashed into anything.

She turned, not wanting to face what came next, momentarily regarding her brother's movements. He was lifting himself up off the ground, still groggy, but otherwise uninjured.

Then she tentatively glanced at the driver's side of the car. The harsh pinpricks of sunrise made it that much more painful for her to face the reality in front of her: her father, no matter how much she hated him, was probably dead.

But, from where she stood, she couldn't see her father. Her mind immediately shouted that it was still an unknown; there was a possibility he rolled around like her and didn't suffer the fate she knew he must have. She didn't want to make it real, not yet.

Then reality gave a weak moan.

She dragged one lead-weighted foot forward, still not seeing him. His side window was also gone.

Another step, his face...

He was breathing!

He turned to look at her, little red pieces of glass clinging to his cheeks and forehead, and he smiled. "Oh, good, you're all right." Each word seemed a struggle.

"Daddy, you're hurt." Her voice quivered.

"I'm afraid," he paused and took a breath, "it's a lot worse than it looks." Another breath. "You need to not freak out, Lex." His eyes flickered as he licked his upper lip, dislodging a small piece of glass stuck there.

Lexi's eyes fell, for just a moment, and then snapped back to hold his gaze again.

"Honey, don't look yet."

Other than his short breaths, his voice was steadier and more certain. As if he was gaining strength, not losing it with the precious life that must be leaking out with every beat of his heart.

"There are things you need to do, and I need you to pay attention." Another breath. "First, come around to the passenger seat." He turned his head in that direction and waited for her to appear there.

Her feet moved more fluidly now, fueled by fear and adrenaline. Gliding around the car's front, she glanced back at the windshield. The driver's side was pulled inward, and a hole shaped like the rough silhouette of an airplane provided the last piece she didn't need of this puzzle.

She continued around the car, although everything inside of her told her to run away. It's what she usually did.

Crawling onto the seat beside him—she had been unwilling to do this before the accident, but her protests now seemed silly—she couldn't help but glimpse again at his mortal injury. A post was sticking out of his gut. On the end of it, a highway sign of mocking irony read "Pass with Care." She looked away, her gaze attracted to the rabbit's foot connected to the ignition key, still swaying—it was the rabbit's foot she had given him when she was a little girl, just before he left them eight years ago. He still had it, all this time.

"Open the front pocket of my bug-out bag," he commanded, "pull out the flip pad and pen."

She did as he asked, her gaze now more comfortably on his backpack and not him. Her probing fingers found the items, pausing over the smooth surfaces of a revolver. She shuddered from its coolness.

"Pay attention, Lex." He jolted her back, causing her to almost drop the pad. "You're going to take my bug-out bag and empty most of yours. Carry only one change of clothes; you don't need more." He took several deep breaths and continued. "Take this highway, west. Get to a store, smaller is better, immediately. My bag will have most of what you need, but you'll also need to buy the following ..."

She waited for her shopping list, but he was quiet. She looked up, pen poised over the pad, making sure he was still conscious. He had his eyes upturned, thinking, just like she remembered him doing when he would tell her stories as a child.

"Write," he demanded.

He proceeded to give her a list of items they would need to buy at a store. He said they would need to prepare themselves for a long journey. They would stop at friends' houses along the way, but ultimately they needed to get back to their home in Tucson, where they would be safe with their aunt and uncle.

She wrote down everything he told her, and listened to the other things as well, paying attention as if she were receiving a vital homework assignment. With a near-photographic memory, she knew she wouldn't forget any of it. Yet, none of what he told her clicked, as her mind wandered, running away from this. It was like an HD movie playing before her while she was recording it in her mind, so she didn't have to really pay attention as she could always hit "rewind" and watch the important parts again.

She couldn't accept what she was seeing and what he was telling her. None of it made sense, especially when her eyes fell from his and caught the surreal image of the sign sticking out of him, the red stain on his shirt a little larger every time she looked.

"Lexi!" he croaked. "Look at me. This is important ..." He paused, and took several more breaths before continuing. His color had been slowly slipping from his face and now he looked terribly pale, even with the bright splashes of sunlight angling through the freckled windshield.

"I don't have long now and you two need to get going. Remember, first get the food and supplies and get back to the highway. Stop at Abe's place. You have the address and inside my bag is a map if you need it. Read it and the other things later when you're safe. Then get back to the highway." His voice, normally booming like a radio commercial, was weak, barely above a whisper. "The highway will take you home."

He paused for a long moment.

"I'm sorr ..."

His lip drooped, mouth holding onto his last word, but would never let it go.

He was gone.

She peered at his blanched face, and then out his door, her vision blurry from her silent tears, her face streaked with black and made more macabre by her runny Goth makeup. Only just then did she notice her brother standing there, head bobbing up and down as he sobbed, eyes just peeking above the door. His hands like hooks, clutching so hard over the opening his knuckles were white. He looked like some morbid bobble-head doll.

Run away, Lex!

This was the only action she could fathom right now.

She reached behind her dead father and pulled out his wallet, just as he had instructed, along with his cell phone firmly held by the ashtray door. These, with the pen and paper, went in the open front pocket of his bag, where they were zippered shut.

She looked once more at this man she had hated for so long, who sired and then abandoned her and her brother, unsure what emotions she was supposed to feel or not feel.

Swiping the car keys out of the ignition, she burst out of the front seat, the bug-out bag already making its way onto her shoulders. Over the roof she barked, "Come on Travis, we're leaving," her voice raw and penetrating.

Lexi threw open the creaky trunk of her father's beloved Plymouth Fury—*perhaps it was the only thing he loved.*

She rummaged through her rolling Hello Kitty bag—an absentee present from him when she was a kid, resurrected from storage for their meeting, as a reminder that she'd grown up without him. She did exactly what he said and removed all its contents but one change of clothes. He hadn't said, but she went for comfort as opposed to the ultra-short black dress, punctuated with Goth boots that she currently wore.

Hurriedly, she closed her bag and withdrew it and her brother's plain rolling black bag and slammed the trunk shut, shoving the rabbit's foot and keys into her father's pack.

They were the keys to my father's coffin flashed momentarily in her head.

"Travis, I'm going to leave you if you don't come." She bellowed in a voice stripped of emotion.

Ripped from his mounting, Travis shuffled over to his sister, stepping beside her, while wiping his eyes and nose with the back of his hands.

"Daddy told us to get moving. Take your bag." She had already set their bags down and extended their handles. She thrust his to him and then turned and walked west, not even looking to see if he would follow.

But he did, silently except for his sniffles and his bag's rollers protesting on the warm asphalt.

She stopped for a moment, Travis in lockstep, and risked a glance. Her father's prized car—*it seemed fitting he would die in it*—shimmered, like some mirage that never really existed and would float away into the growing heat.

She didn't even notice, and would only later remember the orange billowing cloud in the distance, shaped like a mushroom.

Chapter 2

Frank

Frank Cartwright sprang upright, sending his Prepper Brothers book tumbling into the predawn darkness, clanging off the unseen metal staircase in front of him. First stumbling over the coffee table, he bounded to the living room window, his bum knee warning him not to push it any further than he was. As he peered out into the night, his sluggish mind continually replayed the bomb-sound that woke him, trying to determine if it was real or part of an interrupted nightmare. He'd fallen asleep after a full day working on his land, rebuilding the back drainage area in preparation for the seasonal rains and spraying his crops against those damned locusts eating up his corn. The Michelob Light he'd opened just before falling asleep was pouring onto his tile floor.

A distant red glow illuminated soft billowing smoke, which seemed to come from the area where his gate would be, and this confirmed that it was not a nightmare. This was real.

Without thinking (the advantage of years of planning and repetition), Frank slipped on his drop-leg—Beretta M9 already holstered—and then hoisted on his hefty vest, sporting four preloaded thirty-round mags for his AK, and snapped it snugly around his slightly bulging midriff. Finally, he dropped his AK and homemade sling over his head and right shoulder, and mounted the metal stairwell to a portico above. This gave him the visibility he needed to see which assholes were out there intending to kill him.

Three older-model civilian trucks, headlights blazing, bounced along his long washboard-riddled driveway, racing toward his house. This was further confirmation of their intentions. It wasn't a stealth operation, but one of braggadocio. They were coming to kill him and take his stuff. They obviously didn't know him or his unwillingness to go down without taking everyone with him.

He lifted his pre-positioned 7mm Remington Magnum, fitted with a new Armasight Vampire night-vision scope, and the world instantly burst into a hazy green-gray light. He watched the trucks approaching fast and focused on the driver of the second one, figuring he could then immediately fire upon the first truck before its driver would have reacted. At the last moment, he turned on the IR illuminator, making his target clear, and squeezed the trigger. The glorious sound of the seven-millimeter's boom and the truck's instant swerve established he'd struck pay dirt.

In a smooth and effortless motion, he cycled another round, painted the first truck's driver, and fired again. But this time, he couldn't confirm a hit as the three trucks' headlights flashed out the night vision. He laid his rifle down, pulled back the charging handle on his AK, and flipped the selector to Auto—perhaps this was not the smartest move tactically, but he was pissed at this point. Standing up tall and exposed, but still unseen, he flicked on the spotlights. As if lit by the midday sun exploding from a passing flotilla of clouds, the front of his house and driveway were instantly bathed in bright light. There was no hesitation as he let loose a full burst on the first truck. Its brakes locked and it veered hard right, directly into the path of the second truck, which coasted right into it. Now, both the first and second trucks appeared lifeless. Frank knew the occupants were soon to follow.

Swapping magazines, he turned his AK's attention to the third vehicle, already pulling a U-turn twenty yards behind the two dead trucks, and just out of the spotlight's cone of light. The door of the second truck popped open and a passenger bolted out and ran to the third pickup, turning back to glare indignantly in Frank's direction.

Now it was fun.

Frank flipped the selector to *Semi-Auto* and aimed at the running man, squeezing off a couple of shots at a time. But the darkness and the distance assisted the target, making it too hard to get a good site picture. With the magazine emptied in the running man's direction, Frank knew he had missed as the man leapt without effort into the bed of the third truck, which was already bounding back down the drive, and to safety.

Frank slid down the staircase's handrails, having practiced this move several hundred times. But this time he hit the floor hard and icepicks of pain detonated in his unprotected knee—he'd be hobbling for a week or two, for sure.

Limping to his kitchen counter, where he'd left his damned brace, he cursed with every step. Barely stopping, he latched it over his pants and shuffled to his gunroom, where he switched magazines. He threw open the front door and paused.

But for a lingering cloud of dust and a ringing in his ears, it seemed quiet. In the distance, the third truck's engine and bouncing undercarriage were the only sounds. He was sure he had won this battle, yet he couldn't help but feel this war was just starting.

He had been prepping for a moment like this for most of his life, especially the last twelve years. He was sure that American society would come crashing down upon itself at some point, and when it did, he was just as sure that bad guys would show up on his doorstep and try to take what he had. But as far as he knew, nothing had happened. Of course, he'd been working outside most of the day. He hadn't bothered to turn on the TV or glance at his phone for news. So, maybe the world had ended and he was just the last to find out.

He risked a straight run—or rather stumble—from his front door. Normally he would have gone out the back, enjoying the safety of the diminishing darkness, waiting for movement from anything before striking. But he needed to find out who these men were and what was coming next.

With his AK leading the way, he slowed his approach to the first truck, an old Chevy from the late 50s. It was classic, but now filled with punctures all exactly 23.9 millimeters around.

The passenger side creaked open and an unarmed man flopped onto the ground with a grunt, his rapid but shallow breaths his only movement. Frank pulled a Maglite from his vest and illuminated the second truck and then the first to confirm what he saw in his scope; both drivers were dead. Using the bright beam of light, he searched around both trucks, confirming there were no other signs of life.

He slung the AK to his back and drew his Beretta while focusing the flashlight's beam on the only living assailant. He was a well-groomed man in his 20s, wearing paramilitary pants and a T-shirt, with several new holes courtesy of Frank. The man was bleeding from his chest, cheek, and mouth. He didn't have long before he'd be experiencing Hell's fiery grip.

"Who are you?" Frank bellowed at the man.

Gurgle-gurgle was his only reply.

Frank moved closer, his flashlight inches away from the dying man's face. He let the barrel of his Beretta ask the question again, pushing it hard into one of the man's chest wounds.

The man groaned in pain and then said something in a foreign tongue.

Was that Arabic?

"Who are you?" Frank asked once more, thinking the ringing in his ears prevented him from hearing properly. "This is the last time I'll ask." He punctuated this statement by clunking his Beretta against the man's temple, and then shoving it against his forehead.

The man's throaty protest was weak. But then he started whispering something.

Frank put his ear near the man's mouth. And this time, he heard it very clearly. He just didn't want to believe it.

"Allahu Akbar. Allahu Akbar... Allahu Ak ..."

Chapter 3

Lexi & Travis

She was numb. What else could she be after watching the man she hated die?

Lexi focused on the sound of her feet. The clomp-clomp-clomp of her boots on asphalt, heating up under the Florida sun with each passing second. Just above this was the thrumming bray of her brother's incessant pleas to stop, to talk, to cry, and what else she didn't know and didn't care. Then there was her throbbing head from hitting the car's side window. Rounding out the crescendo of clamorous pain assaulting her temples was a shrieking chorus of a trillion cicadas, clicking their own demands for attention.

None of this could crowd out that image of her father bleeding to death in front of her.

So, she focused on her walking. Walking felt like a move in the right direction. She wasn't really walking to some place, but away from another. She was walking away from the accident, away from their dead father, and most of all, away from the emotional agony. If she stopped, she feared this hellish monster of her emotions would catch up and devour her. So, her feet marched one in front of the other, as if on automatic pilot.

After a while, Lexi let her mind go, and the memories of her mom and dad washed over her and drowned out the symphony of her pain. But she couldn't deal with any of it: her brother, her father, what they were supposed to do next. She couldn't deal with herself.

How was she expected to live with both her parents dying, and one of them dying in front of her? It was not right. It was so unfair. Why did she and her sniveling brother have to come to Texas and drive all the way to Florida? If they'd stayed at home, their dad, no matter how much she detested him, would still be alive. Now, both their parents were dead.

And to compound their problems, neither of them had their phones with them. That was the deal: they'd left their phones at home. They'd be together and talk, like *real* people and not have *textus-interruptus*—as he called it—every five seconds. It was just one more thing in the long list of things their father had done to them. Of course, his phone was dead. He probably forgot to charge it before they left. So, Lexi couldn't call their Aunt Sara and Uncle David and let them know they were safe.

Her boots stumbled one after the other, an unconscious limp growing with each mile they covered. And she focused again on the sound of her steps. *Clip-clop, clip-clop, clip-clop.*

Most of all, she just walked, not thinking about where she was going or what she was doing, letting the haze of her anguished thoughts drown out her conscious mind, trying hard to keep it from spending any time on the issues that hurt too much.

After a while, a disordered quiet shrouded her. Maybe the adrenaline finally melted off in the heat. Her thoughts were no longer screaming at her and neither was her brother.

Travis!

She abruptly halted and spun around expecting her brother to be right on her heels, as he had been the whole time. But he wasn't. In fact, she couldn't see him at all. How could she have not noticed her brother had stopped talking? How long ago was that? He was like some dog she was obligated to watch and feed, and she had let go of his leash. The truth was, she realized, she was so into her own heartache, she completely ignored her brother's.

Oh God, where is he?

Her heart banged inside and a tsunami of panic flooded her mind, obscuring her senses. She scanned the highway, back from where they had come, and saw something. She squinted at little dots that could be people by one of the stalled cars in the middle of the road. She didn't even remember seeing that car, as she had passed more than a few stalled cars since walking away from theirs.

It *was* people. She was already hurrying in that direction.

One dot was smaller than the others. She hoped it was Travis.

She was running now, her body desperately trying to catch up with and pass her worries. If this dot wasn't her ten-year-old brother, she didn't know what she'd do.

She could see his cowboy hat, a Christmas gift from Daddy that he wore all the time. Travis was talking to an older couple and they were pointing her way.

Oh, thank you, God. It is him.

No longer galloping, she paced toward him. The strangers had stopped conversing and scrutinized her approach.

Only a couple of dozen feet away from him, she wanted to say something, but she couldn't catch her breath and her vision swam with little pinpricks of light. Anger coursed through her, pushing aside her panic. If she had the physical lung capacity, she'd yell at her brother for stopping and for not telling her that he did.

But panic hadn't fully released its clutches yet.

Who were these people? She wondered. And how had she not even noticed them or the car when she had clattered by a few minutes ago?

The woman had her arm around Travis, bringing fits to Lexi's already unsettled stomach.

When drawing up to him, she did her best to immediately assess whether or not these old people were creepers, even though her emotions were battling for her sanity and she just wanted to run. If it were just her, she could run, but it was not so easy with the new responsibility of her brother.

When their mom was dying of cancer, she had drilled into Lexi the stranger-danger stuff, obviously preparing them for a life without her, and it stuck with her even now. She'd always been skeptical of people, no matter their age. And even though she didn't have much of a relationship with her brother, she felt wholly uncomfortable seeing him with these strangers.

They were smiling at him and then at her.

"Hi, young lady," said the ancient man in a suit and tie, his hand holding back a flop of white hair from blowing onto his face. "Your brother here was just telling us about your father and the horrible accident you were in."

"We're so sorry, dear," said the equally antique woman beside him in a flowery dress, its edges wanting to rise up, her free hand occupied with holding it down. "That must have been awful for you both."

The couple looked down in tandem at their feet, acting uneasy as if they didn't know what else to say.

Lexi concluded that they were probably just nice people who broke down, but wanted to help, and Travis noticed.

Lexi couldn't think of anything else to say either, and the last thing she wanted to talk about with these strangers was their dead father. Apparently Travis had done enough of that for both of them.

Her irritation started to bubble up again.

She grabbed her brother's hand and pulled at him sternly, intending to drag him away if necessary. Then the man said, "I'm Don and this is my wife, Seti. We were headed to church when our car died."

Lexi's eyes darted from Don to Seti and to their car and back to each. Her nerves were shot and she felt a wave of nausea, like she would puke at any moment.

"You're Lexi, right?" said Seti. Her voice was calming and reminded her instantly of her mom, and how she talked to her when she was scared of the dark. The nausea passed.

"We've already met your brother, Travis. We're walking back to Lloyd, to our home. You're welcome to come with us. I'm sure you must be hungry."

She was hungry. They had been driving all night and hadn't eaten since a burger from McDonald's—one more thing their father didn't do, because he was so anxious to get on the road. *Maybe it would be all right to stop for food.*

But then she remembered her father's dying instructions and the shopping list. "They have a market in this town?"

"Yes, Lloyd has a market. We can stop on the way," said Don.

"Okay, we'll come with you."

Seti hoisted a giant purse onto her shoulder and Don slid his hand into hers and they led. Lexi and Travis followed a safe distance away, while Don shot back smiles and stories about them, their town of Lloyd, and so many other things Lexi didn't care about, but she happily listened because that meant she didn't have to think. She learned that Seti got her name from the Search for Extraterrestrial Intelligence program, because her mother was a scientist and involved in it. Seti was a big science fan and Don had met her at the university, in an astronomy class. He was a science buff too and he loved to build things. He said he would show them his inventions while Seti was fixing them food.

It went on this way for about a half hour, until they were standing in front of Simpson's World Market.

Lexi found herself scrutinizing the small store as if it were a threat, while they all waited for her approval.

There were no other buildings beside it, and it was bounded by two roads, a parking lot, and swampland. As long as it had what her father had told her to get, it would do just fine.

"Come on and we'll introduce you to the owner," Don invited as he pulled Seti through the door with him.

Inside, Lexi's senses were flooded all at once. The foreign smells would have been noxious to her in any normal circumstance, but because she was hungry and her stomach was finally settling, any food smells were good at this point. Her eyes, too, were suffering from their own sensory overload, as she tried to take in the tangled mess of paraphernalia covering the walls, or hanging from the ceiling, like an overgrown college kid's dorm. On the walls, each patch of stuff seemed to be separated by flags identifying their country of origin. A surf board from Australia; a bobby helmet from England; a pair of wooden shoes from the Netherlands; and so on. Likewise, the shelves were crammed with foodstuffs from every place imaginable, as well as the US.

Don watched with amusement as the kids took in what the store had to offer.

"Yeah, Simpson picked up all of this *junk*"—he accentuated the last word loudly for Simpson's benefit—"himself, during his world travels. Then he brought it back and opened this market about twenty years ago."

"G'day mates," Simpson said in a not too Australian-sounding voice. His face glowed with genuine happiness, as if he loved what he did and didn't want to be anywhere else.

"I'm Ron. Welcome to my store," he said to the two kids. "Sorry, miss; our power's out, so it's hard to see everything inside. Ah, and I hope you brought cash, cause the credit card machine isn't working either."

"I've got cash," Lexi said, flashing a forced smile.

All watched the young woman with the flirtatious black dress and the blue streaks poking out of short black hair grab a basket and start down the first aisle. Travis hung with the adults.

"Sounds like a lot of things aren't working," Don said while scratching his head. "Ron, did your car start today?"

"No, the damn thing was dead. Hey, how did yah know?"

Seti looked first at Ron and then her husband anxiously before asking, "The blast at Jacksonville wasn't the cause. Are you thinking a separate blast in the atmosphere?"

Don's travel map of facial lines looked more worn from growing detours of concern. "Yes." He didn't want to voice this in front of their friend Ron and the young people. He had started to suspect it when they had passed all of those other stalled cars on the way to Simpson's.

"What blast?" Ron asked.

Lexi slid past the magazines and the car-care stuff, and looked first for the item near the bottom of her father's list: "Small lighter fluid." All Simpson's had was the one-quart size. She tossed that into her basket. The fifth item on the list was bug spray. She found the one with 100% Deet and moved on to the food, first grabbing a bottle of apple cider vinegar, completely unsure what this would be used for. But it was on the list and so she threw it in the basket and moved to the next aisle.

She had heard it was wrong to shop on an empty stomach and now she remembered why. At this moment, everything looked good to her undiscerning palate. In the snack section, she stared into the windowed package of chips with Japanese writing on it and yearned for its contents. But she had a job to do, and she would finish it. Two shelves down, she snatched the only two packages of beef jerky and one bag of spicy Doritos chips. That last item wasn't on the list, but she liked them.

"Shelled peanuts?" She emoted out loud, reading the next item on the list. She searched and found two bags of them, and into the basket they went. She was starting to understand the reasons behind the food list he'd dictated to her. The food was easily portable, stored well, had a long shelf life, and was high in calories and protein. When she'd first scribbled it all down, she had thought it was just babbling from her dying father. But this list had purpose and forethought. She wondered what treasures she'd find in his bug-out bag currently resting at Travis's feet, up front.

Walking past the candy aisle, her eyes wandered over the fruity candies from all over and came to rest on Starbursts Fruit – Tropical. She tossed a glance back up at Travis. He was listening to Don and Ron argue about nuclear blasts. The packet went into her basket. She thought it was a favorite, at one time. Maybe she could use it as a bargaining chip at some point to make him do what she wanted.

Back in front of the store, she walked down the next aisle and compared the packaged and canned food options. The list said "dried foods - Just add water." She snatched the only three packages of dried soups. Beside this were some rice and beef packages. All had instructions indicating "Just add water." Laying them in the basket, she went to canned foods, where she picked up two cans of chili and crossed that off her list.

"Packaged fish? Yuck." This was definitely not her favorite. But she understood what he was doing here: all the major food groups, and ready to eat without a stove. She found some packets of tuna, surprised that they didn't require refrigeration. Equally amazed when turning them over, she found they would be good for sale until four years from this month. She grabbed four of these. She'd hold her nose if necessary.

On the juice aisle, she grabbed some pineapple and apple juice packets. Lastly, she grabbed two gallon jugs of water, struggling to carry those and the now full basket.

All four of them watched her return and lay all of her items on the counter.

"Hope you have cash," he glanced at all the items.

Lexi threw down her wad of cash onto the counter, making a slapping sound to accentuate her frustration at his repeated question.

Simpson took out a yellow pad, looked at his Timex watch and wrote down the amount and description of each item, before adding up the columns of numbers longhand.

"You don't use calculators in this part of the country?" Lexi asked, her sarcasm meant to be as biting as she knew it sounded.

He wrote the total and then spun the yellow pad around to Lexi. "I doubt adding is something your generation could do without a calculator. Besides, that's what I have a cash register for, which doesn't work without power. $67.58," he said with a sly smile.

"Do you have a telephone I can use?" Lexi asked putting the remaining cash back into her father's wallet from where it had come, and then shoved it into his bag. She kept the coins in her hand, jingling them.

"There's a payphone by the bathroom, that way." He pointed toward the back of the store.

The bathroom was clean and the toilet flushed—she wasn't sure it would with the power out. After changing into an old T-shirt and oversized jeans, for reasons unknown to her at the time, she slipped the rabbit's foot and keys into her pocket. The pay phone didn't work; it only emitted a sickly sounding crackle rather than a dial tone.

"Hey, you know your payphone doesn't wo—" Lexi froze when she saw Don and Ron hovering over Seti, who was on the floor. Travis was crying again.

"What happened?" Lexi shrieked. Her panic back in her throat.

"I think she's had a heart attack," Ron said, feeling for a pulse and then starting CPR on the woman. "Does she have a heart condition, Donny?"

The old man shook his head no, holding her hand.

Lexi walked around them, grabbed their groceries and then whispered into Travis's ear, "We're leaving."

They slipped out of the front without being noticed.

It was another quick getaway from death and questions. They had their own problems to deal with.

The sun was high in a sky that seemed angry.

They'd return to the highway. They'd find a tree off the road where they'd stop and eat and maybe nap. She felt so tired.

Travis kept tugging at her hand, each time he'd turn and look back in the direction of the market, which could no longer be seen. He kept mumbling something, but she wasn't paying attention. She was too busy noticing all the dead cars leading up to the highway, remembering Don's conversation with Ron.

When they were back on the highway, the gravity of their situation finally sank in. On both sides of the asphalt, as far as she could see, all the cars were dead and lots of people were walking, although in the opposite direction as them.

Chapter 4

Frank

All his senses knew what his mind argued it couldn't be.

It had to be terrorists. But there were the unanswered questions: Why was he a target? Why on his property? Why in the backwater of Stowell, Texas?

Frank paced through the reasonable possibilities as he plodded back to his house, after making sure his property was clear of any more of the combatants.

"Combatants?" he chuckled at this. It was the term the Army taught him to use when describing the enemy. "Combatants" was duly descriptive, yet very generic, and it was woeful in describing these men and their intentions. The term was perhaps useful in the theater of war, but not on his ranch in Texas.

He'd served three tours, and multiple combat missions, where everything was black and white, where everything made sense. So everything about this situation seemed surreal to him.

He suspected that this was just normalcy bias: an American disease that he now suffered from, that he'd been infected with the moment he retired, and that had incubated through a solitary civilian life for more than a dozen years. He had thought he would be immune to this, and found himself angry that he wasn't.

He felt he was not unlike the media and politicians who were always so quick to report that a violent act committed by someone claiming Islam as their religion to be anything other than a terrorist attack. But always, the inconvenience of the truth became unforgiving: it *was* Islamic jihadists. The dead man's words were his proof of this. Still, this attack was different.

Besides the paramilitary outfits, jihadists usually sought to kill as many targets as possible and usually in a very public place. That way the public would be filled with terror. That was their modus operandi.

Frank's ranch wasn't public, and he was the only soft target on it, other than a few goats and the coyotes always trying to eat them. And in spite of their noisy and boisterous attack, it wasn't meant for public consumption. No one would have heard about this, especially if they had been successful in killing Frank. So he reasoned there could only be one reason for this attack.

Despite its sloppy execution, this was an invasion. It was the beginning of a war.

Both mind and body in sync now, Frank dashed through his already open doorway, ignoring the pain from his aching knee, and bolted to the TV, slapping the remote's on-button as he scooped up his phone. He had this horrible feeling that Stowell, Texas, no matter how dumb it sounded, was the front line of an invasion by Islamic jihadists.

"Damnit!" he swore, realizing that his aging cell phone was dead. After all the work he'd done on his land yesterday, when he finished last night, he'd forgotten to plug the stupid thing in. He snapped it into the wire snaking from the wall and left it on the living room table, already crowded with books and the mostly empty bottle of Michelob Light, its contents drying on the floor.

He glared at his flat-panel TV; a static buzz in the background matched the picture on its screen.

Thinking he must have accidentally knocked it off the satellite, Frank stared at the remote for a long moment, trying to make sense of its multiple buttons before clicking on the one that turned the satellite on. He cursed the damned thing for its complexity. The picture flickered in response, and then displayed static once again.

He switched channels and received the same result from his TV. *Why the hell would the satellite be out?*

Moving more slowly over to a computer perched on a roll-top desk across the room, he stabbed the on-button with his forefinger and watched. His mind begged for the standard annoying Windows emblem. He craved normalcy. The screen splashed the familiar logo and ground through its routine. His mind raced, frustratingly faster than the computer's.

After an excruciating couple of minutes, the computer was fully booted and the web browser window opened, confirming what he suspected. His connection to the Internet was down as well.

"My radio!" he blurted out to the unquestioning morning light flittering thru the living room door he'd left open. Ignoring this he trotted over to the short wave, a time-worn Heathkit that still used tubes, and flipped on the toggle. A low hum told him it was warming up. Everything seemed to take an unbearable amount of time, when he needed answers immediately.

To punctuate his frustration, he walked over and slammed the door for no reason other than it seemed better than just waiting. He dragged a stool across the room and plopped himself in front of the short wave, nestled in his bookshelves. Static blared from the two speakers, spaced on opposite sides of the room. It had last broadcast a church's radio program several weeks ago, a firebrand preacher spouting how Revelations was coming true today. The station, a local one that played mostly Christian music 24/7, which he sometimes liked to have on in the background when he was reading, was noticeably gone. Maybe that preacher wasn't as loony as he had first thought.

Frank spun the dial to another end of the band; the speakers sang out a whistlelike sound with occasional pulses from live broadcast stations. Each was perhaps broadcasting something and maybe telling him that this was just local. But he didn't stop; he was looking for a specific station.

"We return to Peter, who we were able to locate in South Carolina, United States," said a somewhat frantic woman, with an otherwise silky British accent.

"Thank you, Ashley," said a staticy male voice. "I can now confirm through multiple reports that America has been attacked by several nuclear blasts, including two high in the atmosphere, causing electrical outages everywhere in North America. We're told that New York, Washington, DC, and Chicago have been destroyed by separate nuclear devices—"

"Fu—" Frank exhaled, stumbling back, knocking over the stool. He grabbed the mostly empty beer bottle and drank the remaining warm liquid while sinking into his couch, his eyes fixed on the radio.

"ABC Radio thankfully had backup equipment that we were able to broadcast on—"

Frank's phone beeped at him, a tone indicating that it had enough power and had turned itself back on. Then another tone, telling him that he had a text. Then another text-tone.

He scooped it up into his palm, stretching to match the cord's length from the wall and glared at the phone's messages in shock. Like everything else today, it was surreal.

There were two texts displayed on the phone, both from Stan, his best friend whom he hadn't heard from in years.

The first one was dated July 3rd—*yesterday*. "Terrorists will strike. America will fall any day now. Prepare. Taking kids to Florida."

He stared dumbfounded and then gnawed on the next text, "Could happen any time. If don't make it might send kids your way via highway, or Abe's. Please watch—"

There was nothing more.

He looked at his recent calls and saw the last one was from Grimes, probably calling to find out what he knew. But there was no coverage, no cell service.

The phones were down too.

Frank stood up. He had a nagging feeling, like a horrible scratch that wouldn't go away. What if these men came back and brought more of them? He no longer had the element of surprise, working in his favor. If they returned, any time soon, he might not be able to defend himself.

He raced out the front door, as Ashley's tearful voice reported about the millions of American lives lost.

Chapter 5

Lexi & Travis

They woke to a duet of their own screams, Travis reliving today's nightmare and Lexi experiencing a new horror: a bright orange snake fluttered its mocking tongue at her, while slithering across her bare feet. She kicked and pushed away from the small serpent, driven by sleep's disorientation and an abject fear of snakes. Travis giggled at his sister's foolish display, his nightmare already forgotten.

"It's not even poisonous," he said with a chuckle.

"How the hell would you know?" she quipped, already regretting she'd said this; if anyone would know, it was her genius brother, Travis.

"There are twenty-four varieties of snakes in Florida, and only six are venomous. That is probably a salt marsh snake." He looked at her with a wry grin. "They eat insects, so he must have thought you'd be tasty."

"Smartass!" It was times like this when she really hated her brother. "Get your stuff together. We're going in five minutes."

"But ..." He looked around, as if someone was listening, and whispered, "I have to go number two."

Lexi turned her wrist, blindly glancing at her watch—originally her mom's—and then back to him. "Now you only have four minutes and fifty seconds ... forty-nine." She smirked pleasurably. She knew she was being insensitive, but that little boy pissed her off.

As Travis retreated quickly into the bushes with their lone roll of TP in hand, Lexi tentatively looked for her shoes. She'd kicked them off her swollen feet after they'd settled on this place for their rest, savoring the relief. But it was only temporary. She couldn't imagine wearing her Goth boots again. They were ridiculous things with multiple buckles that were designed to be seen in, not to be walked in. She'd only worn them once before, preferring sandals. It was all part of the look she was after, meant to cut at her father for leaving them. It was a dual-edged blade she'd meant to thrust and twist into him: the flimsy dress that accentuated her feminine curves—a reminder that he missed her growing up into an adult; and the Goth style, driven home by the boots and makeup, worn during her turbulent high school years. He hadn't had the pleasure of experiencing that portion of her life.

"Guess you got the last laugh on that one, Daddy," she chided herself.

A thought struck and she carefully waddled—damaged toes bent upright to avoid ground contact—over to their bags, one black boot clutched in each hand. She straddled her father's bag and plopped down on a tuft of grass.

For the first time, she unclasped the main compartment to his pack, or what he called his bug-out bag, and pulled the opening as wide as it would go. It was a hunch and a hope, as she didn't really *know* she'd find what she was looking for. But almost immediately she did: a small red canvas satchel, emblazoned with a stark white plus sign. Carefully she unzipped it and snatched up a white roll of gauze tape, a smile announcing her delight.

Her feet were an angry pink and swollen, but it was the blisters that concerned her: one on each heel, each big toe, and the top-front of each foot. Hopefully the gauze would help.

She sparingly wrapped the front halves of her feet and placed a small strap on each heel, meticulously cutting each strip with a scary-sharp folding knife sheathed on the outside of the bag.

After checking out her work and wiggling her toes for confirmation, she was startled to find her brother had crept up and was waiting behind her.

"You wore those stupid-looking shoes to mess with Dad, didn't you?"

She ignored him and instead of answering reached into her Hello Kitty bag, which somehow had become their food storage, and pulled out a package of peppered beef jerky. After ripping it open, she took out a large piece and handed the bag to him. They both tore into their ragged morsels of meat like ravenous animals munching on a fresh kill.

This gave her some time to search for the next item she needed from his bag, the only article she knew would be there. Her fingers found a folded piece of paper beside a book. It was a printout of a Google map, with navigation on the other side of it. The map side showed two points, one in the panhandle of Florida and the other on the mid-northern Gulf side, with a jagged line connecting both points. Most of that line was their highway, I-10. The lower portion of that line snaked down a couple of unknown roads to the origination point. She suspected the point closer to them was the home of their father's friend, known to her only as Abe. The other location she didn't recognize either, but guessed that was where they had been headed to spend a few days, before the accident.

She flipped to the navigation side and saw it was from the perspective of the mystery location on the Gulf side of Florida, near the far eastern end of the panhandle, going to Abe's house. Their destination was right off the highway they were on. Best she could figure, it was less than sixty miles away. That was doable on foot. They had enough food and if they covered twenty miles per day, they should be there in three. She sure hoped that this was a good idea, and that Abe was the person who could help them. She folded up the map and slid it back into the pack where she had found it. Although she was eager to explore the rest of the contents, she was more eager to get going. They had a lot of ground to cover.

"You ready to go?" she asked, carefully slipping on each boot. They still hurt like hell, and they were impossibly tight now, but her new padding would do until they found a shoe store on the way, where she could buy replacements, along with some socks.

"I'm ready," he said, handing back the jerky.

After some gulps of water, they were back on the highway, heading west. And almost immediately Travis hit her with a fusillade of questions: "How bad did Dad suffer?"

"Why are we walking?" "Why did we leave that nice lady, Seti?" "Do you think she died?"

Lexi's favorite question was "Is Dad in Paradise?" Oh, she wanted to answer this one and tell him no, he was probably roasting away in hell, if there was such a place. But all of these questions were trivial, and Travis, as smart as he was, should have known the answer himself. She was concerned about more important issues, like would she find some decent shoes? Or was their father's friend Abe a bum like their father? And how in the hell would they travel the thousand-plus miles back to Tucson? She was hoping that Abe would provide the transportation, although she wasn't sure how that would work since cars no longer seemed to function: another unanswered question.

Then, perhaps in an effort to tune him out, Lexi considered her greatest concern: radiation. She picked up what she overheard from Don and Ron's discussion: there were two nuclear blasts, and one of them was in Jacksonville, in the direction they were headed by car. Thank God they didn't get closer to there when it happened; they might have all been dead, rather than just her father.

A clear image of her high school project on nuclear nonproliferation popped into her head. She thought of the map she'd examined showing how the wind currents would carry the deadly radiation west to east. So, the blast east of them was not a problem. But if there was another blast somewhere west, say in Dallas, they'd be dead in weeks or months. And then of course there was the second blast, in the atmosphere. Wouldn't that drop radiation on top of them?

She felt her skin baking just thinking about it. In response, she picked up her pace and Travis followed in sync, his one-sided questions continuing. "What about Seti? She was sick; shouldn't we have helped her? She helped us? Don looked really scared. I'm still hungry; can I have something more to eat? Can we stop again?"

Lexi continued to block him out, thinking about Abe, the man that their father was sending them to. She hoped he wasn't like their father. This filled her with more dread. How could they trust this guy too, whose friend abandoned his kids years ago? As a friend, wouldn't you say something?

And who abandons their children for eight years, sending only an occasional birthday card or present, and then wants to have a family vacation like they were some happy family? She was working herself up again.

Their rolla-boards skipped and skidded over the highway blacktop, already sweltering from the afternoon heat.

Then a question from Travis caught her flat-footed. "Why do you hate Dad? What did he ever do to you?"

As if Lexi had run straight into a tree, she abruptly stopped and spun around to face him directly, casting a gaze of fury meant to slap her brother harder than her hand ever could. Then she let loose with her own verbal volley. "Shut up! I'm so tired of your whimpering and crybaby attitude." She raised her pitch in a mocking way. "I'm hungry—I'm tired—I'm—I'm—I'm." Now she was yelling. "What about me? I'm stuck in this horrible place with a sniveling little boy, who is just about to wet his little pants. You're always complaining and whining. And since you brought up our dearly-departed father ... let me tell you a thing or two about that bum. Our mother died of cancer and he couldn't take it, and even though he had a little girl and a little boy, who was just a toddler, he left us. That miserable man, who cared only about himself, shipped us to Tucson on a flight, because he couldn't be bothered to even drive us there, and dumped us like trash on our aunt and uncle."

She paused for a moment, seething with anger at her brother, not really because of anything he had done, but because of her father; because she had been holding this anger inside for so long; because she'd never gotten the chance to tell her father this in person; and because she didn't use the opportunity to tell him how angry she was when she had the chance while he was alive, instead of ignoring him from the back seat during the last of their time together. So, her whining brother received both barrels at once.

"I for one am glad he's dead. I hope he rots in hell!"

She glimpsed only for a moment at Travis, like a hunter who'd fired the kill shot at the prized buck, making sure it hit. And even though she turned away from him and started to march off, she caught enough of a glimpse of him—a clear picture her guilty conscious would gnaw on endlessly—to know her words drew blood.

With each angry step separating her from her brother, left flabbergasted by her words, his image already burned fires of guilt inside her gut.

Travis just stood where he was, gut-shot, reeling, tears welling in his eyes, mouth gaping at this person who pretended to be his sister. Tears bursting like flood waters from a fall monsoon, he bawled.

Lexi was a good hundred yards from him when her pride gave in to her compassion and she stuttered to a stop. Her shoulders sagged and she felt horrible. Her brother wasn't to blame. He was just as miserable as she was, more so because he was confused. She may have hated her father, but her brother didn't know hate. Her brother was innocent and couldn't hate anyone. He loved his father and looked at him entirely different than she did. Even the years of separation, with only a birthday card to look forward to—often signed by someone other than their father—didn't sway Travis's opinion of him. And until now, Lexi had stayed out of it, only occasionally responding to his questions of "Aren't you excited to see Dad" with curt "no's" or "I don't care."

As far as Travis knew, their father was a good man who left for the right reason, and Travis had waited for the day when he would return, even though he really never did, and now, never would.

Lexi realized she had been standing hunkered over, crying for herself; crying for the father she never knew, and never would; and crying for the pain she inflicted upon her innocent brother.

She *really* was "a bitch." That's what the popular girls had called her, first in high school, then later in college. And she knew she was that way to most people, but she didn't need to be that way with her brother. He may have been smarter than most adults, but he was just a little boy who didn't know any better. Her lips curled into a crooked smile and she quipped to herself, "Yeah, a little boy who already knows calculus, and will someday find the cure for cancer."

She slowly turned around, fully intending to offer up some sort of apology to Travis. She was never very good at apologies, even when she was dead wrong, like now.

She fixed her gaze on the place where she had left Travis in a heap of emotional wreckage, all happiness eviscerated by her. But he wasn't there.

"Not again!"

This time he was *really* gone.

This time, she didn't see anyone on the highway, her eyes darting everywhere. A hundred yards or so away, she saw a small object lying in the middle of the road.

It was Travis's cowboy hat.

Chapter 6

Frank

F rank felt as tortured as his wrecked gate, a testament to this morning's invasion.

He had hoped a more careful examination would reveal that some part of it was salvageable. Unfortunately, it was totally destroyed. To prevent his unwanted visitors from driving right up to his home, until he could figure out what was going on and find a more permanent solution, he'd have to create a temporary barricade. He could use the small dirt road that crossed a neighbor's property for ingress and egress; the terrorists weren't likely to know about this.

His antique tractor was the solution. It hadn't worked for years; its wheels were rusted in place and it wouldn't be functional without a complete overhaul. It was his father's and he had always intended to bring it back to some utility, but time and its lack of practicality scuttled that idea. So, it sat in back, a rusted monument to his father.

Using his truck, he dragged the antique from the back of his property and deposited it right in the middle of the broken entrance, its rusted-in-place wheels burrowing a trail the whole way. It would take an adversary several crucial minutes to move this, giving Frank time to hear and respond.

He walked one last patrol of all fifty acres and the main road, just to see if he missed something and to think through all his options. He was more careful this time, but he marched with a sense of urgency—he knew they would be back again.

He had been prepping for this moment, when the US would collapse, most of his life. Since 9/11, he'd thought a highly coordinated attack from terrorists was a possibility, albeit a remote one. He had thought a much more likely occurrence was a plasma burst or CME from the sun, which would lead to a societal and economic collapse. All his preparations were centered on this type of event.

He'd built shields of Faraday-like protection using a combo of steel bars and mesh all around his house and garage/workshop. Besides protecting his electronics and his two electronic-ignition-system vehicles, they created an almost impenetrable physical barrier against any potential invaders, whether terrorists or the run of the mill B-and-E. His solar power system had circuit and battery protection from an EMP's surge. With his well and septic, and over a year's worth of food set aside, he was ready for the worst the sun could throw at him.

The actual attack may have not been from the sun, but it was just as deadly, perhaps even worse. Although nukes destroyed the major cities of New York, DC, and Chicago, it was the two separate nukes exploded in the atmosphere that brought America to its knees. The EMPs from those two detonations probably fried most unshielded electronics from Canada to South America and from coast to

coast. Many late-model cars, appliances, TVs, some cell
phones, and pretty much everything electronic, especially where the EMP was closer, were probably damaged
beyond repair. But, this would only be the start of the end.

The American grid would be down, which he confirmed with the lack of Internet and satellite service. In
spite of years of warnings to Congress that serious up-
grades were needed, the network of transformers that
made up the electric grid was fried either from the EMP
or from the system's overloaded capacity. The result was
a cascading failure that would take years to fix, if indeed
it ever could be. Its effects on the machinery of America
would be systemic and result in failure of everything:
power, water and sewer delivery, food production and
delivery supply chains, medicine, communications, and
emergency and security responses. He knew that as food
stores would dry up quickly, in the next day or two, those
that didn't die from the bombs would eventually starve to
death or succumb to diseases once thought no longer a
problem. Chaos would reign supreme.

All these things Frank dreaded for his country, but
he still prepared for them as he grew surer with each
year's passing that the systemic risks of a collapse became
far greater than during the previous one. Many of his
buddies, even those whom he served with, thought him
paranoid. Even after COVID. Frank knew they suffered
from the same normalcy biases that most Americans did,
but then evidently he did too. In spite of his warnings
for them to prepare for the worst, he was also sure they
would be blindsided by this event.

He suspected that the Pentagon had been blindsided as well. None of their Middle East enemies had the capabilities to launch nukes. So, that left the North Koreans, the Chinese, or the Russians. He figured one of them must have taken advantage of the situation, though any one of them would have made an odd bedfellow with the Islamists. At least, he was pretty sure of this fact: Islamic jihadists were behind this attack on the US. One man's dying words proved this to him. For his own immediate safety, he had to figure out why they were in his home town and why they had targeted him so early.

Frank once again examined each of the bodies and what they were carrying on them. They were all dressed in the same camo-colored paramilitary outfits, and all carried brand-new AKs and lots of ammo. These of course he would add to his inventory, along with one of the trucks.

Vehicle one, a beautiful 1958 red Chevy, was only good for parts—he'd shredded the engine during his successful campaign to stop it. The second was a '79 Chevy C/K, and it was in perfect shape except for the bullet hole in the windshield and reddish brain matter spattered all over the inside of the cab. The fact that both vehicles were older, without electronic ignition systems, wasn't lost on him.

There was no identification or anything useful on any of the three bodies, their tactical vests, weapons and ammo already salvaged. Frank dragged each body about two hundred yards away from his house and down wind. He would let nature's scavengers clean up this mess.

After careful inspection of the vehicles, he found no identification in the cabs or glove boxes. Not even registration or insurance. It wasn't until he went underneath the seat of the newer one that he found a useful clue: a yellowed receipt from Stowell Grain & Feed. The name of the purchaser on the receipt was Bart Maldonado. Frank knew Bart and his family pretty well. They didn't see eye to eye on some things, but he certainly didn't expect this kind of behavior from any of the Maldonados. So, probably the truck had been stolen or purchased from Bart. Most importantly, he had a place to start, which was far better than waiting around for them to attack.

After moving the terrorists' trucks around the back of his detached garage, behind his house, he parked his truck inside and loaded up his ATV.

He would head down the mostly dry river bank that bounded the back of his property and follow it all the way to Maldonado's. With any luck he'd find out why these terrorists invaded his property and his little community in Texas. If they were there, maybe he'd reap a little American justice and send these bastards back to Allah, gift wrapped Texas-style.

Chapter 7

Lexi & Travis

O ther than his well-used cowboy hat, there were no other signs of her brother anywhere. It was like he'd melted into the pavement, leaving only his hat in his place.

It was the same place where she'd been yelling at Travis only minutes ago. Of course, he wasn't there now.

Lexi twisted her head around violently from one side to the other, making sure she hadn't missed any clues.

He must have walked off into the heavy growth on either side of the road, but where?

It was no use yelling for him; she knew her brother well enough that she was sure he would be sitting and stewing for hours if left on his own. One time he'd disappeared for almost a whole day because Lexi yelled at him about something stupid he did—he was always doing lots of stupid stuff. Uncle David, Aunt Sara, and Lexi had gone off searching for him, hollering his name to the limits of their voices, and together they searched over a five-mile radius around the house. They had knocked on doors, scoured washes, walked miles of roads without any sign of him. When they returned to call the police and plan for the worst, he was there, watching reruns of his favorite

TV show, *The Walking Dead*. After his aunt and uncle promised to not turn him into a zombie—she wasn't going to let him off that easy—he fessed up: He'd been up in the large tree out back, watching their search, and saying nothing. No, he'd remain quiet if she called for him, and in fact, Lexi believed her pleas for him would only fuel his resolve to maintain his silence. She had to think like her brother and find him.

She stood right where she was, facing west, in the direction she had stomped off. Sliding his hat onto her head, the brim still warm with his sweat, she pretended to sulk and cry and channeled her inner Travis. He was right-handed and was on the westbound side of the divided highway, so he probably turned right, dragging his feet across the pavement. She mimicked this as well.

When her feet crunched some loose gravel on the highway's shoulder, her head down as she imagined her brother's would have been, something caught her eyes in the recently cut thick grass right off the pavement, before the green wall of heavy growth. It was the matted down tracks of either a very small adult ... *or a ten-year old boy!*

But beside these were other tracks, made by wider shoes with broader gaits. There were many footsteps, in fact, leading through an opening in a wall of maples.

Lexi took two steps into the dense growth, plunging her into near darkness from the shade. She squeezed her eyes shut and reopened them, trying to get her eyes adjusted to the low light levels. She heard him first.

"Stop!" he said, a sort of muffled yell that almost seemed to echo from under the trees' canopy.

Two men had hold of Travis. One restrained his arm and muffled his screams. The other was rifling through his backpack and then he hunched over and started into his rolla-board.

Frozen like a statue for a few moments, her feet were welded to the soft ground by fear, her always clear mind clouded and unsure. She felt like a small girl compared to these two big men. Without thinking she shouted, "Stop!"

The one rifling through Travis's bags halted his theft and looked up casually, as if his number had been called at the post office and he just wanted to get rid of his package and move on. A smile broke onto his bearded face, as if he had just remembered a funny joke; Lexi suspected that she was the punch line.

He stood, the smile turning malevolent as he started to walk toward her. "Come here, little sweet thing. We ain't goina bite," he taunted her in a gravelly southern voice, a little pointy in places like crushed granite.

She stumbled backward, out of the canopy, into the brightness. Forgetting the highway's curb, she tripped and fell hard onto her tailbone. Righting herself immediately, she shuffled backward down the other side just before the grass strip median. Just then, she remembered her father's gun in the front pocket of her pack. Swinging the pack around in front of her, she struggled to unzip the zipper, before reaching in and searching for it frantically.

She didn't remove her gaze from the oncoming man, only a few steps away.

Got it!

Releasing the pack, she clutched the gun's cool heaviness, thrust it out toward the man, and unsteadily shambled back some more. Her hands and arms wobbled as she tried to aim it at him, hoping desperately he would run in fear. She had fired a similar gun—Some-Number-Magnum—with a pink handle, owned by her aunt, who took her to the range to fire it. Although it was intended for a woman's slenderer hands, when she fired it, the recoil was so bad she'd almost dropped it. In spite of her protests to stop, her aunt and uncle forced her to fire almost twenty bullets at a paper silhouette of a man, like this one. They said she was a natural at it. But at this moment she vividly remembered the loud bang, the painful vibrations in her hands, and her swearing she would never fire the damned thing again. It didn't matter then; it mattered now.

The man kept coming, seeming almost surer of his step. "Whada-think you goina do wi dat?" the man gloated, as he maintained his advance, having reached the shoulder of the highway.

Lexi continued her scuttle backward, almost into the eastbound lane of I-10. "Leave me alone!" she demanded. It came out as a whimper.

This man kept coming, his beard pointing east, pushed by the wind. Now that he was fully in the sunlight, she could see his clothes were covered in dirt. He and his buddy must have been sleeping off of the road when Lexi and Travis had come along and she woke them with her yelling.

She caused this.

He was in the middle of the westbound blacktop, not hesitating or slowing his progression toward her.

She didn't want to see what came next.

She turned her head down, scrunched her eyes closed (hoping that would muffle the explosion she'd hear next while knowing it would do no such thing—she wasn't stupid, just hopeful), and squeezed the trigger. It blasted and her hands whipped back. But this time she held tight.

She looked back and saw she must have missed because the man was now running at her, only a few feet away on the grassy median.

It was a panicked reaction of adrenaline that forced her hand. She quickly pointed again; this time she kept one squinted eye on the sight and the man—just like her aunt had taught her—and squeezed once more. Before she could fully feel and hear the effects of the eruption, she threw herself sideways to avoid the man, who tumbled past her and onto the asphalt.

He clutched his gut, a dark red dye spreading out past his fists. He looked up at her, his face twisted in confusion, then pain, and then anger. "You shot me?" he mumbled.

She ran back to the opening in the trees, not sure what she'd do, just knowing she had to be there. The other man was still standing, but was no longer clutching her brother, who had moved behind a tree several yards away. Lexi and the man stared at each other for a long moment, but his gaze kept falling on her gun which he had surely heard go off.

She lifted the gun, which felt like an iron weight, and pointed at this other man, fully expecting him to rush her as well. She wouldn't miss her first shot this time.

The man spun on his heels and dashed out of sight.

She remained in place and waited, the heft of the gun forcing her arms down. But the man was gone. Travis stood up from behind a tree, mouth agape, and just stared at Lexi, who shrugged her shoulders as if to say "Who knew I had it in me?" Feeling confident the man was gone, she walked up to Travis and asked in a businesslike tone, "Are you hurt?"

At first, he said nothing, as if he was in shock. Then, "N ... no," he said with a sniffle.

She collected the items on the ground that Gut-shot Man had pulled out from his rolling luggage, and shoved them back in. "Come on. Let's get out of here before that man comes back."

He slowly at first picked up one thing, then another, then moved quicker with each second. No doubt he too was afraid that the man would return while they were cleaning up.

Within a minute, they had collected everything, zippered it all into his bag, and were racing down the road. First running, then trotting, finally walking at a fairly decent clip.

But they had to stop.

Lexi bent over uncontrollably and heaved the remains of last night's hamburger and this afternoon's beef jerky, until all that was left was a long line of spittle, and nothing else.

She heaved again.

She had never shot anyone before. She never watched a man die either, except for her father.

She shuddered at this thought and heaved again.

Chapter 8

Frank

As when waking from a nightmare, Frank was filled with an overwhelming nervous anxiety that couldn't be explained. He halted his ATV, but couldn't stop his disquiet.

The afternoon air clung to him, a wet blanket that dampened everything, and yet his skin was cool and prickly. His heart pounded in his chest and a fire grew in the pit of his stomach. These foreign feelings were unsettling for a veteran of numerous combat missions. It wasn't fear, an emotion that he had long ago conquered but had seen possess many men like an evil specter. And it wasn't adrenaline, which was his faithful servant on the battlefield. This sensation was something with which he was wholly unfamiliar. He pulled on the reins of this bucking bull, desperately trying to regain control.

What the hell was going on?

At one time, in multiple theaters he'd been considered an expert at killing enemies, including some of the vilest creatures vomited from hell itself, but he was always able to perform his duties dispassionately. It was his job of course, and he was damn good at it. More than this, for Frank, it was a simple matter of separating himself

from the weight of emotions which were normal when a
soldier was forced to take another human's life. He looked
at his emotions like a heavy winter coat that he'd hang
up and leave at home before going into battle, and that
he could always put back on when he needed to feel
again, which wasn't often. After a while, it was just easier
to leave the coat off. This probably explained why he
was alone. Yet, all this was necessary: avoiding emotional
entanglements kept him and his men alive.

But there were some emotions he couldn't separate
himself from, such as that time in Fallujah—his last battle—when all those kids died from Army grenades. After
that he had given up battle and taken retirement.

But that was a long time ago.

Since retirement, he'd allowed himself to become mentally and physically out of shape for battle.

He sneered at this thought, and gave a self-deprecating
pat to his belly, slightly bulging under his tactical vest. It,
like the rest of his body, had grown flabby from a diet of
beer and the laziness born from his retirement from the
Army. Yet, even when he was at the top of his game, this
exercise was decidedly different than all of his previous
missions.

It was anger.

He was fuming that some group of assholes had tried to
kill him, on his own land no less. More agitating was that
these pricks were Islamic jihadists, raised in a brand of
Islam he had experienced first-hand. He'd always thought
if the Middle East, and perhaps the world, was ever going
to survive this plague, Radical Islam would need to be
eradicated. But, what filled him with rage was that these

religious nut-jobs attacked his country without provocation, and would probably end up killing a hundred million of his fellow Americans by the time their nuclear dust settled.

That must be the reason for the uncontrollable earthquake of emotions rumbling inside of him.

He couldn't shake off his emotional coat this time. In fact, he didn't want to. This time, he'd zip it up and feel its warmth. It would be like a partner in a three-legged race, a race with a prize much larger than a home-baked apple pie. And if he did embrace his mate, he might just be able to vanquish his enemies and avoid getting himself killed.

Knowing this now, Frank forced his warrior self—and his new partner—to focus on his plan, tempering his fury. His mind started to chew at each morsel of his strategy, like individual peas at a Sunday family dinner. His purposes were simple. He needed intel about his enemies: What were they doing in Stowell? Why did they attack him? What do they have planned next? As a bonus he would pacify his vengeful partner with the opportunity to annihilate a few terrorists.

Retribution!

He drove a few hundred yards more, parking a mile away, under a dense tree on the bank of the Spindletop. Even though his heavily muffled exhaust system was designed to be stealthy, in a world of loud silence, absent all mechanical noises, he needed to be sure they didn't hear his approach.

He marched purposefully through the heavy growth and mud, considering what he might find at Maldonado's while he scanned ahead and around his perimeter with his AK 74.

It was over twelve years ago, when he completed his last operation.

He felt every one of those years in his body. He was not in good shape any longer, and he had a bum knee—lest he forget, it reminded him with each step. Still, he figured he was just as lethal up close as he was before, and certainly better than any damned rag-headed terrorist.

Now that his friend adrenaline was kicking in, he was instantly reminded of the pleasurable rush he'd experienced just before going into battle. He was ready.

He crept up to the end of the thick weeded area, cleared of trees years ago, and knelt—on his good knee—before the Maldonados' walled pool area and their usually manicured yard leading to the back of their sprawling ranch-style home. The property looked out of sorts through the Aimpoint PRO scope.

He'd been back here only once, right after he'd retired and moved back into his residence full-time. Bart and Samantha Maldonado served Frank over-the-top hors d'oeuvres and expensive wine, as if they were trying to impress him. He'd have been happier with a Bud and a burger. The presentation of their pool and manicured grounds were impressive then.

Now in the green water of the pool a moldy-looking seat cushion floated with other debris, and the grounds looked like they'd been untouched for months. It was as if no one had lived there in that timespan. The only sign of life was on the patio area leading to the rear slider. A large space on the tiled patio was cleared away and looked recently swept, with debris and trash pushed to the sides. In the middle were several oriental rugs lined up, three by three.

He made a mental note that all were aligned east-to-west.

After scanning the terrain, he moved up the south side of the property and toward the front of the home, keeping inside the tall growth, unseen. So far, he had spotted only two men. Both wore paramilitary garb, similar to what the men wore who'd attacked him last night. Each was at a different point around the home, patrolling the grounds.

He worked his way around to the other side of the overgrown grounds, back toward the rear where he had started his surveillance. Within a few steps of a small shed, by the pool, the familiar but cruel smell of death crept into his nostrils. He peered through the shed's little window, dusted over by the elements, and saw the Maldonados. Their corpses were dried out like mummies at an Egyptian exhibit. The uniform holes in their heads confirmed their deaths had been quick.

They had been there for several months, meaning these men had probably been here that long, unnoticed all this time and yet very likely associated with those who attacked the US. This made him boil even more. He wanted to kill these bastards and he wanted to do it now. But patience was a virtue here. Because he didn't see any vehicles, and there had to be more men than just these two, he would come back in the evening, suspecting any others would return by then.

Frank made his way quietly to the river bounding the rear of the Maldonados' property, making sure that he had not been heard. The ATV was exactly where he'd left it, covered over by leafy branches from the ubiquitous river birches which stood at attention at each side of the river's banks. He mounted it and drove slowly south holding closely to the banks of this mostly dry small stream bed, soon to be bursting from seasonal rains.

He was anxious to get back home and gather what he needed. As far as Frank was concerned, it would still be Independence Day and he was anxious to start the fireworks.

Yes, he thought to himself, *an explosion would be wonderfully poetic irony for these bastards.*

☾ † ✡ ☯ 🦅

H assan Hameed was still seething, several hours after the American pig had thwarted his plans and killed three of his men, forcing a hasty retreat.

"Like dogs we ran," he emoted passionately to his men.

Hassan considered his failure as he and most of his remaining men marched down the highway toward Cartwright's compound.

This morning's mission should have been easy, as it was the last piece of their plan to secure a ten-mile corridor from I-10 and Stowell down to the Gulf. Hassan obtained the automatic gun records of all Texans in this area from a bribed records clerk at the Houston office of the ATF, who taxes and oversees ownership of older automatic weapons. He snickered at the stupidity of Americans to allow themselves to be restricted to only ancient automatic weapons and to have those tracked by their government and available for the taking.

From what he gathered, only one man had an automatic weapon—and that was Frank Cartwright. And although Cartwright was ex-Army, Hassan hadn't been worried, because they had the tactical advantage.

In the three months they had been living among the community, using American names and pretending to be relatives of the Maldonados', they learned a lot: Cartwright was mostly a loner, with no visitors. He came to town twice a month to share breakfast with a few other elderly men and gossip like old women. The few who knew him spoke of a nice man, who wasn't a hazard. Still, Hassan was given instructions to take out anybody with weapons sufficient enough to mount a fight against them.

Based on all of this intel, Hasson decided to take only a third of his men, sure that a retired elderly man, living alone, would be easily overpowered by their own firepower and numbers. They had planned to burn his house down if they couldn't shoot him or if he locked himself inside. County tax records listed it as a wooden ranch-style home. It should have been simple.

What Hassan didn't expect was that Cartwright had a fortified compound, and he was prepared for their attack. Only later, after it was too late, did Hassan realize their attack was too overt and without sufficient manpower.

Now, he would finish the job and get his revenge. Hassan grabbed his remaining men, leaving only two at the property to patrol in case anyone might stop by, even though no one had since they'd taken over the property from the previous occupants. And with the American electrical grid down and many vehicles incapacitated by the EMPs, he expected no one else would.

They parked their two remaining trucks a mile down the road—no one was likely to question this with abandoned vehicles everywhere—and walked to Cartwright's, watching for anyone who might pose a threat to them.

This time, when they quietly arrived at the house, it appeared empty as a tomb. And if he was there, it soon would be his permanent place of rest.

Immediately upon arrival, Hassan could see another problem. The house appeared to be a giant steel cage that they couldn't break into without more powerful explosives or an acetylene torch, neither of which they had. The windows were bulletproof and the doors were hardened, capable of withstanding even an RPG's blast. And yet Cartwright was nowhere to be seen.

Hassan's sniper had a Baher-23 sighted on Cartwright's tower, if he should appear. He never did. He was either inside hiding, or he had left.

A deep, tooth-rattling boom sounded from in back of the house; a thick swirl of smoke signaled its location. Hassan ran to it and saw four of his men—or rather pieces of them scattered from the blast. Cartwright had set up an IED by the back door and in the process killed more of his men.

"Ahhh!" Hassan screamed. "Burn it down. Burn it all down."

The one of the five remaining men who'd been carrying an open canister of gas splashed it every ten feet onto the side of the house. Others lit the splashes, creating a spider web of flames that crawled up the sides of the house which then widened until the entire house was ablaze.

"We're out of gasoline sir. We can't burn down the garage," said the man with the canister.

"Leave it," Hassan said. He turned to the rest of his men. "We need to leave. Cartwright is probably inside." He signaled and they started to walk briskly away from the house.

In the back of his mind, he knew it wasn't over. But he had to prepare for the next wave, and he couldn't afford to lose any more men. When the next wave came, none of this would matter as all the infidels would be brought to their knees.

Chapter 9

Lexi & Travis

Lexi and Travis plodded down the middle of the highway, their heads weighted down by gravity, fatigue, and insurmountable grief. For hours they'd been marching side- by side in silence. The only sounds in and around this highway were the squeals of their spinning rolla-board wheels and the cicadas chirping their songs of summer.

After their escape from the clutches of the two bums and her inadequate apology to Travis, they headed west on the highway, just as their father had instructed. Surprisingly, they found no one else on the road. Only the occasional abandoned car. This was just fine with Lexi. She couldn't deal with people right now; her brother was barely tolerable

Their plan was simple; walk west to get to Abe's house, figuring it would take three days to cover the sixty or so miles by foot. They didn't know why they were being sent there, only that it was safe and it's where their dad, in his dying breath, had sent them.

She was in no mood to talk or plan their next meal or to think about anything, for that matter. She was completely spent.

They stopped once, for what Travis called a potty break, then to hydrate and consume a quiet brunch of beef jerky and chips. She was already tiring of the jerky's taste and it made her thirsty, and that made her worried they'd guzzle their water supplies too quickly. *Too many worries for a little girl,* her mom would say.

It was during this stop that she decided to explore the reaches of what was now her bug-out bag. She finally understood what this term meant as a book inside it, called the *Prepper Brothers Guide to the Apocalypse: Surviving the First Seven Days After an EMP,* told her this was applied to a backpack that someone paranoid about an EMP-caused end-of-the-world event would use to survive in their attempt to make it back home. Ironically, this was exactly what they were trying to do. She didn't feel like flipping through more, intending to read it later, as her father obviously had this specific book in this pack for a reason.

There was also an iRonsnow radio with a hand-crank to generate power, and cords to charge a cell phone. She had Travis slowly turn the crank, while she attempted to get a radio station, and they powered up their father's cell phone. After a few minutes, she realized finding a radio station was futile. Perhaps they were too far away.

The cell phone turned on, although it only had a 7% charge. But right away, she could see it wouldn't matter. "No Network" told her what she needed to know. Either they were outside of cell service, which she didn't believe, or cell service was down. A dull fear crept into her then that maybe all services everywhere in the US were down. Maybe readers of the book she now carried weren't paranoid after all. Maybe this really was the end of the world. She shook her head free of these worries—*like I need more*—and tried to explore her daddy's phone.

So that she could fiddle with it, and because Travis continued to toss impatient gazes her way, she handed him a small, rectangular wood box that clanged when she shook it. "Why don't you see if you can figure out how to open this." She then set her sights on the phone, hoping maybe his phone book or texts might shed some more light on who he really was. She vaguely remembered him playing with it just before she nodded off, and just before the accident.

Unfortunately, this too would be fraught with frustration as his keypad was locked and she had no idea what four-numbered code to try. And with ten thousand combos, she'd have to play with it later. It was time to move on. They had a lot of territory to cover.

"Wow. Look Lex, there's medals in here!" Travis's eyes were wide as he held it out for her to see.

Lexi snatched the opened box from him. She should have given him the phone to figure out instead. "Not now, Travis. We need to get moving." She slid the box closed, and placed it and the other items back into the pack, where she had found them.

They continued their trek in silence.

With all the questions and images running through her head, Lexi couldn't dislodge the vision of the man she might have killed—or probably had killed—from her mind. No matter how much she hated her father for abandoning them, his dying in front of them both was more than enough death for either to deal with. But then she'd had to send a man to his eternal rest, and it was still the same day? She longed to be home and away from all this heavy thinking.

Travis had his own worries. He kept his head down, probably fearful to say anything again and receive another dose of his sister's wrath. He no doubt replayed the mental movie of his father dying in front of him, and then the old lady croaking too, and then his sister shooting one of the bad men stealing from him. Of course he lost his shit, forcing them to stop again.

Like the unstoppable surge of rolling tsunamis, with a first wave, and then another, and another, Travis did nothing to hold back his emotions and let loose with his little boy tears.

Once more, she was forced to stop and wait for him to finish. At one point he became inconsolable, unable to even acknowledge her.

She stood in front of him, her arms folded, barely tolerating his outburst, angry at her father for putting her into this mess and annoyed at her brother for not controlling his emotions better. She knew she should do the sisterly thing and wrap her arms around him, and comfort him, but she just didn't have any love to give. She didn't hate her brother, but she didn't really care for him much either. He was more of an inconvenience than anything else.

She approached him, desiring to offer comfort, not for him, but for her: she just needed him to shut up. She couldn't give him what he wanted.

Finally, she patted him on the head, like she would a dog who was worthy of her praise or sympathy. It was the most compassion she could muster.

He peered at her through foggy eyes; his quivers of sobs were slowly replaced by sniffles. With both longing and confusion, he examined this person with whom he had no relationship, their only connections being their blood and the hallway separating their rooms in the same house for years. He glared at her with equally cold eyes.

"Help ..."

Both of them held their collective breaths for a moment and listened.

A light breeze caused the thrumming cicada tune to crescendo and then fall again.

"Help," called a weak female voice, so close the "p" in "help" sounded like a soft bubble popping from a fresh piece of bubble gum.

"Come on Travis, we need to keep moving," Lexi said in a monotone voice. She turned to show she was going to walk away again.

"What about ..." He sniffled. "She needs our help."

"We can't help everyone, Travis." She searched her clouded mind for a reason. "Look what almost happened with that elderly couple. They would have slowed us down if ... Let's just keep moving."

"Help, please," the female voice called out again.

Travis was stalwart, remaining in place. His eyes bored holes into her.

"Please, I know someone is there," the voice pleaded.

"No, Travis," Lexi called as the boy started off toward a little tree on the side of the road, to the voice.

Reluctantly, she followed, not about to lose him again.

They stood at the edge of the road, near a BMW, and stared down at a slender woman in a business suit, who was momentarily startled to see them standing there.

"Oh, thank God."

She was lying on her back, somewhat propped up against the tree, under its shade. "Please help. I think I broke my ankle," she said softly. "I was walking after my car stalled and I wasn't paying attention and I fell. I'm so thirsty; I haven't had a drink since this morning's Starbucks. Do you have any Evian? I'd settle for a Perrier at this point."

Lexi lifted her head, ignoring the businesswoman's pleas. She had heard something else.

She fixed her gaze to the east, and watched an object flutter in the distance. It had no form; the heated air wafting off the baking pavement made it ghostly. Then the sound, very faint at first and then louder, until it was obvious to all of them; it was coming their way.

"It's a car?" Lexi asked incredulously. Something that had been so commonplace only this morning now seemed foreign and disturbing. "Come on, Travis, we need to hide."

"Hide? Are you crazy?" the businesswoman said. "That car may be our ticket out of here. I'm most certainly not going to hide."

Lexi grabbed Travis's arm and led him down the embankment as the vehicle's engine noise became predominant.

The woman pulled herself up into a sitting position. "Hon, you mind getting my shoe? I lost it dragging myself here. They're Bruno Malis, very expensive." She stressed the shoes' name as if to punctuate their importance.

The approaching vehicle was only a few hundred yards away.

Lexi snatched up the woman's shoe and handed it to her.

"Thanks ... Hey, wait, what are you doing?" the woman begged.

Lexi had grabbed Businesswoman under her pits and yanked her behind the tree. "Come on Travis. Back here with us."

He trudged over and all three looked from behind and through the tree, waiting for the car to pass.

"So, why are we hiding?" Businesswoman asked.

"Shhhhh."

"That car can't hear us," Her voice elevating as the vehicle was just about to pass. "It's going to—"

The Jeep Willys hit its brakes hard, sliding to a stop and leaving thick black tracks on the road.

The driver pushed himself up so that he was standing in his driver's seat, and looked directly at them, like he was trying to find them.

"He must have seen us," the businesswoman whispered, but much too loud for comfort.

The Jeep's driver swung himself out of the car and quickly walked their way. Right away, they could see he wasn't looking for them; he was only interested in the BMW.

☾ ✝ ✡ ☯ 🦅

Rodie figured he had enough time for one or two more hauls before he had to return. Clyde and the others were spread out. After he had realized what had happened—that all new cars had died on the road—Clyde saw an opportunity for himself as well as each of his lieutenants. They'd first take from the cars that had stalled on the main roads and the highway. Then, tonight they'd hit some of the houses. Rodie found that most of the cars were slim pickins because most folks took everything they had packed with them when they left their vehicles behind, but it was Clyde's idea, and no one argues with Clyde. Plus, they got to keep half of their haul, and have the full protection of their gang. And if they found anything or anyone special, "there were perks," he had told them.

The only two cars that yielded anything interesting so far were the rentals. Their owners must have abandoned them figuring they'd get help and then return. So they had left their bags locked in their trunks. The red BMW caught his eye and he was happy to see it was a rental. Maybe there was something good in there.

He reached onto his Jeep's floor and grabbed the crowbar. Some of these locks took finesse and some of them force. BMWs were often real easy. He walked to the front passenger-side window and calmly smashed it in, and then dragged the tool around the window frame to clear away the excess glass. Leaning in, he hit the trunk release, which gave a satisfying click.

Inside, he found several pink bags. The first one opened up easily, revealing makeup and meticulously packed clothes. He held up an itty-bitty thong with his thumb and a forefinger and smiled at the image of the woman who must have worn these.

"Hey, leave that alone. That's mine," hollered a female voice behind a tree, off the road.

Rodie squinted to see, walking toward the sound, still clutching the panties.

As he caught a glimpse of a barefooted woman in a business suit, his smile spread over his whole face. "Whoa, yah a looker aren't yah? Let's go back to my place an party."

With this, she screamed, looking behind her as if someone was going to come and help her.

"You're far mo valuable dan any other cargo. You better come wit me. Clyde will want to meet yah."

He dragged her kicking and screaming to his Jeep. Really, she offered only minimal resistance until she started biting, then he let go of her. Rodie pulled out a radio and spoke into it, very businesslike. "Hey dis is Rodie, I've got a hot-looking bid-ness woman fo Clyde, but she too much for me to handle. She nearly bit off my finga. Bring some guys to mile makah sixty-seven?"

He glanced at the woman, who was trying to crawl away into the bushes.

"10-4, Rodie. I'll be there in five. Over."

"Shit!" That was Zach, Clyde's asshole brother. He'll probably not even mention to Clyde that he was the one who found her.

"Thanks for your good work, Rodie," boomed Clyde's voice from the radio.

Rodie smiled at that. He then wondered how he could make it better for Clyde. He would prefer she'd have the proper clothes. So, he went back to the BMW, retrieved the woman's bags and his crowbar, and tossed them back into his Jeep.

☾ ✝ ✡ ☯ 🦅

L exi and Travis sat quietly in the thick brush, about twenty feet from the road. They had receded there when the woman yelled. Lexi held the revolver in front of her, following this man who called himself Rodie with the barrel.

Travis whispered to his sister, "Are we going to let this man take her?"

"Yep," she said.

While they waited for the other men to arrive to complete the woman's abduction, they did nothing to stop it. Lexi reasoned that this highway was now like their lives, and the lives of everyone who used it. It gave them a route to some nebulous place that might provide them safety and survival. But it also led to death and the evil men who laid claim to it. And because of this, the more time they spent on this highway, the less likely they would survive.

Every moment that passed as they waited for the men to disappear made their destination seem more unlikely. They were running out of time. They had to find some way to get to Abe's place quicker than their feet would take them.

Chapter 10

Frank

With each churning swirl of smoke rising in the sky, the burning pit in his stomach grew. Yet, he approached his property slowly, careful to not crash his ATV.

There was only one reason why there'd be so much smoke: house fire. And because his nearest neighbor was a mile away, he knew it was his house that was burning.

Anxiousness turned into full-fledged worry as he considered what this could mean for him. Not only was he probably homeless, but with the fire, he may have lost all of the life-giving supplies that he had assembled over the years. Everything on his prep list may have been reduced to ashes.

He should have been ready for this.

Besides his military training, Frank had become fairly prepared for an EMP, guided by many sources, including a series of *Prepper Brothers Guides* that got him started on prepping for different types of apocalypses. Since he was already covered for EMPs, prepping for a CME was easy. Then he prepped for a pandemic; then nuclear attack; then for economic collapse. He tried to consider every contingency. Aside from a zombie outbreak, which he thought was as stupid as stupid could get, he had prepped for everything. Well, except for this.

Frank cursed himself for not having thought of this obvious tactic and for not having done a better job securing his supplies. He should have gone underground or gone all metal or metal-lined concrete, like his detached garage.

Maybe that was still intact. He could only hope.

As he neared his burning home, his mind riffled through all the ways he could have done a better job. As each yard passed, he craned his neck upward to try and see past the growth that obstructed his view. Instead, his dread rose with each billowing cloud that filled the heavens.

And with each self-excoriation, Frank began to realize the biggest problem wasn't something for which he could have prepared. Oh, he knew he couldn't have prepared for everything. But there was something noticeably absent that affected all his preps. It was something that he hadn't had to worry about in the Army.

He was alone.

If he had had a companion, that person might have been able to defend his home before it was destroyed. But he had no one. Right after he retired from the Army, his wife couldn't stand the cold unemotional man he had become, and she took off for California. Then, Frank hid from his life, in Texas, comforted by his own lie that he didn't need anyone else. And although he kept a few friends in town, he never had anyone come to his house, fearful that they would accidentally tell others what he had. Fearful that one day, someone would try and take his stuff. Well these asshole terrorists did one worse than that; they destroyed his stuff, and likely with it, his life.

A thundering boom pulled his attention once again skyward. He yanked hard on the ATV's brakes, stopping abruptly. His jaw slacked; his anxiety was at full throttle as he watched a thick, mushrooming, mud-colored cloud blossom over his house, or what was left of it. His propane supply most likely fueled that sickening sound, which confirmed to him and anyone for miles around that his house was destroyed.

He popped the clutch, spun his wheels and was back up to a slow seven miles per hour, about as fast as he'd dare travel along the river bed. Then he heard smaller explosions. First a few, then hundreds of them, so rapid as if was if they were igniting almost at once; like giant bags of popcorn popping from a microwave, only much louder. That would be either the primers or his actual ammunition.

In spite the roaring sounds coming from Frank Cartwright's home roast, and even though his ATV was suppressed for noise, Frank still parked a half-mile away and approached quietly on foot, hoping to surprise a few of these bastards and make them pay for what they'd done.

Before he even ascended the small rise to his back yard, he could easily confirm his house's destruction. The only good news, from what he was seeing, was that except for a few random marks from the errant bullets, it looked like his garage was intact.

Frank had the selector of his slung AK on Auto and he pointed it wildly back and forth with each step closer, hoping that he could kill just one more of these guys.

A small smirk crawled onto his face as stepped over the severed hand of one of his enemy. A few steps farther, he could see more body parts: a foot, a leg, and finally the killing field's origination. It was his booby trap. It would have gone off when they tried to break in, and by the looks of all the carnage, it took out at least three of them. He was hoping to have been more personally involved in his revenge, but this small reward was better than nothing.

At first glance, there didn't appear to be anyone here. They had once again left him to pick up from the havoc they'd left. This seemed strange, because he'd have thought that burning down his house was a diversion to get him to return so they could finally kill him, for whatever purpose they had. Just in case it was a trap, he gave his burning home a wide berth and focused his attention on places where the enemy would be hiding, waiting for him to amble by.

But there was no one around; he was sure of that.

As Frank stared at the bubbling lacquer finish on the burning sign, a recent gift from his godson that said "Casa De Frank," a thought sprang up in his mind: they must have assumed that he was trapped inside his home and so they burned it down, hoping to kill him in the process. As he was without supplies, they might ultimately succeed—just a little torturously slower than they had thought.

After circling around the flaming metal shell of his home, he proceeded to his garage. There was no food stored there, but he did have his bug-out supplies already packed in his truck, and some extra cans of fuel. So, he could leave. But where would he go? This was his home.

None of this mattered right now. He could figure out his accommodations and food later. There was a much larger problem he had to address. He needed to neutralize these men who had not only attacked and damaged him, but had attacked and damaged his country. Yet with almost all his ammo and firearms burned in his home, he lacked the firepower to take them on.

He had just two weapons on him: his AK and Berretta 9mm, and maybe one-hundred-fifty rounds of ammo for each. He had stupidly tossed the salvaged guns and gear from the early-morning attackers into his now smoldering home. It was barely enough to defend himself. Certainly it wouldn't be enough to mount any sort of offensive. And he just couldn't do it alone.

He was pretty sure no one else even knew these terrorists were here. So, it was up to him to do something about them even if he died trying.

Once again, he felt the tug of obligation. His country was depending on him. Every terrorist he let live would be responsible for the death of more Americans. He couldn't let them live any longer. It was his responsibility to end their lives, so that others could continue with theirs.

Still, Frank knew he needed help. And he knew right where he'd get it.

Chapter 11

Lexi & Travis

L exi's anxiety grew with each step they took.

Every moment she thought she'd heard another approaching vehicle of murderers and rapists; every growing shadow threatening to leap from the brush, an assault from men who wanted to harm them; every abandoned car, a monster that would open up and consume them. Yet, with each step, she was sure their only path to safety was getting to the home of their father's friend, Abe. And the only way to get there was this highway. So, they marched as fast as her injured feet would take them, while they each dragged their baggage.

She had no idea of the time, nor did she care; she only knew that it was late. Each glance at the darkening sky reminded her of this, further adding to her mounting anxiety. They had to find shelter for the evening and then find bicycles and then get back on the highway and then get to Abe's.

A residential turnoff to a small housing development presented them with a possibility of solace, and maybe even transportation. Perhaps someone would take them in, or there would be a park they could sleep in; anywhere would be fine, as long as it was off the highway, where danger lurked with every footstep.

The first house they approached was a fairly new single-story, with an empty garage, open and inviting. Gift-wrapped were two bicycles, a man's and woman's, lying against the clutter in back. They felt to her more like morsels of cheese in a giant mousetrap, luring them in.

Was it worth the risk?

After trekking up the inclined driveway, they stood at the garage entrance, hesitant to take a step inside. Lexi glared at the dead garage door as if warning it not to close on them.

Two sets of light stains on the concrete told her that both the occupants and their vehicles were probably away, and perhaps never returning.

"Someone forgot to shut the garage door when they left for work this morning," Travis observed, probably accurately. Then he perked up and pointed at the back wall.

"Look! Two bicycles; one for me and one for you," Travis looked up to his sister wearing a huge grin and wide eyes, his face pleading for them to walk into the trap.

What the hell.

She was exhausted. If it wasn't a trap, it was a sanctuary. She almost didn't care which at this point.

As they both softly treaded into the garage, Lexi noticed the door at the back was ajar, its frame busted inward. She hesitated for a moment, tossing around in her mind their chances with each potential action. The safe thing to do would be to take the bikes and run. But, they needed a place to sleep; it was dark, and she was hoping whoever had broken in had taken what they wanted and left. And if she was right, and the homeowners were stranded in broken-down cars, they may have lucked into a semi-safe place to sleep.

Swiftly, she unslung her backpack, withdrew the revolver and flashlight, and flung it back, now wearing the straps over both shoulders. She tilted her head to Travis and whispered, "Stay behind me and be prepared to run if I tell you. We need to make sure there's no one else inside."

The door offered no resistance.

"Hello?" she called through the opening, afraid to say anything too loud. The darkness was foreboding, causing prickles on the back of her neck as she led them inside. As soon as she clicked the button, the flashlight bathed everything in front of her in a white glow. She steadied the gun on her flashlight hand, and then realized why the protagonists of all cop shows did it this way.

Their footsteps were dull and quiet. Thankfully that was all she heard.

After checking out the entire house, her nerves calming, Lexi felt satisfied they were alone. Several of the drawers and closets were upended, presumably by whoever broke in. She wondered what they were searching for; probably money and guns.

Maybe she had been riding on adrenaline the past several hours; maybe it was a momentary feeling of safety, when every moment since the crash she felt like they were in peril; maybe it was all of the walking; regardless of the reason, Lexi was beat. Travis yawned, telling her he too was tired.

"Safety first!" That was on one of the pages she saw in the Prepper Brothers book in her father's pack.

Without electricity, the garage doors posed a safety problem. First the main garage door. She noticed the small handle on the cord and wondered if it would be as simple as pulling on it to close the door.

"Yes, that's what the handle is for," Travis said with a giant bear-about-to-hibernate yawn.

An aluminum ladder she took down from the wall provided her the boost she needed to reach the handle, but it wouldn't budge. She shot him a glance that said "Help me!" Travis just shrugged his shoulders in a wordless "Got me."

The only thing she could think to do was hang from the rope and use all her one hundred pounds. She bounded off the ladder, clutching at the handle like a trapeze. On her arc downward, the rope snapped and she landed on her hip hard on the concrete.

Epic fail.

"Bet that didn't go as well as you thought," Travis said with a slight smile and then headed through the door into the house, leaving her to figure it out for herself. He was going to find a place to sleep.

"At least take the bicycles inside," she huffed, while rubbing the newest place on her body that hurt like hell.

While Travis rolled each bicycle inside, she set her mind on securing the door to the house, giving up entirely on the garage door. She rummaged through some drawers in a chest, abutting a wall with precisely mounted pegs of tools. Next to this was a table saw, covered in sawdust.

She wasn't sure what she was looking for, but knew she would find some solution in this handyman area.

A wedge!

That sprang to her mind, maybe from the Prepper Brothers book she thumbed through earlier or her own memories. By the table saw, in the corner of the garage, were dozens of little pieces of wood in a pile of sawdust, scraps from a project the owner would never finish.

She snagged two wedges with 45-degree angles. After kicking both under the door, she pulled on the handle and thought it might be secure enough. She checked the two other exits, the front door and back slider. They were locked and secure. She moved the bikes from where Travis had left them, and leaned them against the wall by the slider. If they needed to run, they'd exit there with their new bikes.

She hated the thought of stealing, but reasoned that the bikes would be taken by someone else soon enough. More importantly, she was excited that they could cover the distance to Abe's in as little as a day, instead of the two or more they were facing if they continued by foot. Her feet would be happier too, as they ached like they never had before.

They both felt weird about sleeping in the owner's beds, especially after taking their bicycles, so they agreed to sleep on the living room sofa and love seat. Once the decision was made, Travis immediately flopped into the love seat; sleep came to him almost instantly.

Lexi examined the living room more closely. The owners were baseball fanatics. Their walls were plastered with their passion: baseball pennants adorned the stuccoed surfaces everywhere, with pictures of individual players and teams—all autographed—filling the spaces between. A lone baseball bat rested with reverence on two clawlike braces above the fireplace mantel. It was autographed by an Evan L-something. The blue or black—she couldn't tell with her flashlight—etchings were almost illegible. Like monks praying to their elevated deity, baseball caps with the initials TB filled the mantel space below.

She slipped the revolver and flashlight into their proper places in the pack and kicked off her God-awful boots. Then she sank into the soft leather cushions of the sofa. Left with the company of her own thoughts, she wondered about some of the unanswered mysteries. Why was there no power anywhere? Why were all the cars broken down? She connected the conversation of Don and Ron at Simpson's World Market and the cover of the Prepper Brothers guide, the lone book she was carrying. Emblazoned on its front was "EMP" or electro-magnetic pulse. Was it possible that this was the cause of everything breaking down?

It struck her as a little too coincidental that if it was an EMP that caused all this, the only book her father happened to be carrying in his pack was about how to survive one. So far everything he had done seemed to have purpose, in the clarity of hindsight: the list of things to buy, the so called bug-out pack of stuff that included a revolver—the only type of gun she'd ever shot—and a book specifically about *Surviving the First Seven Days After an EMP*. Her head swam with a myriad of chaotic thoughts.

Travis startled her slightly, mouthing something from a nightmare for less than a minute, until his breathing returned to a peaceful rhythm.

She wanted to think more about their situation, or read more from the book her father left her, but she was too exhausted to entertain any more thoughts. Quickly, she fell asleep.

She dreamt of an orange mushroom cloud, growing before her. Its billowing form grew larger and larger, enveloping the whole sky. In a moment of panic, she realized that she was going to be consumed by these billowing and fiery clouds. Just before the blast's flames hit, her father appeared and jumped in front of it. He flashed his familiar crooked smile at her and then wrapped his arms around her as protection from the conflagration. She scrunched her eyes closed, to protect them from the molten prickles trying to force them open. She knew she shouldn't look, but she couldn't help herself; she cracked a lid open and peeked. But the sun's single searing eye gazed right back at her.

Then the blast punched at her and talked to her, and when she thought she might pass out from its unending brightness, it punched her again and yelled at her, "You alive?"

A sharp pain hit her chest and then her eyes flicked open into the beam of a bright flashlight and a gruff voice demanding, "Hey son, you alive?"

Terror once again consumed Lexi as she was prodded by what at first felt like a metal rod, but which she realized was the barrel of a shotgun.

Chapter 12

Frank

F rank pounded so hard on the security door that it seemed the tiny single-story home it was attached to shuddered in response.

"Gunny Sergeant Aimes, I need you on the double," He yelled at the door and then stepped back and waited so that its alarmed occupants could see him.

The scent of something sweet and familiar wafted through the door's screen.

Fresh baked cookies.

Footsteps sounded from the clatter in the kitchen and approached, out of sight. A small, but broad framed man appeared abruptly. Although the screen obstructed much, Frank could easily see the man's bald head, close-cut gray beard, and the prominent tattoo on his thick bicep, an eagle perched on top of the world, with an anchor mounted in it, and the letters USMC below.

"Major Cartwright, what a nice surprise," the man said, unlatching and pushing through the security door an arm with a small white plate on which sat a single chocolate chip cookie. "Susie just made them; nothing better than cookies right out of the oven."

Frank accepted the cookie and immediately tore into it. He'd just become homeless, their country'd been nuked by invading Islamists, but it didn't mean he couldn't stop and enjoy one of Susan's freshly baked cookies.

After her stroke a couple of years ago, she took up baking as therapy. In a short time, she perfected the cookie. Then the doctors diagnosed her with some unnamable variation of Parkinson's. So she baked even more, although not without help. To make extra cash for the doctor's bills and meds not covered by insurance, Gunny sold them in town. Susie's cookies were a big hit among the community, not only because they were helping the Aimes family, but because they were so damned good.

"I know," Aimes said, seeing the delight on his friend's face. "I'm just glad we've got a propane stove and solar power. My neighbors are down, and best I can figure, so is the rest of the town. Did you hear we were nuked?"

"It's far worse than that, Gunny," Frank said as he popped the last morsel in his mouth and licked off a hot chocolate chip stuck to his finger. "They got at least six nukes off, and two at high altitudes. Three major cities are gone."

"Holy crap, sir. Where?" Aimes propped himself against his doorway. He knew Frank had a shortwave and no doubt he would vet his intel, so it must be credible.

"DC is gone; we probably won't know who's in charge for weeks."

"Damn." Aimes's face crumpled in disbelief.

"New York City is also gone, so is Jacksonville—"

"—Jacksonville?"

"Yeah, the base. And Chicago is toast. There were a couple other bases, but I haven't been able to find out which."

Aimes whistled at this. "Who got us, Sir? Was it the fricking Chinese?"

"No, it's Islamic terrorists, and ... they're here."

"They're here in Stowell? You mean, right now?" Aimes hurried out of the propped-open doorway, letting the security door clank closed. At the edge of his porch he peered down both directions of his street.

"No they're out at the Maldonados' place, a couple of miles from mine. They torched my place, but I've killed at least six of the bastards."

"Oorah, sir."

"That's why I'm here. I want to get the rest of them. I don't know how many more there are, but I can't do it alone. They burned down my house and destroyed most of my guns and ammo. I've only got maybe one-hundred-fifty rounds for my AK and Berretta. I need at least a couple more guys to send these bastards back to Allah."

Gunny's shoulders drooped, along with his whole demeanor. "You know I'd like nothing more than to kick Bin Laden's ass, but ..." He looked toward the house, and lowered his voice. "Susie has gotten pretty bad, as I told you last week. I don't like leaving her for more than a few minutes, anymore. I'm all she's got ..." His gaze drifted to the ground and then sprang back up. "Have you talked to Grimes?"

"I visited him first. He broke his leg this morning, falling off his roof. He said he saw the flash of one of the nukes—although it would have been too far from here ...

Anyway, he lost his balance and, well he's not much good for a special op, in his condition."

"Look, Major, sorry for stating the obvious, but we ain't exactly spring chickens anymore," he said, glancing at Frank's brace, which he had usually left at home each time he'd get together for lunch in town with the guys. "What about Sheriff McCullum, and his deputies?"

"Already tried. Of course, the dispatcher can't reach them because the radio doesn't work. Besides, this is not some two-bit drug gang. These are well-armed and probably well-trained terrorists. They need to be killed, not arrested. The sheriff and his men would be out of their element and probably cut down as soon as they showed up."

At that instant, Frank knew this mission of his was probably a mistake. Gunny was right. What the hell was he thinking, trying to take on a bunch of terrorists himself?

A long pause continued as both men awkwardly stared inside themselves.

Frank thought, *Oh screw it.*

"Thanks Gunny. I understand. Please give my best to Susie." Frank slapped Aimes on the shoulder and handed back the plate. "Another amazing cookie," he said as he carefully navigated down the front steps.

"Major, you're not going out on your own, are you?"

"Take care of that wife, Gunny, and keep your eyes open," Frank said without turning to look at his friend. He hobbled into his truck and drove away.

Unlike Aimes, Frank didn't really have anyone that depended on him. The only family he had left were his two godchildren and his best friend, but they had each other; he wasn't likely to see them—it had been many years, in spite of the texts promising otherwise. And even if they did visit his ranch, there was nothing to see, and they would be in peril if these terrorists were allowed to continue using his neighbor's property as their base.

His reasoning led him to one conclusion: He'd take care of this himself. With a little help from above, he wasn't about to let these bastards take over his country without a fight. He'd take out as many as he could, and if he died in the process, so be it.

He felt his old friend adrenaline start its familiar course through his veins, preparing him for the inevitability of his fate. Plunging the accelerator down, he steered north on Smithy Road, toward the enemy and his destiny.

☾ † ✡ ☯ 🦅

Hassan listened to the radio carefully, dialing the transceiver to the five different designated stations. His army would be arriving soon and so he was required by Farook to listen between 8 and 8:15 every evening for the call. It would be repeated once every three minutes on one of the five channels.

He looked at his watch. It was 20:17. So, it wouldn't be tonight.

He dialed to their pre-selected channel and then keyed the mic. "One-Foxtrot. This is one-Tom-two." He let go and the radio spewed a staticy crackle.

After a minute he tried again, "One-Foxtrot. This is one-Tom-two."

Crackle.

Just before he was about to try again, a deep voice sounded, crisp and without static, "This is one-Foxtrot, go ahead."

Hassan clicked the mic harder, his heart beginning to race. "Package is not being delivered tonight. Repeat, no delivery tonight."

"Copy that. One-Foxtrot is out."

He turned down the volume, making sure the crackle of static was still audible, just in case Farook called him later. Otherwise, he was done for the night. His pulse slowed as there was no chance he would upset his superior this evening. He wasn't about to report the fact that six of his men had been killed by some insignificant infidel. There would be time enough to report this to Farook.

He'd heard stories about Abdul beheading his own soldiers in the field when they disappointed him.

No, he would wait till after Phase Three had begun and there was no time to find a replacement for him. He would prove himself on the battlefield during Phase Three, and then he would tell Farook.

There was a knock at the door. "Excuse me, sir," said Sayeed, who stuck his head through the doorway first, then his body. Hassan beckoned him closer so that he could see him better, as the mesh of the metal cage he sat in obstructed everything in the room. He spun his chair around to face the cage's open doorway and waited until his number two man appeared. He watched Sayeed tentatively walk past each corner. Hassan couldn't help feel like he was some prisoner in a high-tech jail cell, waiting for his daily beating—that was another place. He just didn't want to hear of any more setbacks.

"Sorry to interrupt, Hassan, but now that it is night, how many men do you want to put on watch?"

Relieved at such a simple question, Hassan thought about this, rubbing his burning eyes, attempting to massage the fatigue out of them. It had been a crazy day, from the jubilation of taking down the American grid and confirmation that their nuclear strikes were successful, to these two setbacks at the hands of a single American. He couldn't afford any more failures.

"Post four on six-hour staggered shifts, allowing up to four hours' sleep for those not on watch. Tell the men I will shoot them myself if I catch anyone sleeping on watch. I'm going to get some sleep now. Wake me up in four. Don't wake me before then unless it's important."

"Yes, sir," Sayeed said resolutely. He jogged around the cage and slipped back out the door, clicking it closed.

Hassan got up from his chair and shut the steel mesh door behind him with a metallic clunk. He glanced through at the radio equipment, locked in for the night, making sure once again that the volume was high enough if Farook should call. It was probably unnecessary to shut the door, as there shouldn't be any more blasts and their ensuing EMPs. But being a cog in someone else's battle plans meant that he would never know and his orders were to keep it closed at all times.

He trudged over to the small cot at the far corner of what was once a bedroom. His bed was a lot more austere than the palatial American bed that had been here. His was just a piece of canvas stretched between four legs. His headboard comprised cases of new AK-103s, a newer version of the ubiquitous AK-47s, that would be used for the next wave of destruction he would lead if Allah so willed it.

He reached down and withdrew his hand-held radio from its charger and made sure that the volume was up high enough that he would hear if his men called him, and put it back so it would continue receiving a trickle charge.

He tumbled onto the hard surface and bunched the single pillow underneath his head. Reaching over to an open crate that served as a bedside table, Hassan grabbed his well-worn Quran. He thumbed to Surah 4:57, a verse he knew by heart. After the first sentence, he was fast asleep, dreaming of the virgins he would soon enjoy in Paradise.

☪ † ✡ ☯ ☸

Frank crept as silently as he could, as his right leg wasn't cooperating too well. He more or less had to drag it and hop with the other. If he hadn't been wearing his brace, he'd be unable to walk at all.

The warm, moonless night was perfect for an evening op. If only he were younger and in better shape, he might have looked forward to what was coming. But as Gunny reminded him, he was no spring chicken. God knows he felt every one of his 57 years with each labored step.

Once he could see the house's light and his first target, he slid into the heavy brush. Branches slapped wildly at his face, darkened with a mud he'd created and then smeared all over to help him blend into the night. After each step he'd stop and listen to make sure no one heard him. It was a slow process, sneaking up on a kill. He just wished he could have retrieved his AR-15 with suppressor so he could take each one out from a safe distance. He still had his AK at the ready, but that was purely for defensive purposes as it would eliminate the surprise. The AK was perhaps perfect for this; its short barrel didn't get entangled in the brush, and it never jammed. And although heavy, its weight felt comforting to him, like a favorite sweatshirt during the winter.

When he was only a few feet from his target, he slowly slid his weapon around to his back, and withdrew his SOG Seal fixed-blade knife from its sheath.

For a minute or two, he was motionless, listening to the light breeze rustle the leaves, an orchestra of crickets chirping at the night, and the slight snore of his target, somehow sleeping while standing up. He inched forward, forgetting his knee, all his systems operating at maximum efficiency to complete his mission: killing this man silently.

He reached out, slowly at first and then rapidly, like a snake striking, grabbing the man's mouth to muffle his scream, and then driving his knife deep into the man's neck, severing his carotid. The man offered almost no resistance, just a slight stiffening when a deathly realization woke him. He folded over into a heap on the home's overgrown lawn. Frank's body mimicked the man's as he kept his hand over the man's mouth, intending to flex his knees to let the body land silently on the ground. But his right knee wouldn't respond to his mind's command, and his brace did its job and stopped his progression downward, sending him forward. Now off balance, Frank let go of the man who hit the ground with a resounding thud, and metal struck rock, making a startling cymbal-like crash in the calm.

Frank tumbled into the dying man, his wrist connected to the knife's lanyard, handle still protruding from the man's neck. His mind pictured him rolling over the man, like some circus performer, and perhaps he would have except for his arm had gotten stuck under the body. Without any grace whatsoever, he landed hard on top of it, yanking his arm in an unnatural way.

Unnerved, he withdrew his knife and flopped onto his back, his AK jamming into his side, causing a jolt of new pain into a different part of his body.

Holy Christ, this getting-old shit really sucks, he yelled in his head.

A detached voice called to him from the darkness.

He lay motionless, trying to get a mental bead on the voice, while wiping his soiled knife against his stomach and sliding it back into its sheath.

The voice called again. He recognized the language instantly. It was Farsi. It was coming from the back of the property, and it was closer this time.

Frank rolled over onto his front, away from the approaching voice, to release his AK. Then he rolled back beside the dead man, using him as cover, his rifle pointing in the direction of the approaching voice. Knowing he was about to make some noise, he quickly examined the perimeter of the home. There didn't appear to be any other combatants, just the oncoming voice.

He could see the form approaching. It called again. The words sounded somewhat familiar, even though Frank's

Farsi was pretty rusty at this point. "Mohammad, are you sleeping?"

Frank had the man dead to rights. But before he could squeeze his trigger, he heard a click behind him and a command in a British accent. "Don't shoot or you're dead." The muzzle of a rifle racked into his neck to prove the Brit behind him had the means to carry out his threat.

"Hassan, sir. You're up. What are you doing?" asked the approaching man in a plaintive tone.

"Silence, fool. There may be others," barked Hassan, who pushed the muzzle harder into the back of Frank's neck. "Hands! I will not ask again."

Frank's hands rose quickly. *How had he not heard this man coming up to him?*

He heard someone else approach from behind and knew it was now or never.

Frank's left arm whipped back to the muzzle pressing against his head. He grabbed it and was about to pull back hard to knock Hassan off balance, when two loud shots rang out right next to him and then several suppressed rounds farther away. As Frank yanked at Hassan's rifle, he looked up to find the approaching man had already fallen. As Hassan's weapon came free, Frank spun around, grabbing his rifle and swinging it to bear on Hassan and the other approaching man, but Hassan collapsed right in front of him. In the background, a few meters away, he heard a suppressed rifle firing again, and again.

Training his rifle on the thick bald form appearing in the darkness, behind him, he knew instantly it was his friend, Aimes. He couldn't see his face, but he imagined he wore his usual big smile.

"Are you all right, Major?" Gunny whispered, kneeling next to him.

"Damn glad it's you Gunny. That Grimes doing his thing?"

"Of course. Do you know how many more—"

They heard two more sets of boots, running from the back of the property. Frank had already spun around and was about to fire, when Grimes's rifle erupted with two more precise hits. One man flopped face first, all life removed from his body; the other jerked in mid-step, knocked sideways by the powerful round that ripped off much of his shoulder blade, and then he continued his run in their direction.

Frank felt and heard the suppressed rifle, Gunny's .45 handgun, and his AK all assault the man with a salvo of rounds. As if the man hit an exploding wall, his body appeared to bounce backward in a black mist.

"That was fun. Any more Hajis to kill?" Grimes asked, as he hopped their way from the darkness.

Still on the ground, Frank had already swung back to face both men, now leaning over him, eager to hear his orders. They'd never served together, but after sharing stories over the years, he'd imagined what these men would be like in combat, and his assumptions had been correct.

"I suspect that may be all or we'd probably have heard them by now, but be on alert." He didn't need to thank them for showing up. That was for later, over beers.

"So these are the bastards who torched your house, Major?" Gunny asked.

"What's left of them," Frank answered while he frisked Hassan, who he suspected was the leader.

Using a small but powerful Maglite, Frank inspected the body from head to toe. The face looked familiar, although he had only seen a flash of it earlier; he suspected it was the same man who had jumped into the third truck during the initial assault on his compound. Hassan was dressed in civilian clothes: jeans, a button-down Oxford, and leather loafers. He grabbed Hassan's wallet and a set of keys and shoved those into his vest for later inspection. When he grabbed the man's rifle, also an AK, he instantly knew something was different about it from every other AK he'd ever seen in the battlefield: it was unfired, still smelling of its packing oil.

"It smells brand new, Major."

"Yeah, I noticed that too. Come on; let's have a look and see if we can figure out what these pricks are doing here." Frank took Gunny's offered hand and was pulled up on his left leg. He put some weight on his right and a burst of pain erupted. He'd definitely screwed it up more. Well, at least half his body worked all right.

The three of them trudged carefully to the back of the property to look for clues about why these men were here and what they had planned to do after the nukes.

Chapter 13

Lexi and Travis

"Get up right now!" demanded a voice eager for violence.

The flashlight's bright beam lost strength as the man holding it backed away, perhaps in an attempt to get a better angle to shoot from.

Lexi swung her bare feet to the floor, her hands reflexively searching for her father's pack, and the revolver inside.

"Ya lookin fer dis?" The man cast his light on her bag below him, along with both their roller bags. "Anyone else in da house?"

"No, we're alone," she responded in raspy words, barely recognizing her own tired voice. She rose to her feet and caught a glimpse of his face for the first time; a shot of recognition hit her like an ocean wave. It was the driver of the Jeep, who had abducted the businesswoman earlier. Rodie.

"Ya better not be lying bout dis ... Say, how old are ya?" he asked, his light blinding her again. It moved up and down her body, from her face, to her chest, and back to her face.

She thought she might hyperventilate as she knew where his thoughts were going.

The man walked up to Lexi and grabbed her chin, and inspected her face like she was a T-bone he wanted to sink his teeth into. His filthy hand roughly turned her gaze away from him and then back. The foulness of his breath was unimaginable. Then he let go and grabbed her chest, squeezing a breast through her shirt.

She slapped him away, revolted.

"Woah, ya woman ain't yah?"

Even in the glare she could see his disgusting, toothy smile.

"I thin I found Clyde anotha." He released her and walked away, before flashing his light at her again. "Ya best sit down now and wait for me to return."

He kept the beam on her, waiting for her to respond to his command. "Sit-da-fu-down!" he hollered.

As she fell into the couch, she shot a glance at Travis, who sat wild-eyed, unmoving. Then she caught a glimpse out the window of a large truck—the same one she had seen earlier today that had pulled up to help Rodie drag the businesswoman away—parked in front of the house on the street. Two men proceeded up a walkway, toward the house.

Rodie marched to the front door and fumbled with the lock. Lexi guessed that he must have entered through the garage door and that her wedges didn't work. Rodie put his shotgun down and stuck the flashlight into an armpit to free both hands.

Something snapped inside of Lexi. Perhaps it was the realization that she would only get one chance at this, or maybe it was the horror of what would come if she did nothing. She leapt off the couch, hopped onto the hearth, and grabbed the autographed bat from its display. Like some psychotic barefooted ninja, she practically flew to the door, lifting her arms back, ready to strike. Rodie was just pulling the door open when she put her whole body and arms into it.

Home run!

She wasn't sure what sound she expected. Perhaps her mind anticipated the crack when bat meets ball, sending it out of the park on a warm summer afternoon. But this bat connecting with Rodie's head felt and sounded like striking a ripe watermelon. At first she thought the bat would bounce back, but it sailed through and splashed warm wetness all over her. The inertia from her bat propelled him forward into the door with a louder thunk.

Another man was just entering from the other side when the door crashed into him, knocking him away. She clawed at the lock attempting to bolt it before they could try to open it again. A muffled voice yelled profanities about his nose being broken.

"Come on, Travis, grab your bag and run out the back!"

Lexi seized the shotgun, figuring it would be handy, and dropped the bat.

"What about the bikes?"

"Leave them. There's no time," she barked, gathering her boots, bags, and yanking open the slider.

The front door banged, a muffled voice yelled more profanities behind it, and a dark face appeared at the window and flipped on a flashlight, illuminating the empty living room.

They bounded outside, clutching their belongings, and ran straight for the back of the property, careful to not stumble in the darkness.

Lexi heard a crash from the house, but she didn't look back. They just ran into the night.

☾ † ✡ ☯ 🦅

"**H**ey, Zach, look at poor ol Rodie," a short man pointed his flashlight at the crumpled figure on the floor. "He look like his head bin squished under da wheel of a cah."

"Shut up, Pete," growled a tall man, clutching his bloodied nose. Then to the rest of the house, bristling with harried activity, he screamed, "Find those damn kids!" They scrambled all over the house, away from Zach like rats running from a fire.

"Whoever gets me the little shit who broke my damn nose might live to see tomorrow."

☾ † ✡ ☯ 🦅

After an hour of hiding and then walking and hiding again, they found themselves on the small residential road leading back to the highway. The clear view of the subdivision let them see the vehicles driving slowly down the street, flashlights shining into each of the houses and under bushes and in trees, looking for them. When the vehicles moved to the highway, so did they.

They walked for what seemed like hours. The adrenaline had long since worn off. It was only fear that kept them on their feet. They wanted to put as much distance between them and this gang as possible.

At some point, late into the night, they heard engine noises approaching. There were no headlights. They had scurried into the bushes and waited for the vehicles to pass, just out of reach of their flashlights. The large truck turned around and came back, again stopping maybe a hundred feet from where they had slipped into the bushes. The vehicle idled there forever, or so it seemed. Lexi and Travis listened to the men inside argue over which way to go, until the voices drifted off as they fell asleep.

Chapter 14

Frank

"It's a Faraday cage."

"That's what one looks like? It's more like a ... a jail cell for a tech-nerd," Grimes said as he hobbled after Frank into what had been the house's master bedroom. A box-shaped sub-room of framed-metal bars and wire mesh occupied most of the space. Inside of this was a portly desk covered in radio equipment, a laptop, and scattered papers.

"This one must have been set up to protect their radio equipment against the EMPs. I have one of these around my entire home ... at least I used to," Frank said, staring at the radio equipment inside from which a crackly hiss beckoned him.

"So either these bastards are preppers like you, Frank, or they knew what was going to happen and that means they must have been involved with the atmospheric blasts you said took out our grid?" Grimes locked his fingers through the mesh and peered at all the equipment, and contemplated the meaning of this new clue.

"It sure looks that way."

They both turned back to address the bedroom doorway and a familiar set of heavy footsteps approaching.

"You guys in here?" Aimes called to them as he rounded the entrance. "Whoa, Haji has a jail cell."

"It's a fairy cage, Gunny," said Grimes, a slight smirk on his face.

"Don't let the fairies out then. We've got enough of 'em in this world already."

"Better get in there; they like baldies, I hear," Grimes responded.

"Report, Gunny," Frank chimed in smiling. He genuinely missed this kind of idle banter among men right after battle; the fervent chiding of each other and the enemy was common among their band of brothers in an overt attempt to ratchet down the tension level.

"Perimeter is secure, Major," Aimes responded.

The three of them had already searched the entire house, each clearing different rooms. It appeared that they had killed all the combatants. Aimes volunteered to do a once-around the perimeter to make sure they weren't going to be surprised by anyone. Not yet having seen this part of the home, he wide-eyed the enormous cage that rose from the floor to just below the ceiling's blinking light fixture.

"They've got a giant genny in the garage and lots of gas in jerry cans to feed it. I had wondered where they got their power." He stepped beside the others and examined the cage's interior. "The garage door was open a crack, possibly for venting, but I'm not sure how none of them had died of carbon monoxide."

Frank clumped around the cage's right side, careful to not bump into the rows of supplies lining the walls, anxious to check out what was on the desk of this terrorist cell's operation center. It would have been nice to have found one of them alive, and to extract actionable intelligence. But then, they might not have had this room to examine, because any of the living would have had orders to burn down the house and all of its secrets within. He opened the chamber's steel door and stepped inside.

"You know you have two stiffs in the pool house?" Aimes continued.

"Yeah, that was the owners, the Maldonados," Frank answered from the swivel desk chair, carefully riffling through the loose papers on the desk.

"Shit, I know them," Grimes added. "A bit obnoxious if you ask me. Very full of themselves ... Whoa! Look at this, guys." He was standing over an open gun crate, next to a cot. Behind both at least twenty more crates lined the back wall. Grimes withdrew a brand-new AK-103. "Haji has some new toys, brought to you from Kalashnikov Concern in Udmurtia, Russia straight to Stowell, Texas, all for the purpose of killing Americans."

"Hope these Hajis are shitting mud bricks about now, realizing Paradise wasn't all they were told," Gunny said, adding his usual colorful commentary.

"But why so many crates of guns for"—Frank looked up to the ceiling for help with the mental calculations—"fifteen terrorists?"

"Here's the answer." Aimes held up a gallon-sized, plastic zip-lock bag, stuffed full of little round pills. "There must be several thousand Amps here."

"I don't get it. Are they selling drugs too?"

"No," Frank answered, not looking up from his examination of the papers on the desk, "ISIS commonly jacks-up their suicide fighters on Captagon before they go into battle. That way they feel indestructible and less likely to run away from their mission of blowing themselves up, or in this case, shooting people."

"Then, it looks like we've stumbled onto the tip of a much larger arrow." Grimes mused, while pointing to each crate. "Fuck me! That's over two hundred Kalashnikovs. In our little town? They're planning an invasion."

"Precisely!" Frank added. "Hello." From the mess of loose papers he pulled a single printout. It was a satellite image of *his* compound, with *his* name written on the top. Below this was, "AK-74 #AB 29 3 001," and below this, "Remington 7MM #E6875669," and "Beretta 92FS #BER314397Z."

"Major?" Aimes said over Frank's shoulder, "Are those the serial numbers of your guns? How the hell did they get that kind of intel?"

"Yes, and I don't know. My AK has the ATF stamp, so the feds would know about that one ... but even if they somehow got access to ATF records ... you got me on the others."

"That's why I bought my guns from third parties. No reason to let our government know about my private collection," Grimes offered gruffly. He sat on the cot, adjusted the splint on his broken leg, and then rose to join the others.

"We have a bigger issue than the government trying to grab our guns, Lieutenant." Frank examined a yellow pad with lots of scribbles, to the left of the microphone. At the top of the page was "Phase Three" and below it, lots of doodlings of palm trees, little pig silhouettes with "Abdul" written inside each, and dozens of furry looking things, which he suspected were women's pubic areas.

"This guy must have been some sort of perv," Grimes said, echoing his own thoughts.

Frank tapped on a hand-drawn box on the yellow pad, surrounding five sets of numbers, expecting Grimes knew what they were. He was the electronics expert among them.

"Frequencies," he said decisively. "Specifically, they're five different ham radio frequencies on the 20-meter band."

Frank twisted the volume control on the transceiver, and the static blared.

All three stared at the bisecting line's location on the large display.

Frank wrote this number on the top of the pad.

"When we're done here, I can monitor these frequencies from my setup at home."

Frank turned to Grimes. "Thanks, Lieutenant. That's what I was hoping you'd do." He returned his attention to the pad. "Now what do both of you make of the date, July 8th? There's a question mark by it, as if Hassan, wasn't sure about it."

"They obviously chose our Independence Day as the day to blast their nukes ..." Grimes mused out loud.

"My bet, it's the date they're getting more fighters. And when they arrive, they have guns and Amps for each."

"That's good, Gunny. I think you may be corr—" Frank stopped thumbing through the yellow pad and cocked his head at a sheet of paper in between its pages, folded in half. He pulled it out and opened it. A satellite map, like the one he'd found of his own compound—only bigger, with many buildings on a triangular section of land, bounded by large fencing and a navigable river. On top of the page was typed "Abdul Raheem Farook," and his address in Florida.

"Do you suppose he's the pig or the twat?" Aimes quipped.

"I ..." Frank caught a hand-written note on the bottom corner of the page: a set of numbers. His eyes flashed to the frequency he just written on the top of the pad. It was the same. "I suspect this is the location of the head pig."

Chapter 15

Lexi & Travis

July 5th

"**I** wore these damn shoes for you, Father!"

They woke to a vehicle zooming past them at high speeds. Lexi had been dreaming that they were back at the accident and she was yelling at her father, who was pinned to his seat, bleeding to death. He seemed completely uninterested in her attire, which was true before the accident. But this time, in her dream, she was yelling at her father for not noticing her dress and boots. Before he died, he told her, "You'll always look beautiful to me, no matter what you wear."

She smiled at this lingering thought. It wasn't real, but it felt as real as anything she could let her mind settle on concerning their father.

"I'm hungry, Lex," Travis whimpered.

"Hang on, Travis, let me just—" Lexi stood up, intending to sneak a peek and see if the coast was clear, but she fell over as her feet shrieked in pain. She couldn't go any farther, not until she did something about them.

It felt like late morning and the spot they had found themselves in wasn't too bad; it was protected and yet they could see the highway and anybody searching for them. They'd have to stay there a while longer.

"I need to fix my feet first. Why don't you peek and see if anyone is coming?"

His head bobbed up and down in agreement, before he stood up and stuck his head tentatively outside the canopy of green.

Lexi tried to slip out of one of her boots, but it felt like she was ripping skin off her foot in the process.

"Damn it to hell!" she cursed at herself, letting the first one fall, then the next. Why did she have to pick the most uncomfortable shoes in her closet to drive home a point? Hiking boots would have done the trick.

She didn't dare look at her feet. But after building up her courage, she did, and was terrified by what she saw. Both were swollen like grapefruit. Each heel had been overtaken by two giant blisters: one swollen like a gorged tick, the other already popped and oozing. But the most grotesque was the gauze. Most of it had come off in the boot. Her right foot was still connected to the boot by a bloody umbilical—that's my blood. It had dried like an epoxy that became part of her skin. An inch or so of gauzed skin reluctantly came loose when she pulled harder, leaving behind a rawness that made her stomach turn once more.

She didn't think she could do this.

Usually, when she felt completely out of control and her only option was to cry, that's what she did. And someone, normally her aunt, arrived to help her pick up the pieces.

This time, no one would come and save her. Her father and mother were dead. Her aunt and uncle were a couple of thousand miles away—as good as dead. And to make matters worse, her brother was completely dependent upon her. As much as she wanted to take her seat on her treasured pity-potty, she had to figure something out, on her own.

It took a while, but she gradually worked off the remaining bandages, leaving most of her skin intact. She even managed to lightly clean her destroyed feet, being very judicious with their water. Although they had stocked up a little at the house from which they had made their swift late-night getaway, she didn't know if they'd get another chance before reaching Abe's place.

Her bare feet almost felt good, wiggling dry in the warm morning air.

She wondered if there was anything in the Prepper Brothers book that dealt with first aid, especially blisters. Leaning over to her father's bug-out bag, snorting again at the strange name, she dragged it toward her by a shoulder strap.

It was the first time she had actually taken the time to really examine the book. Yesterday, she had hurriedly flipped through its pages, stopping to catch only a few sentences. This time, she carefully thumbed through each page, letting the words tumble through her fingers from the back to the front, stopping and consuming a few paragraphs every couple of pages. On the book's second page, normally just a blank filler page, there was some writing she hadn't seen.

She glanced in stunned silence as the words connected, making sentences in her brain. When she finally grasped that this was a message from her dead father, her head flew back as if she had been slapped, and she looked around as if someone else might read it before she did.

Travis was sitting cross-legged in front of her, guzzling water from one of the many full water bottles they'd found last night, like a horse gorging itself after a long walk in the desert.

She read.

Dearest Lex,

I had always intended to teach you myself how to prepare for an emergency or something far worse, but here we are, another unfulfilled promise of mine. If you're reading this, it's because we didn't make it to Florida. And so I'm leaving this book as a substitute for me, to help you and Travis survive the next few days, before you make it to one of the addresses I've left with you.

I'm sorry I wasn't there for you and Travis. I purposely stayed away to protect both of you.

I will love you always,

Dad

Lexi closed the book and looked at it again, blinking back tears. How could she have any left?

After a couple of minutes, having regained her composure, she whispered thanks to her dead father and opened to the back of the book under the lists section for "On The Road." Under "The First 24 Hours Shopping List," the fourth item down was apple cider vinegar. This had been on her own shopping list, given to her by her father, although at the time, she didn't know why.

In parentheses, beside it was "uses": After "Cleaning" and "Remove Stains," there they were. "Injuries" and, equally good, "Heartburn."

"Hand me the vinegar," she directed Travis, who was studying the food choices in her Hello Kitty bag. He held the bottle out to her, his eyes begging for the go-ahead to dig into one of the items inside. Bet he'd even eat the tuna at this point.

She unscrewed the top and took a whiff, crumpling her face at the smell and considered what she was about to do. Lexi held the bottle out to the air as if for inspection and said, "Here's to you, Daddy."

She took a gulp. "Oh God, I'm gonna hurl." She slapped the dirt with her other hand in protest, waiting for the nastiness to fade.

She'd live with the heartburn.

"Do we have any paper towels in there?"

Travis handed her a small napkin from Simpson's World Market. He had grabbed a few of them when no one was looking.

She grimaced away the taste, took the little cloth and used it to dab a bit of vinegar on each of her wounds. Each dab was like jamming a hot poker into the already damaged area. But after the pain quickly subsided, each actually felt better. Once more, she wrapped each foot in gauze. When it was completed, she gingerly slipped on the monstrous boots and tentatively tried out her handiwork. Perhaps she could actually go on, although she certainly needed new shoes soon if they were going to make it to Abe's in the next day or two.

Now some food.

They needed something more substantial than the beef jerky they finished yesterday. Surprisingly, Travis was all-in for the two chicken, noodle and vegetable MREs from their father's bag, instead of one of the items they had bought from the market. She had no idea how long they had been in there, but heard they would practically last forever. It was pretty cool that she only had to pour water into one package and that would heat the packets of chicken. Both their stomachs growled in anticipation.

While they waited, she gave Travis the condiment bags to play with—each contained Skittles candy, and she investigated the other food packets. It only took a few minutes and then she poured the deliciously hot contents of each bag into their cups; Travis had pulled out spoons and jabbed one in each cup, so that each was standing at attention.

They scooped food into their mouths, *mmm-ing* their delight, and were done in seconds.

While Travis cleaned their cups, she packed up their bags, figuring they'd eat the rest of the MRE's contents on the road. Lexi wanted to get moving if there'd be any hope of making it to Abe's house in the next day or two.

A mile further down the highway, while popping the last couple of candies in their mouths, they saw a sign for Greensville. She didn't want to stop, but her feet were hurting a lot. They still had some cash. Maybe this town had a shoe store.

The fire's smell arrived before it was even visible. Neither gave it any thought until breathing became difficult and then they noticed the smoke was all around them.

The main drag bisected the "downtown," and they stood there, dumbstruck. It looked like one of the nuclear bombs had gone off here. The street was carpeted in debris, surrounded by several smoldering burnt-out cars. Over half the stores were leveled and several were still glowing. Their eyes watered from the thick haze which hung around them like a soupy morning fog.

"What happened?" Travis asked.

"It was a riot," crackled a male voice behind them, causing Lexi to jump. She turned to face a very old man resting on a cane—*there sure are a lot of old men with canes in Florida.* "Ma and me hid out last night while a bunch of kids looted and rioted our town. That's our home." He pointed to a white house with a wrap-around porch and a white picket fence. "I saw you two out here staring and thought I'd come out and see if I could help."

"Hi, I'm Travis Broadmoor." The boy thrust his hand out. "And that's my sister, Lex, I mean Lexi."

"Do you have a shoe store?" Lexi barked, not moving to reward the old man's offered hand with hers.

"Sotheby's shoes. And I think it's one of the few that didn't burn down. I'll walk you there." He thrust his cane into the pavement and lurched forward one step.

Great, she thought as the man hobbled one slow step after another.

Their pace was painfully sluggish. *This could take all day.*

"That's all right, I'm sure we can find it." Lexi burst forward.

Her brother pulled her back. "Thanks, mister, for being so nice to us."

They waited for him to catch up. "Don't you have any police around to stop these kids, as you called them, from destroying the town?"

"Haven't seen the police since the bombs went off."

"You mean the new-cue-lur bombs, right?" Travis offered, following along.

"Nuclear, Travis," she corrected.

He shot her a scowl.

"Did you see any mushrooms?" the old man croaked at both of them, but he was looking at Lexi. She remembered seeing one in fact, but bit her tongue.

After a minute of no answers, the old man continued, "One of our neighbors, a ham radio operator, said that there were multiple bombs exploded around the coast and two in the sky. That's what killed everything electric.

We have an old Westinghouse that still works, but so far, all we're hearing is mostly static.

"Say, you two really look like you could use a shower and some food. Ma will be cooking a big meal, always too much for us. After we get you some shoes, you wanna come back with me? I have a gravity shower set up outside that you can use; already rigged some curtains around it for Ma's privacy."

Lexi turned the offer over in her head before answering. Although it would do them good to have a shower and a big meal before they continued their journey, she wanted to get more miles under foot. Yet she was already feeling fatigued. Maybe after finding shoes they could rest some more. And maybe he could help them find bicycles. She just hated the idea of depending on anyone, most especially a stranger. They had depended on their father, who was family, and look where that got them.

"Can we, Lex?" Travis begged.

"Okay, thank you," she said curtly.

Walking through town, it looked worse than when they were outside looking in. She remembered seeing video footage her aunt had showed her of when her hometown Wildcats won the championship and the town went nuts. Some of the students overturned and burned a police car. Her aunt and uncle were very agitated about the whole thing complaining that the kids came to school here, from privilege, and yet they rioted and destroyed property from a celebration over a sport. Lexi remembered the image of the overturned burned-out car and the garbage in the streets. This town looked far worse than that.

"Dammit! Looks like they got the bakery. Ol' Hoff-steadler will want blood for that one."

Lexi saw a smoldering lot with a giant oven in the middle of it and a pile of burnt rubble. Literally, everything had burned but the oven. Any other day, she'd laugh at the irony.

"Looks like they spared your shoe store, though ..."

Lexi excitedly gawked at the brick facade on the other side of the street. Its lofty sign read Sotheby's Shoes. Then her heart sank. Its two front windows and double doors were missing; the looters had already had their way with it. She was starting to feel desperate, like she'd almost be willing to steal shoes off of someone already wearing her size.

Her feet crunched on little bits of shattered glass; images of their accident flooded her mind. It seemed like it had happened weeks ago, but it was only yesterday.

She withdrew the shotgun she had captured from Rodie last night and secured her bag around both shoulders.

Two of the front shelves were overturned and boxes and shoes were strewn everywhere. She stepped around them and walked through the women's section, which was mostly bare. She headed toward the back of the store, where the children's shoes were kept. She may have been 22, but she was "petite" and could actually wear a large kid's size, so she sometimes shopped in the kids' section. Past Infants, she saw a display with one boy's hiking boot, which looked like the correct size. She laid the shotgun down and then lifted her right foot and compared boot print to boot print. It looked good. She had considered getting tennis shoes, but those were all gone. There were only two boxes below the boot display. The first box held tiny boots made for what looked like a three-year-old, but the other had the mate to this one. *Bingo*.

She grabbed both and found a chair in front of a mirror. Carefully pulling off and tossing aside the monster boots—for good, she hoped—she slipped on each hiking boot. They felt the correct size, and she knew instantly that this was an improvement. After lacing them up and tying them snugly, she walked around, exaggerating each step to fully test them. *Perfect*.

"Hey, I found my size!" she bellowed in joy. Her feet were still sore, but they felt great in these things.

Before she took a step, she glanced at Travis and the old man, just outside the store. Both were animated, and both were rubbernecking toward the highway.

A loud rumble roared up to the door. A large truck squealed to a stop right in front of the old man, its doors already opening. Lexi stepped closer, stumbling over boxes and furniture, her anxiety building up again. She recognized the truck instantly, having seen it multiple times. She chomped at the air, wanting to yell something to her brother, but nothing came out. It was too late.

A man walked around from the driver's side of the truck, his face obscured by the old man, but she knew instantly who it was. Then, the man walked around the old man and Travis, and stood glaring over his bandaged nose right at Lexi.

It couldn't be!

The old man stepped in front of him, yelling and shaking his finger at him vigorously, and then holding his other arm out to block entry to Broken Nose and another man beside them. The old man shot a glance to the back of the store. It was a helpless face, full of fear. But it wasn't fear for himself, it was for Lexi and Travis.

The old man turned back to Broken Nose just as several thunder claps exploded.

The old man collapsed in the doorway.

Lexi screamed. She didn't want to, but she did anyway, unmoving.

Travis dashed to the old man, bawling, "Noooo!"

The old man, breathing heavily, held out his hand. Travis grabbed it, his eyes filling, dreading the inevitability of another death.

Broken Nose pointed into the store, right at Lexi, who was petrified to find that she hadn't moved the whole time. She was literally paralyzed with fear. She should run, but where? Her brother was caught. She couldn't leave him. The other man ran directly at her. She felt different than yesterday when she was angry and able to react. Now, she felt helpless. And just like that, all her energy left her. She toppled over to her knees, onto a tumble of boxes, only a few feet from the door. Her plummet continued, helped along by her heavy pack. She landed on her belly just as the man reached for her, roughly clawing at one of her arms, pulling her back up.

"Look what I found, boss," said the man, practically carrying her.

Broken Nose smiled broadly, watching her approach.

"We've been searching for you all night. Clyde's got some great things planned for you, and so do I."

Her gaze drifted down first to her brother, then the old man, his eyes weakly fluttering, perhaps for the last time. His chest was a bloody soup.

"What about the kid?" the man dragging her asked plaintively.

"Leave 'im. We have what we came for," answered Broken Nose.

"Lex," her brother wailed.

The old man gasped, "Ma will take care of him."

It was as if their lives had just been decided for them: she would go away for good and Travis was to spend his days at some strange old lady's house. It wasn't right.

Tossed into the front of the truck like a bag of feed, her right arm snapped back, nearly dislocating it from her shoulder; her wrist was handcuffed to the roll bar above the door. "Zach don't trust you," said the thug who manhandled her, before slamming the door.

Broken Nose Zach entered the other side. "You're pretty, just like I thought." He punched her in the face with a grunt, spinning her head around till she was facing the store again.

Lexi watched the periphery of her vision fade. Like darkness consuming the daylight at dusk, blackness spread across everything; a shrinking black picture frame, with her brother's portrait in the middle, standing over the dead old man, alone and crying, watching her sister being taken away.

They weren't going to make it to Abe's.

They weren't going to make it home.

Then there was only blackness.

Chapter 16

Abe

"CQ CQ, this is Whiskey-Bravo-Nine-Zulu-Mike-Oscar calling from the Chicago hot zone. I'm looking to talk to any survivors out there," pleaded a gruff voice laced with cigarettes and desperation.

"Whiskey-Bravo-Nine-Zulu-Mike-Oscar, this is Whiskey-Four-Alpha-Alpha-Mike, in Miami. Whoa, surprised, but thankful to hear anyone is alive in Second City."

"Hey Chicago and Miami, this is Jonathan in New York. I'm northwest of the Manhattan blast. Just glad to talk to someone."

"Hey Jonathan. You can call me Walter," said the gruff voice, becoming a little more animated. "What about you, Miami?"

"Hello guys, this is Cindy. How are ya doing? Are ya able to stay out of the radiation?"

"Hey Cindy ... Ah, not so good here ... this is Jonathan in New York. This is ... was my son's radio. He talked on the damn thing all the time. He went on a science field trip to Manhattan with classmates, when the bomb hit ..."

Cindy's mic was obviously clicked on, but she was quiet for a long pause. "What about you, Whiskey-Bravo-Niner in Chicago?"

"It's Walter. I'm in a western suburb of Chicago, so we were outside of the blast area, mostly. The local emergency station told us to stay inside and to protect against radiation. I've taped up all the windows and have enough food or water for a while. But I don't think I did so good. I have a Geiger counter too, and it's already in the red. I guess I'll probably be dead in a few days. I'll take a bullet of course, rather than puking blood from radiation; I hear that's pretty unbearable."

It seemed as if no one was going to say anything more.

"So tell me, Cindy or Jonathan. Before I leave this earth, I just want to know, have you heard if we've started taking it to the bastards who did this to us?"

"Umm ..." It was Cindy answering. There was a sound of a nose being blown in the background. "I think the country's too in shock right now to take action. I mean they leveled DC too. The good news, if there can be any in this darkness, is that I've heard talk of only a few of our bases getting hit, but nowhere else. I've only been able to confirm that Jacksonville was destroyed. And a neighbor-friend of mine, who is a scientist, tells me that the radiation is blowing east, so ..."

Cindy paused again. She had mentally concluded that the radiation from the Chicago blast would eventually hit Jonathan in New York, but she probably didn't want to say it.

"I'm sure that once we get on our feet again after we figure out how to bring back the power, we'll find out who these terrorists are and we'll send them back to hell, where they belong."

There was another long pause as Abe considered her words, his fingers poised over his radio's controls. Like everyone so far, they attributed these blasts to mere terrorists.

Cindy continued, "I'll pray for you both" (she blew her nose again) "but I have to go now; my battery is running low and I need to keep a charge for emergencies. God bless you both. Whiskey-Four-Alpha-Alpha-Mike out."

Abe switched off the radio. He had heard enough. The smattering of reports from ham radio operators—those whose units were protected against the EMPs, who were always ready for emergencies—reported the same thing all over the country: power down, most vehicles didn't work, some electronics burned out, those that worked had no Internet or network service, and few had supplies of food. They had no idea what was coming; hunger, disease, and death awaited most Americans in the weeks and months that lay ahead.

It wouldn't be this way for him. He was prepared for this. He had lots of supplies. He lived away from the radiation, so his water was fresh and plentiful. He had solar power. He even had a plot of vegetables, so he and his family and others living on his property ate fresh produce daily.

There was a knock on his door, and it cracked open to reveal a man whose dark skin and clothing stood in stark silhouette to the brightness outside.

"Excuse me," the young man announced, his eyes cast downward out of respect. "Sorry to interrupt, but I hear a truck coming down da drive."

"Thanks, Leo. I may need your help with this."

He closed his door to his radio shack—that's what ham operators called it, but it was hardly a shack—behind them. Before walking between it and the next building to meet the vehicle in the drive, he glanced at the river dock and the cigarette boat tied to one of its posts. His mind wandered just a little bit, in spite of the urgency of their guest's arrival. Had he been born into a different world, he would have enjoyed spending his days on this river, fishing and trapping wild game, or reading his books in the sunshine. It was a splendid place, full of natural beauty everywhere. But his life was meant for greater pursuits, not following his own desires. He had responsibilities. He had men and women who depended on him. And he had a mission to fulfill.

He turned back to the driveway, the noise of the on-coming truck already drowning out the river's soft lapping sounds and the constant banter of the tropical wildlife it supported.

He reluctantly walked to the drive, away from the river and the life he'd like to have led.

A war was coming, and he had limited control over what happened next. He could only do his job and react to his environment. In the weeks and months that would come, this world would change, regardless of all the planning he'd done; he could only use his skills to react to what came at him next.

The truck pulled up to him, a small plume of dust arriving a few seconds later. The door groaned open and a dark-skinned man hopped out, and smiles of familiarity lit both their faces.

"Good morning," he said, welcoming the driver.
"Yes, it is."

☾ ✝ ✡ ☯ 🦅

The potholes jostled Lexi awake, although it was
more like a familiar nudge as she could have been
back in Tucson, where the city's or county's roads were
always blanketed with broken asphalt. Her uncle con-
stantly cursed the "monkeys in government" for not fixing
the endless potholes, allowing some to grow so big they
threatened to eat whole vehicles. The jarring of her arm
and the stabbing pain in her wrist and her nose reminded
her that she was not in Tucson any more. She flicked her
right eye open, careful to not flutter the left one or move
any other muscles in case he was watching her for a sign of
consciousness. As best as she could see and feel, she was
still handcuffed to the truck, and they were still moving,
now on a dirt road in a forest, or perhaps a jungle. Every so
often, the cover of green would open only a few feet and
reveal a river, several yards beyond. Then just as quickly,
the leaves would close in again.

They slowed and turned around in the driveway of
somebody's property. There were multiple houses and
men waiting for them. She closed her eye again lightly and
continued to pretend that she was unconscious, hoping
to learn something more about her captivity and her captors.

That image of Travis flashed into her mind. He was
standing over the body of the elderly man who was nice
to them. Travis's eyes were swollen with sadness, his

shoulders heavy with grief, and he reached out for his sister. Her brother needed her and she had treated him like a non-entity. Pangs of guilt tore at her already shaky gut as she remembered the years of indifference she had for him.

How could she be so heartless? She wanted to cry, but she couldn't.

The truck's stop pulled her off the seat so that she was somewhat cantilevered over it. The driver's side door quickly squeaked open, the truck jostled, and then the door slammed shut indicating the driver had gotten out. *What was his name? Zach!* The man whose nose she broke. It felt like he returned the favor as her nose throbbed in pain, and she felt dried blood caked on her lips and chin.

"Hey brother," a muffled voice sang outside the window. "What ya bring me besides your busted nose?"

She desperately wanted to open her eyes, but she didn't dare.

"Yah, that's another story. But the boys scored, Clyde. We raided a neighborhood a few miles from here and grabbed a lot of food."

"Great work, Zach." She heard some footsteps coming closer. "Who's that?"

The hairs on back of Lexi's neck stood up as she could feel them both looking her over.

"Oh, *dat's* da reason for my busted nose. Bitch broke my nose wit a door, right after she bashed in Rodie's head wit a baseball bat.

"That little thing done all that?"

"Yup. We've been searching for her all night. Found her dis morning in Greensville. I brought her here for you. And if ya don't like her, maybe a public hanging; ya know, something for da men to enjoy?"

"Not a bad idea. But I didn't care for Rodie. He was careless and obviously paid for it. She looks like she was pretty before you busted her up. No, I'm thinkin we just give her to the boys. Let them have fun with her."

She felt her face flush and her nausea return.

Clyde whistled, like he was hailing a New York cabbie. "Hey boys, before you unload, put this one in my house. Lock her up to a table or something."

Her door squeaked open and she felt the warm, wet breezes work at her hair.

Someone—she didn't dare open her eyes to see who—released her wrist and she let her arm fall into her lap. Without the door to hold her in, her meager weight poured out the door. She was toppling into the air—*hope the bastard catches me*—when she hit something soft and pungent.

"Damn boss, you musta hit her hard. She's still out," a deep voice said much too loud beside her ear.

Strong arms hoisted her up, without effort, and yet they seemed to regard her with care, as if she might break. She so wanted to look and see where she was and who carried her. Her head was cradled in his arms, softening every footstep.

"I got her," said her carrier, his arms squeezing tight, almost protectively.

"Why does Big Mike gets to play with her before all of us?" said a new voice.

"No one gets to play, yet," answered Clyde. "You lock er up in the house and come right back, ya hear?"

Lexi felt the arms release somewhat, and heard his feet grinding over a gravelly surface. After a short time, she felt him move her weight higher onto his biceps, while his arm reached out. A door's hinges squealed for maintenance. She instantly knew they were inside and she carefully squinted her right eyelid once more, to let in the light and get her first view of the man. He was black as night and he had a hangdog face—that's what her Aunt Sara would have called it—that was naturally sad. His eyes flitted down and then back to where he was going and she shut her eyes, hoping he hadn't seen she was awake.

The inside was almost comfortable, the air not as heavy as outside. A loud fan in the background must have been the reason for the breeze she felt against her skin.

She almost flinched as he laid her on a cool tile floor. Then she felt her left arm being pulled gently to one side, the sharp circular metal of a handcuff clicked snugly around her wrist. At least it wasn't the other one, which ached.

"Sorry little missy, gotta do this." His voice was wet with tenderness. Not what she expected.

She listened to the heavy ramble of his steps behind her, the door's hinges crying out again before it slammed. She listened for any other sounds and heard none. When she was sure she was alone, she opened her eyes to see she was attached to a heavy-looking wood chair, pushed under a table. Moving herself around, she could see this was a small house, and she was in the middle of a big room that held the dining, living, and kitchen areas. It looked old and in dire need of maintenance, but it was mostly tidy, and appeared clean.

To this point she had been somewhat calm, although she didn't know why. Maybe she was too busy assessing her surroundings to focus on her future. But now, locked up in a house surrounded by bad guys, not knowing where she was or where her brother was, and knowing what Clyde intended for his men to do to her; she was starting down the path of full-out panic.

Calm down, Lexi. You'll find a way out of this.

It felt like her father talking to her. But it wasn't, it was from the pages of the Prepper Brothers book, which said to *relax and to think logically* when in a life or death situation, *because there are always options.*

She did start to calm down, as she considered her options for escape. And as she looked around, a plan started to take shape when the door screeched opened once again.

Chapter 17

Ft. Rucker, Alabama

One Day Earlier

F ive olive-colored trucks with US Army markings on their sides approached the gate. As the lead vehicle slowed to a stop, the others followed suit.

Private Shields bounded out of the command unit, excited to see more soldiers had arrived. After the attack, the base commander said that more troops would come eventually and in the meantime to be vigilant on watch. More than reinforcements, which they didn't really need for a base that mostly serviced and flew drones, Shields was anxious about getting information. When the public grid their base shared with Enterprise Alabama went down, so did their power. And other than the single radio broadcast they'd received from a base in Georgia after starting one of their gennies, and the constant feed from the BBC, they'd had no other information. There was so much they wanted to know: Who did this? Why? When was the US going to strike back?

Shields was so excited about the convoy's arrival, in fact, that he didn't even notice that the trucks were over twenty years old and had been out of Army service for at least the last ten years. These were the kind of details he was supposed to be aware of. He only knew that they must be carrying troops and they must have information from the outside world.

Shields remained at ease waiting for the window of the lead truck to be rolled down.

"Damn good to see you gentlemen," he said while standing his position for a copy of their orders. But the driver was busy talking to his passenger in the cab. Shields couldn't help himself, forgetting all protocol, and blurted, "What can you tell me about what's going on out there?"

The driver turned to Shields, a little perplexed and then spun his head back to his passenger. The passenger leaned forward so that Shields could see him. He had a giant nose, red like raw meat, and an unshaven face, which was not common for an officer. "Sorry Private, but my driver has laryngitis and can't speak. We're here with some troop reinforcements from Ft. Benning. What's your status?"

"Oh, we're pretty much dead here, Sir. Our power is out but for a couple of gennies we have running right now. One of them powers the radio room, which is how we knew you were coming. I heard they got us pretty good." Private Shields finished his stream of consciousness and then fell silent, realizing he was doing all the talking. But he felt uncomfortable just standing there staring at the man's honker, and worse hating that he was going to have to remind his superior that he needed orders.

"I'm afraid so, Private. Please let us pass, so we can give you the reinforcements you need," said the giant-nosed man.

Shields glanced over to the other side of the gate; PFC Johnson was waiting impatiently for the sign to open it up. Shields turned back and found himself staring at the business end of a rifle pointed right at his face. At first, he thought it was a mistake or a joke, so he just gaped at the large-nosed man, dumbfounded.

"Sorry, Private, but if you don't signal your man to open the gate, we'll shoot you and your man in four seconds ... three ... two ..."

Shields gave an overly enthusiastic thumbs-up to Johnson, who nodded and unlatched the electric gate. Johnson grunted, putting his whole body into the heavy section of fence that no longer opened except by human exertion. Thankfully, this was the first time he'd had to open it up.

Shields looked back up to the cab of the truck, and didn't even register the suppressed round that entered his forehead.

Johnson made the opening wide enough for the convoy of trucks, and then looked to the lead vehicle which had already started its move forward. He was looking forward to some information from Shields via this convoy, and relief at the gate would be nice, too. The base had a minimal deployment—their whole base had been on the chopping block because of cutbacks, and would have been dead by now were it not for the drone program—of only a hundred men and women, mostly pilots and support staff.

Johnson noticed something strange. There was a form on the road, like someone's discarded garbage, and he no longer saw Shields. Then it hit him that he was looking at Shields's body. As he glanced up at the convoy's lead vehicle, which had already passed, a man hopped out from behind a flap of canvas at the back, smoothly trained a rifle at him, and fired twice. Only the birds fluttering in a tree nearby noticed.

The man who had exited the truck ran over to Shields's body and dragged it past the fence line, before doing the same to Johnson's. He removed Shields's shirt, hat, and gun and closed the gate. The trucks drove down the road, headed to Ft. Rucker's command center.

The Shields stand-in took his position at the gate.

Frank

July 5th

It was a six-hundred-mile drive, and Frank spent most of this in a staticy silence; his mind, like his radio, crackled with a flurry of disparate thoughts, which struggled to connect amid the noise.

His truck radio had been switched off long ago. Finding an operating AM/FM station proved fruitless. His HF rig—set up by Grimes so they could communicate the longer distances—resonated a gurgling constant hiss the whole journey, only a few times bellowing out a familiar voice. He mentally moved the clock forward, anxious for the next update from Grimes, on their predesignated frequency. Until then, it droned on, adding to a headache that started yesterday.

This long wait to get there and the lack of information were making him nuts.

They were witnesses to the third world war, started on American soil, and yet they really knew so little. Grimes's last report had been less than an hour ago—it felt so much longer—and the news so far was not good.

There had been almost no radio or television broadcasts inside the US. He could only find two local stations which broadcast that annoying tone along with the emergency broadcast message that hadn't changed since yesterday. None of them expected the Emergency Alert System to be silent. It was as if FEMA's NARS on Mount Weather was taken out as well.

What they learned was broadcast from outside the US.

The BBC was their only source for updates about their country, although it provided no more than what they knew already: the US had been attacked by multiple nuclear warheads and no one knew who was responsible. Fingers were being pointed everywhere. The few new details Frank picked up were about what was going on outside the US, and none of that was good either.

All the world's stock markets had collapsed; all exchanges had halted trading indefinitely. There were runs on every bank, and riots in most major cities. Around the world, countries were terrified that the same would happen to them. But in fact it had, without the bombs.

This was a breakdown of the world's economic machinery, and America was the monkey wrench thrown in to cause its collapse.

And just like the bullies Frank expected to fill the power vacuum within America's cities, already there were opportunistic nations that used America's current weakness to their advantage: Russia was making incursions into Poland, Yugoslavia, and the Czech Republic; China had just invaded Taiwan; and there were reports of a million soldiers marching into Seoul, South Korea, from the North.

Meanwhile America was silent, as if hibernating because of its wounds. There was one report that American naval ships were being recalled from all over the globe, but that may have been just speculation. If American forces were planning a response, there was no evidence of it.

Grimes said that he had tried several of the known US Army and US Coast Guard radio frequencies, including Ft. Rucker's, and found no communications. It was like they were purposely under radio blackout. Ft. Rucker's silence was most puzzling, because they had a special system hardened against EMPs. Furthermore, Grimes's son, Porter, was stationed there as a technician. Because of Porter's friendship with the radio operations officer, they had worked out a system of radio checks that allowed father and son to converse regularly via Ft. Rucker's radio. But Grimes had heard nothing since the attack.

The only actual on-the-ground reports from within the US came from a scattering of ham radio operators. Most repeated the same assumptions and non-news they had heard from others or the BBC. Very few, other than those close to the blast zones, knew anything. As far as Grimes could tell, no one had electricity in North America, with power grids all down from Canada through Mexico.

Ironically, only Grimes, Aimes, and Cartwright seemed to know they were under attack from jihadists, and that the enemy was already on US soil. It was because of this that they all agreed that it was time to bring the US Army directly into the fight, if they weren't already.

With actionable intelligence about Farook's base in Florida and the known terrorist cell in Texas, Frank was headed to Ft. Rucker to personally deliver the physical and testimonial evidence they had to the brass there. Frank's plan was to hand over the intelligence and hope they'd take it from that point. Between the cases of guns—one of them in his truck—and the papers they'd found, many of which Frank had brought along, they had an irrefutable case. Frank would then come home and focus with Aimes on recruiting others in Stowell to protect it from what they feared was the next phase of the invasion, coming in a few days.

They disagreed initially over reporting this intel to an Army base that was closer to them. But they feared that nothing would be done immediately, until that base was able reestablish communications and kick it up the command chain. That would take too long. Because Ft. Rucker was located directly north of the main terrorist cell led by enemy number one, Abdul Farook, Frank thought they might be more prone to quick action if they received the intel by hand. He didn't have to convince Grimes, who wanted Frank to go to Ft. Rucker, Alabama for another reason: he'd use the opportunity to try and collect Grimes's son, Porter, and bring him back home.

If, however, Frank was not able to convince the US Army to act, he would take the case of guns and recruit individuals locally to join a militia of fellow countrymen and take the fight directly to Farook. This was Frank's last choice, and he would do everything in his power to convince the Army to take on this burden themselves.

While Frank was on the road, Grimes was also attempting to do forensics on Hassan's laptop, although he had so far been unsuccessful. Only Hassan's notes gave them any details, and even that was not clear: the first phase was nuclear, phase two they didn't know, but it was to occur on or after July 8th, and phase three appeared to be the invasion. Finally, Grimes monitored all the noted radio frequencies, listening for any enemy chatter. So far, he had heard nothing.

Aimes's work was no less difficult. He was trying to recruit a militia for Stowell. It helped that everybody knew him, having tasted his wife's incredible cookies. So, he worked on every able-bodied man and woman, with plans to prepare them for the invasion they thought would happen on or after July 8th. So far, Aimes had over a dozen recruits, although they had hoped for a lot more. Each would be given one of the captured AKs and Aimes had started training on how to use them.

Jihadi invaders and preparing for the next invasion weren't the only oddities of this war.

Frank had witnessed many sights he didn't think he would see at any point in America, even after all his years preparing for the end of his world. He'd only seen a half-dozen moving vehicles on the road, and thousands of dead ones. Some were burning or had been burned. In fact, there were smoke plumes everywhere, like the land had been reborn into a pyromaniac's utopia.

Then there were the walkers. Hundreds of people, mass migrations of folks: individuals, couples, and whole families, all walking along the highway, probably all trying to get home.

At least they had a home.

At the 231 turnoff, north to Fort Rucker, he couldn't help but feel that he was driving the wrong way. He was no longer going toward the action; he was driving away from it. The distance between him and Farook's base—perhaps the nucleus of this virulent malignancy taking over his country—was growing with each mile closer to Ft. Rucker.

On highway 85, leading directly into the base, he had to hit his brakes hard.

Right in the middle of the intersection with another major road, there laid a cluster of debris blocking passage from all sides. In the middle of the wreckage was the rudder of an F-16, blackened by a fire that had since gone out. From its direction, it looked like it had just fallen right out of the sky, short of its runway maybe a mile away.

He spun his steering wheel hard left and navigated into an open field, following a large set of tire tracks made by someone who had the same idea, and then turned back and drove over the connecting road, circumventing the whole mess. After another field and a back road, he was once again back on I-85.

After passing Daleville High School, only a dozen car lengths from the public entrance to the base, a sign stood vigil in the middle of the road. Its hastily written message warned: "Because of the recent attack, this base is closed to public traffic. Turn back or face arrest."

Frank slipped his truck around this, ignoring it completely.

Even before he saw the sign, or the dead cars lining the road to the fence line making exit impossible, alarm bells were going off inside his head.

But still he drew up to and stopped before the gate. Almost immediately two men in Army uniforms dashed toward his vehicle with guns drawn. His window was already open, so the sounds of their approaching boots poured in with the humid Alabama air while he waited.

For a moment, Frank considered driving away, but abandoned that idea knowing his truck couldn't outrun their bullets. His mission had just gotten more complicated.

Thankful that the case of weapons and ammo were secured unseen in his locked truck bed, Frank quickly slid his weapons and a folder containing Hassan's papers—their evidence—under his seat. He slowly raised his hands in surrender.

The lead guard, wearing the rank of Private First Class, hollered at him to get out of the truck. The top unbuttoned portion of his shirt fluttered with his agitated demands. The second guard ran around his truck, loosely inspecting it. Both were tense and looked—as his ex-wife would have said—as out of place as ugly curtains in a pretty home.

"Come with us," the first guard bellowed and then motioned toward the gate with his rifle.

"What about my truck?" Frank pleaded, more to hear their reply than out of worry for his truck's safety.

"We will bring it in. Now move."

Again Frank obliged without protest, although as part of his performance, he exaggerated his limp for full effect to give himself time to be aware of everything going on around him. They marched him half a mile from the gate to what looked like the base's largest public building, an Army museum.

Frank had been quiet the whole time, even though he had many questions and everything he had experienced was completely unorthodox for a US Army base. Although he suspected these two held similar ranks to the insignias they were wearing and therefore wouldn't provide the answers he wanted, he was sure of two things, without asking questions: this base was no longer under the control of the US Army, and he was their prisoner.

"Can you tell me where you're taking me?" he finally asked.

"You are being placed under arrest until our commander can interrogate you."

Chapter 18

Lexi

P lans are always executed much more smoothly in one's mind then they are in real life.

And so it was with Lexi's escape plan. It felt solid and complete and she was ready, until Clyde slammed the door. Then the plan just unraveled like an old knit sweater when you pull on its loose threads.

Still, she tried to remain motionless, to make him think she was unconscious, as he watched her. Her eyelids were frozen, her fascial muscles relaxed, even though her busted nose still pulsated pain. Even her breaths were controlled. All the while she listened and waited for him to make his move.

"I know yah awake—I saw you jump when I slammed the door. Besides, my brother doesn't hit that hard, even when he's pissed."

Shit!

He dropped two heavy objects on the floor and shuffled toward her, his steps purposeful.

Yet, she kept her eyes cemented closed, her free hand ready to plunge the pen she found on the floor into his jugular. That was her plan. But then doubts instantly scuttled the whole thing: what if she missed? If he didn't die, would she ever get the chance again? What if she succeeded—how would she get out? The complicated weave of her little plan just unwound completely until, she let go of it altogether.

His hand cupped her jaw and roughly squeezed her cheeks, while yanking her head up, "Come on honey. Open those pretty blues," he said just inches from her. His breath reeked of cigarettes.

She flicked her eyes open, glaring her scorn at him.

"There we go. Yep, Zach was right, you have some good-looking peepers."

He had been stooped over, his face in hers. Then he released her, stood up, and sauntered over to the kitchen area, opened the refrigerator and grabbed a Budweiser, like he was a normal working man coming home after a long grinding day. He twisted off the cap, carefully placing it in the trash below the sink, and swigged down a large gulp. She watched him as he swept up her father's bag by the door and he and the bag plopped down in a dining room chair facing her on the tile, as if he were waiting for her to serve him his well-earned feast.

After taking another gulp, he placed the bottle down on the table, its savory taste almost within reach. Drops of condensation slid down the bottle's surface. It was pure torture to watch and he knew it.

Her eyes shot up to the ceiling to a light, only just now realizing he had power, even though she had seen and felt the moving fan when she first arrived.

"Yep, I got solar power," he said with an annoying little snicker.

Modified plan: plunge the pen into his eye. She smiled at this thought.

Another swig and he slammed down the bottle on the table, making her jump. "Don't suppose you want to tell me your story, do yah?"

She just glared at him, not willing to give anything away that he could use against her.

"Let's see what the cat drug in." He unclasped the top of her father's bag, turned it upside down and emptied its contents out on the table. A small roll of black duct tape escaped the pile, bounced twice on the table, and once on one of her outstretched legs, before rolling off onto the floor and under the living room couch a few feet away.

At least it had the sense to run away.

"We have ourselves a prepper chick." He held up an MRE. "You ever eat this shit? I prefer to make my own and vacuum seal em."

She said nothing.

He rustled through the pile and picked through its contents with his dirty mitts, fondling each to show her he had the control: the tarp; the first aid kit; the tin full of string, needle, fishhooks and other items; then the book her father gave her. Her heart sank when he rifled through its pages, fearful he would read his personal note to her. "This is a good 'en," he said, holding up the Prepper Brothers guide, "although I like the one about nuclear war prepping better. Certainly more useful now."

As he violated each of her father's things—her things now—her anger increased like an untended pot of boiling noodles ready to burst over its sides. She was handcuffed to a table, separated from her brother, and this man was going through her stuff like it was his own, and all for show.

"What the hell do you want with me?"

"She speaks!" He smiled a sly smile, full of himself. He had no intention of answering her.

He held up a piece of paper, the one with Abe's info on it. "I know this place, on the other side of the river heah." He motioned with his head. "Old Man Roberts sold it for a bunch of money to somebody I never met. Is this where ya were going?'"

He folded it up and put it into his shirt pocket and then grabbed the wooden box, the one with the medals. He slid open the unlocked chamber—the one Travis had figured out with ease. "What do we have heah?" He pulled out the Purple Heart and held it up to her. "Why are you walking around with this? Yah a little young for the Army, aren't yah?"

"Those are mine! You have no business in my stuff." She swung out with her uncuffed hand and tried to lunge at him, the sharp metal of the cuff biting into her other hand as the chair she was attached to screeched across the floor. Spittle erupted from her curled lips.

He yanked it just out of her reach.

A knock on the door startled her. Looking past Clyde, she could see a form behind the curtained entrance.

"Come in," said Clyde shaking her father's medal box at her, like he was toying with a cat. She wanted to sink her claws in him and rip him to shreds.

The grating door slowly opened, revealing that hulking giant of a black man, with his head down. "Sorry to bother you, Clyde, but Zach wanted to talk to you some mo."

"All right. Thanks, Big Mike. Watch this one for me, wouldya? She's feisty."

"Sure, Clyde," Big Mike answered as he lumbered through the doorway. The man's shoulders were so broad, he had to turn sideways to fit himself inside.

"Don't get too settled, Blue Eyes." Clyde was talking to her, but she was ignoring him and staring at Big Mike. "I have many more questions for yah." He dropped the box on the table, grabbed his beer, and slipped past the giant black man, out the door.

With his back to her, Big Mike peeled back the curtains and studied the world outside for a long time. Then he suddenly pivoted and strode to her quickly, like an athletic football player, not as heavy-footed as he looked. "I'm so sorry, missy, fo what dey done to you." He reached down and released her from her handcuffs.

Lexi rubbed her pink wrists, while gazing at him. "Thanks, but ... why are you helping me?" She stood and tilted her head upward to face the man. He was nearly two feet taller than her.

"Nuff talking. Pack yo bags. You best be leaving now." He dropped a car key on the table, and sprinted back to the door.

She didn't need any more nudging. She scooped up all of her belongings on the table into the bag, leaving the duct tape for someone else to find, and darted over to Big Mike. "Aren't there a lot of men out there?"

"Wait and when I run out this door, follow behind me." He continued to study the outside, calculating.

Lexi's eyes wandered down to the edge of the kitchen counter top where she was waiting with nervous anxiety.

She noticed a Bic lighter and a pack of cigarettes. She didn't smoke, but she had tried them once before. She grabbed both anyway.

Movement caught her eye. It was the kitchen curtains, fluttering from the fan in the corner. Her gaze darted to the wood paneling and the living room curtains and the stack of books in the other corner of the room.

"How much longer?" she asked Big Mike as she slid her pack off her back and onto the floor, shoving in the cigarettes. Her thumb rolled over the striker wheel, creating a spark, which ignited a blue flame at the lighter's tip and at the same time, a smile on her lips.

☾ † ✡ ☯ ☪

"**W**e're not going to soil her just yet, brother," Clyde said to Zach, his arm around his brother's shoulder on the edge of the dock where their voices couldn't be heard by their men.

"But Clyde, I promised da men they'd have der fun tonight afta yah was done wit her." Zach said as he picked at the bandage over his crooked nose.

"I know, but she may have some information about that place we were looking at across the river. They may be well stocked. Besides, this chick has a story to tell and I aim to get it out of—"

Gunfire.

The men both looked up, searching for where the shots had come from.

More shots erupted.

"There!" Clyde pointed at his brother's truck bounding down their driveway, away from the house.

"And look, brother, yo house is on fire," Zach pointed thru the stand of trees, mostly blocking their view.

☪ ✝ ✡ ☯ 🦅

L exi pressed hard on the gas pedal, her head barely above the monster truck's steering wheel. Her heart raced faster than she was driving. But she also felt the exhilaration of escape, and just enough of a feeling that she might have made it. She shot out of the stand of trees, and the giant truck leapt onto the highway's pavement, fighting for traction. She had to pull heavy to the right on the wheel, struggling to stay on the blacktop, but she straightened out and found herself headed in the correct direction.

Just before the bridge, she jammed both feet against the brake pedal, screeching the beast to a halt.

What are you doing?

It was right there. Abe's place would be right across the river. She knew this based on what the map said, forever etched into memory, and Clyde's confirmation. All she had to do was get to Abe's place, and he would take care of her. She would be safe.

But what about Travis?

"Damnit," she yelled and pounded the steering wheel with both palms, bruising two of the few uninjured parts of her body.

She couldn't leave him, in that town, all alone. He was her brother for God's sake. He had no one else but her.

And like that, she changed her course.

She gassed the engine and jerked hard on the wheel, pointing the truck sideways. Grinding the gears once more, she found the forward gear and punched the gas pedal again, driving the truck back in the direction she had just come.

She'd get Travis and then she'd go to Abe's. Her eyes nervously glanced at Clyde's private road as she passed, knowing that any moment Clyde and his men would be coming through those trees.

☾ ✝ ✡ ☯ 🦅

"**W**hy aren't we going afta her?" Zach yelled at his brother, beside himself in fury.

"My house first," Clyde said to Zach. "Pump!" Clyde then hollered at his two men pushing and pulling on the seesaw lever of a manual pump. "Pump!" He pulled the hose farther inside his home and doused the remaining portion of his blackened kitchen.

It looked like his collection of books and the kitchen were the only areas damaged, mostly from the water. Clyde assumed the blue-eyed devil lit a couple of paperbacks, then used some sort of accelerant to burn his kitchen. A part of him admired her tenacity. He would enjoy making her pay.

"Okay, turn it off."

"Yah goin to let her get away," Zach whined.

Clyde dropped the hose on his tile floor, reached into his front pocket, and pulled out the folded satellite map he had taken from her bug-out bag. "No, I'm not. We know exactly where she's going. Let's get this cleaned up and then get the other trucks ready."

Chapter 19

Frank

"You expect me to believe that you were just stopping by to say 'hi' after your country was bombed?" The man wearing Colonel Jones's uniform—a fake Jones for sure—glared at Frank over his tomato-sized nose.

"Well, not exactly." Frank sat up a little straighter in his chair, handcuffs clanging against it. "As I told you, Colonel, I stopped by to see my nephew, Private Harry Simpleton." Frank repeated his lie. "He was supposed to be stationed at this base; something having to do with drones. Then, after visiting, I was going to go back to my home in Florida."

Frank's gaze slid down from the colonel's face to his shoulder, and then to his chest; the man's eagle insignias and nametag confirmed his position and name. But, this man's accent and mannerisms, along with what Frank had witnessed thus far, argued against it.

They were certainly keeping up appearances, just like regular Army. But he knew that he was not in the company of the Army, at least not the US Army. Outwardly, to the casual observer, they looked normal enough in their Army uniforms. But there were so many clues under the surface that were obvious, if you looked: the lack of formalities for everything, including salutes; the hushed conversations among their men; and the manner in which he was being interrogated. Plus, Jones's eagles were facing the wrong direction.

Frank wasn't sure what to expect at first. He thought he might be tortured right away, but these people, who he was sure were associated with the terrorists who had nuked America and also captured this base, had chosen something less ... physical. It was as if they really didn't seem to know how to account for the likes of him, assuming most visitors would have turned away at the warning sign, before the gate. Frank guessed by the fifteen minutes of questions, Colonel Jones or whatever his real name was had orders not to harm visitors, until he could report his suspicions. Someone else was calling the shots, perhaps even Farook. Everything was way too coordinated. But at some point, when they realized that they weren't going to get any information from Frank, they'd get orders to either lock him up or kill him. Frank wasn't planning on waiting around long enough to find out which.

One thing was for sure, based on their nonaggressive questioning: they hadn't found the case of their own AKs and ammo in his locked truck bed. If they had, he suspected they would be beating him to a bloody pulp about now; at least they'd be trying to.

Frank just pretended that he knew nothing, playing the part of the amiable, albeit lame older man. He found it was always better to pretend stupidity in the face of his enemy. He knew this ruse wouldn't last much longer.

After a long pause, Jones reached across a table where the contents of Frank's pockets lay, scooped up a worn leather wallet, opened it, and pulled out a driver's license. He held it inches from Frank's face. "Then why does your driver's license say that you're from Stowell, Texas?"

Frank didn't miss a beat. "That's my father's address. He and my mother, who are dead now, have lived in the same place since I was born." (At least this part of the story was true.) "I've always used their address because I travel often and needed a permanent address for my license and truck registration."

Jones just scowled at Frank. It was an acknowledgement that this line of questioning wasn't working. If they were going to get any further information, it would have to be by more violent means.

And Frank couldn't wait forever for them to open his truck bed and find the fully automatic rifles, or check his cab and find his own weapons and the further incriminating papers under his seat from their dead Texas cell-leader Hassan's operation's center.

He would need to make his move soon.

Another man wearing an officer's uniform entered the room and plaintively beckoned Fake-Jones to the back where they spoke in whispered tones, accented with animated hand movements. Both looked at Frank and then the other man rattled off a run-on slurry of words to the other man. It wasn't English. The man, now even more agitated, raised and aimed his rifle at Frank.

Jones marched over to Frank, withdrew a pistol and pointed it at Frank's head. Never moving his eyes off

Frank's, he leaned over and released Frank's handcuffs from the chain attached to his chair.

Normally, this would have offered him the opportunity to look for an escape. In close quarters, he could easily disarm Fake-Jones, grab his gun, and shoot the other man. But he still didn't know what happened to Porter Grimes, as well as the rest of the men and women on the base. He would find them first before he would make his move. He would be patient for just a little longer.

"We'll figure out why you're here, if we have to beat it out of you," Jones threatened, pushing the pistol barrel into Frank's back with a grunt of frustration. Frank rose from his chair and out the door.

"Where are you taking me?" Frank screeched, trying to sound distressed.

"We're going to lock you away with the other prisoners until I'm told what to do with you."

They walked outside into the bright sunlight. Feigning detachment, Frank noticed his truck was parked just to the side of the building; the truck bed was still secure. It was surprising that they hadn't jimmied it open yet, and he could only figure that they simply didn't see him as threat enough to inspect further.

After passing two buildings, they walked to the back of another, labeled Army Museum Administration. Jones pushed the door open for him and they walked down a long hallway, with doors on both sides. At the door marked Meeting Room, they stopped. The other guard sprang from behind them, unlocked the door, and pushed Frank inside.

An auditorium filled with close to one hundred sets of eyes glared at him.

It felt like he was the star speaker they had all been waiting for, very impatiently. But these were not faces filled with interested expectation; they were afraid.

It was an eclectic group for sure: a combination of soldiers, wearing only olive T-shirts and boxers—this explained where Jones and the others got their uniforms; reserve officers, in their fatigues; and the other half of his observers in their civvies. All were silent, as if interrupted mid-sentence.

An older man, wearing a pressed olive tee and boxers and the look of a senior officer, emerged from a conference broken up by Frank's entry. He approached with others following behind him.

Frank saluted. "Major Frank Cartwright, US Army, Retired, Sir."

"Captain Danbury, sir." Danbury returned the salute. "I'm the senior officer here, since they executed our base commander, Colonel Jones. Where did you come from, Major?"

Frank quickly glanced around before answering, finding what he wanted. Hurrying to a jar of pens and paper on a front table by a podium, Frank withdrew a pen and wrote, "Can they hear us?" At the same time he spoke very loudly, "I stopped by to see if a nephew was stationed here."

The captain read Frank's note and shook his head vehemently "No!" and then said softly, "No worries, Major. There's probably someone by the door, but they won't be able to hear us; the door and walls are well insulated so as not to interrupt those in offices next door."

More of the men wearing the olive T-shirts and most of the reserves swarmed around Frank to hear the two senior officers discuss what they knew. Only a couple of the civilians stayed in their seats.

"Great," Frank said, resting himself against a first-row desk. "I'm from a small town called Stowell, Texas. I uncovered a group of terrorists who, to their misfortune, selected me as their target. Luckily they didn't know I was Special Ops and a prepper. A few friends—also retired military—and I sent them all back to Allah!"

"Hooah" resonated from a few voices around him.

"Thanks. But the reason why I'm here is that we found intel that leads to the head terrorist: one Abdul Farook, just south of here in Florida. I have a case of their guns and a map showing his exact location. I came here to give this intel to the U.S. Army."

"Of all the shit-luck, sir. These bastards got us with our pants down yesterday," said Danbury.

One of the reservists spoke up. "Sir, isn't Camp Mabry closer to you?"

"True. But you're closer to Farook's base and I was hoping to get this actionable intelligence to an Army base that would be able to directly respond. And with communications down or nonexistent, I didn't want to wait around while trying to get orders from brass in some bunker somewhere." He paused to see the faces chewing on what he'd told them. "I'm also here to find the son of one of my friends."

"Who's that, Sir?" Danbury asked.

"Corporal Porter Grimes."

"Several heads scanned the group, to see if he was here.

"Sir, we haven't seen SPC Grimes since they took the base."

☾† ✡ ☯ 𓅓

"**H**ave you been able to reach 1T2?" the fake Colonel Jones asked the young prisoner, an Army corporal they charged to operate the radios for them.

He pulled his headphones off. "I'm sorry, Colonel, what did you say?"

"Corporal Grimes, I asked if you were able to reach 1T2 on the radio." Grimes had heard him the first time, but he always acted a little slow to try and get more information. Grimes knew that 1T2 was code for the head of one of their cells, but he didn't know the real name of the man, only his code name. It was the same for all fifty-two of the listings on the piece of paper he'd been handed. The only thing he could guess, based on their position on the paper, was perhaps their hierarchy; Grimes guessed that the first code name on the list, 1F, was the head of the top cell. But it was all just a guess, because nothing else made sense.

"Corporal Grimes," Jones hollered impatiently.

"No, I have not, Sir. And there's been no chatter on that frequency."

"Okay, then try the frequency of the first listing and give me the microphone after you have reached him."

Porter Grimes looked at his captor, and wanted to ask more questions, to learn more. At least he wanted to defy his master, to be less amenable than he was. He detested the fact that he was helping the enemy. Then, he looked down to his feet at the previous radio operator's death trail, a streak of dried redness that ran the floor to the storage closet across the room, where his friend's festering body was starting to stink up the place. "Yes, Sir." He quickly twisted the dials to the frequency on the list in front of him and called 1F, wishing he could find out who this man in charge of them all was. "W4ZZ, this is WI5IS, 1A requesting discussion with 1F. Over."

Colonel Jones turned to the lone guard and barked an order, and the guard zipped away, presumably to fulfill his demand.

"Okay, Colonel, I have 1F on the radio," Grimes pushed his microphone over to the colonel and offered the man his headphones.

☪ † ✡ ☯ 🦅

"Look, time is short for me, and perhaps for all of us." Frank interrupted the torrent of questions being thrown at him. He understood their anxiety. But there was little time to act. It needed to be now. He held up his hands to quiet their voices.

When he had their silence, he continued, "What I want to know is if you've made any escape plans."

Danbury spoke first. "That's what we were just discussing before you arrived."

"Sir? First Lieutenant Wallace, sir. But, we don't have any weapons," barked a young woman, with intense eyes, who gazed sternly at her captain, and then at Frank. Besides being the only woman who was part of the active duty soldiers in this room, she was also the only one not stripped down to her underwear. This was curious, because Frank's experience with Islamic jihadists was not good when it came to women. Fake-Jones must have told them to behave, keeping her clothed so as to not tempt his men.

Frank received an irritated glance from the young officer when he stared at her for too long. "We have all the weapons we need right here. Plus, we have the element of surprise. And if we get prepared quickly, we may have access to a case of automatic rifles and ammo in the back of my truck, by the museum."

"With all due respect, sir," argued the woman with the intense eyes. "What do you mean we have all the weapons we need?" Her ponytail whipped back and forth as she scanned the room in mock inspection. "I see no M4s, no grenades ..."

"First Lieutenant Wallace believes we should wait out our time here," Danbury offered as an excuse for his officer's insolence.

"Still," said Wallace, "I'd like to hear how the major thinks we can fight back with a pile of Ft. Rucker bandanas and novelty pens."

"Let me show you," Frank bellowed as he jogged up the auditorium steps to the back, grabbing a stack of bandanas and directing two olive-shirts to grab some of the other supplies. These they piled on the large table at the front of the auditorium. Everyone, including the civvies, surrounded Frank as he demonstrated the fine art of improvising weapons out of common materials.

☾ † ✡ ☯ 🦅

P orter stood up straight but tried to act as if nothing interesting was being said when the man wearing Colonel Jones's uniform mentioned "Stowell, Texas," where his father lived. This was mentioned in the same sentence as 1T2. He overheard the concern in the colonel's voice as he told his superior that they could not reach 1T2 and yet, coincidentally, a stranger from Stowell, Texas shows up at this base pretending to be looking for a nephew named Private Harry Simpleton. Since this name wasn't on the base's duty roster, Porter guessed this stranger was not telling the colonel the whole truth.

Then, Porter heard something that made his blood boil and freeze at the same time. The colonel made a whispered request that his superior allow him to shoot all the prisoners, including the mystery man. There was too much at stake and they needed to eliminate any threats.

As he was saying this, the colonel turned his head slightly to Porter to see if he was listening, before continuing. "I only need to keep one of the men, because he's the only one who can work the equipment. I lost my radio man when we took the base."

There was silence as 1F was responding to the request.

Porter shot a quick glance at the colonel, who was not looking at him, his head nodding in the affirmative.

While Colonel Jones seemed to be receiving confirmation to murdering everyone but him, Porter slipped into the next room where a long electrical cable snaked inside to the radio equipment from one of the two gennies grinding away outside. Porter quickly stuck his head out the window, yanked off one of the cables attached to the genny, and tossed it under a cabinet, out of sight. The genny sputtered and died, just as Porter slid back into place at the doorway.

The room's lights flickered twice, and then went off.

Colonel Jones pushed up and down on the microphone's button, figuring he had done something. He stepped away from the radios, looking down to make sure he hadn't kicked out the cords. He turned to Porter, who had his arms folded and was looking up at the lights above as if he were surprised by their change. Porter looked back to him apologetically, before nodding. "I'll check the genny, sir." Porter ran out the door and around the building to the generator, pretending to investigate the reasons for the generator's sudden silence. But he didn't stop at the genny; he kept running.

A detachment of five men with guns arrived at the door of the radio room from another direction.

The colonel marched past them. Projecting his voice back, he announced, "Come with me. I've been just given orders to shoot all the prisoners."

☾ ✝ ✡ ☯ 🦅

Frank finished one more bandana, just like he'd shown them earlier. "Ft. Rucker paperweight in the middle of the bandana; then fold in half; then roll the bandana from apex to base; then fold it end to end." He had held it up to show the group what the lethal bandana looked like.

"Do you really think this thing will do much damage?" First Lieutenant Wallace had asked, looking at her sap incredulously.

Without missing a beat, Frank stepped over to a globe resting on a pedestal beside the lectern. "Pretend this is your enemy's head." Frank swung his improvised weapon around and connected hard with the globe, burying the sap deep within the metal orb.

Wallace didn't say another word.

No one did.

They took the next ten minutes to construct their improvised weapons. When everyone had one, Frank knew they were as ready as they could be. He wished he had more time, especially to coach the civvies; they hadn't even had Basic like the officers and reservists.

"Look, we don't have much time. Remember, you're going for the head or the knees, even if they're holding a weapon." Frank said this while walking over to Danbury, who nodded at him as they stopped at the door.

"All right everybody, fall in," Danbury ordered, waiting behind Frank.

The others did as their captain ordered. All were carrying something, even the civilians. Some had rolled-up base newspapers, taped in the form of a bat with pen-spikes sticking out of the end. Many had the bandana and weight combo. Danbury, already an expert at hand-to-hand, just carried a pen.

Frank, using two paperclips—he always kept them on his person—worked on the lock as everyone waited for the moment.

A click told them it was time.

Chapter 20

Lexi

When you're panicked, it's basically impossible to think straight.

Lexi dashed from the truck into the store to see if by some odd chance he was still there. But both Travis and the dead elderly man were gone. Only a red stain from the man's blood remained. She hovered over the spot, hands on hips, mentally beating herself up for not having done a better job to stay with her brother. She'd left him again when she trotted into the store to find her shoes. If they had both gone in, they might have been able to slip out the back before being seen. The panicky feelings returned and her head began swimming, knowing as she did that at any moment Clyde and Zach were going to pull up and kill her for burning their house down.

Breathe and calm down, Lex!

She tried desperately to think of where her brother might have gone after she was taken.

Then she remembered.

She drove the monster truck to the front of the white house with the wrap-around porch that the old man had pointed to. She put it into park and watched for movement. On any other day, this slice of Americana would look inviting. Red, white, and blue banners sashayed the length of the porch, and an American flag proudly flew from a long pole jutting off the front of the house. Before the apocalypse, it would have had kids running around the front yard, sparklers blazing in little hands, and giddy laughter filling the air. *So much has changed in a day.*

Now, the home looked foreboding, another trap waiting to catch her. The front door was open wide and she could see inside and almost all the way through the house. A burrowed trail of blood ran from the grassy front lawn, to the front sidewalk, and up the stairs. Death had fallen upon this home.

Lexi withdrew her pistol—she now considered it hers and not her late father's—out of the pack and mounted the steps. The blood stain continued over the threshold and into the house. Her body and mind stopped, hesitant to go any farther. Her heart leapt from her chest when a crow grated a warning from the large oak outside and flew away. She wasn't sure her nerves could make it through another day of this.

Calm down, Lexi, she told herself over and over, before finally stepping inside.

The blood pooled by the entrance, but then abruptly stopped. Around the pool were a flurry of bloody foot-prints—one small and one only slightly larger—and some scratch marks. And by the staircase, two sets of shoes rested beside each other, socks inside each.

The smaller set of shoes belonged to Travis.

Stepping around the gruesome pond, Lexi pro-ceeded on tip-toes down the long hallway to the back. The staccato beat of her heart filled her ears;

thump-thumb-thump. And there were other sounds out back.

She raised the gun higher as she approached the back door—it too stood wide open. At the threshold, she saw him.

Travis was sitting in a chair, sipping from a glass of yellowish liquid, while an elderly woman knelt beside a mound of dirt. The woman laid flowers on top of it and whispered tear-filled words.

Lexi shoved the gun against the small of her back, beneath her shirt, and walked down the back steps.

He was safe.

☪ † ✡ ☯ ☸

After saying their goodbyes and collecting their bags—Travis had somehow held onto them—Lexi and Travis sped out of Greensville and back onto the highway. Lexi couldn't drive fast enough, sure at any moment now Clyde would be on their tail or in front of them, blocking their passage.

But she also couldn't help but look at Travis, who sank deeper into the passenger seat with each mile they drove. He hadn't said a word the whole time and just stared out the window, despondent. Perhaps he was in shock.

He was like that at the old lady's house. Lexi tried to give him something solid to hold onto, because everything around them seemed so transitory and death so close to them. So she gave him their father's Purple Heart.

It didn't seem to help.

Before too long they drove by the dirt road that led to Zach and Clyde's place. She was driving so fast, she almost didn't notice it. But when she glanced that way, a camo-colored truck erupted from the growth's dark opening and bounded toward the highway and them.

"Shit!" Lexi jammed her foot into the accelerator, and the old vehicle lurched forward in response. They were going slightly faster, but was it enough?

She watched attentively for their turnoff, making sure she didn't miss it. The map was forever etched into her memory. But in a panic, her memory-map didn't seem to match up with reality too well.

"How close are they?" she shrieked in an almost shrill voice. The wind roared through the open cab of the truck. She wasn't even sure if he said anything so she yelled once more, "How many lengths of this truck are they from us?"

From beside her, he bawled back, "About fifty trucks." He was kneeling on the seat, peering behind them.

They crossed over the vast expanse of the Apalachicola River and then she saw it. Their turnoff was marked by a crooked mailbox off the highway. She took her foot off the gas.

"Thirty trucks," Travis yelled, his voice breaking up from fear and the swirling wind.

She spun the wheel, barely slowing down. She felt her side of the truck lift up, the driver's side wheels finding air. She corrected, and left the dirt path. Jamming her brakes, she corrected once more, almost flipping it the other way. She hit the gas again, bouncing onto the dirt road.

"Twenty trucks!" he yelled.

She looked at her side mirror and could see them already on their road, close behind, as if they didn't even slow when they hit the turn. The side mirror exploded.

"They're shooting at us!" Travis screeched and sank to the floor.

She glanced at him and felt deep compassion for the boy. Hell, she was terrified as well. "It'll be okay. We'll get to Abe's and he'll protect us," she hollered so he heard.

She hoped that was true, only assuming that Abe was a prepper like she guessed her father must have been. *Oh God, I hope Abe's house is close.*

They zagged away from the river and then zigged back at it. The truck lurched and gagged.

Then it died.

They rolled to a stop in front of a large fence, the bumper kissing it.

"Get out, grab your bag and get onto the hood of the truck."

Lexi leapt out of the truck. Looking back she couldn't see their pursuers, but she could hear them. She tossed both bags on the hood and jumped up, using the knobby tire as a step. After tossing her two bags over the fence she grabbed Travis's bag and tossed it, and pulled him up so he could climb over. Although, he didn't need the boost because he climbed better than a monkey.

The camo-truck zagged toward them. She could see Clyde and Zach in front and two other men in the truck bed.

She hoisted Travis over the fence and he tumbled to the other side. She sprang fast, without thinking where she would fall, and landed hard but safely. She grabbed their bags and started to run. Looking to her side, she was happy to see Travis was there. She guided them into the thicket and out of sight from the road.

Several shots thundered behind them, but they didn't look back to see where.

Lexi and Travis crashed through the heavy growth, having no idea where they were going or if safety awaited them.

"Go get them," Clyde yelled to the two men in the truck bed.

"When I catch dat bitch, I'm gonna fillet her hide," his brother screamed at the windshield.

"You get 'er, brother."

Zach had already jumped out and leapt onto his truck's hood and over the fence like a lion after its prey. Their two men followed just behind him. Clyde jumped over last.

Travis was falling behind even though she was carrying all their bags.

"C'mon, buddy. I need you to be strong for just another minute or two."

She looked away just long enough that she didn't see the tree limb at chin level until she hit it full force, knocking her on her back.

"Lex, are you okay?" he begged looking down on her, with concern.

She felt a little light-headed and wondered for a moment. Her chin throbbed—matching her constant headache—and it felt like it was bleeding.

Then, she heard approaching noises, the cracking of branches and thumping of footsteps telling her that those men were just behind them.

She jumped up, ignoring the pain and her blurred vision, and moved forward. They were running again, branches and giant leaves whipping at them, but they both ignored their stings.

Lexi could see the area opened up in front of them slightly, and then they were in a wide open area with a driveway leading to several houses, and a river.

In front of them was a man on one knee pointing a rifle at them.

They froze in their tracks, starring at this man who didn't flinch or move a muscle.

She could see his finger wrap around the trigger.

He fired twice.

Chapter 21

Dallas, Texas

Two Days Earlier

I t was the feeling of inevitability that haunted him.

Agent Stanley Broadmoor glanced at the vehicle tailing him, several car lengths away. Hameed's men, led by his assassin Yusuf Habib, were waiting for him to pull off to a quiet side of the road, where they would pass slowly and fire their automatic weapons into him until he was dead.

But Stan kept his white Toyota steady, pointed north at a tedious sixty-five miles an hour. The last thing he wanted to do was pull an unsuspecting motor cop into this. His route, if he continued down this path, would lead to Kansas as he had told Hameed over the phone. That is, he—Malik the Terrorist—would visit an arms dealer there, to purchase more weapons for a large planned attack, coming soon. But he didn't intend to go all the way to Kansas, and the car behind him would never let him get that far.

Stan looked at himself in the rearview mirror, brushing his filthy hands over his full beard, finally yanking at his mustache to remind himself that all this was his real mug. He still didn't recognize this face he'd worn for the last five-plus years. His all-consuming hunt for Farook had come so close to an end. Almost eight years of undercover work, trying to catch the man who killed his wife while taking down terrorist cells in the US, had yielded gains. But it had also taken so much: eight years away from his kids, growing up without him, and the life of his wife, all stolen by Abdul Raheem Farook. Then his plans changed in an instant.

Stan—playing the part of Malik the Terrorist—had been working a young boy named Bilal, who was part of Hameed's Texas cell. He couldn't have been more than 16—maybe five or six years older than his own son, Travis. Malik befriended the boy, providing a father figure that the boy had never had. Malik had Bilal questioning his loyalties to the cell, especially after Malik found out that Bilal was being molested by Yusuf Habib, one of the most bloodthirsty men he'd ever had the disappointment of meeting. Bilal overheard much from Yusuf's bed and recently started to report what he heard to Malik. Three revelations changed everything.

Yusuf was in constant contact with Hassan Hameed, somewhere in a rural part of Texas. This made sense because Hameed was the head of the Texas cell and gave direction for their smaller cell in Houston. But Yusuf also spoke directly to Farook, even mentioning his name. Bilal described the killer actually becoming rigid when he spoke to Farook, so he knew it was him on the phone. In a conversation two days ago, Yusuf let slip that Farook was in Florida. So now they had active intel that Farook was in the States, and in fact in Florida. Agent Broadmoor was able to pass this along to his superiors, and the statewide hunt was on for Farook. Then yesterday, Bilal revealed something that would ultimately lead to Stan's own death.

After raping and brutally beating Bilal, Yusuf received a hurried phone call. By his stiff body language, Bilal knew it was Farook on the other end. Yusuf went to a special locked room, where no one else was allowed. Bilal didn't know exactly what was in there, though once he had caught a glimpse of many maps on a wall. During yesterday's phone call, Yusuf said, "I knew I recognized him" and then later, "Does this change any plans for Phase One on July 4th?" and then he closed the door. Bilal said that he was sure something big was happening on that day, but he didn't know who Yusuf recognized.

Stan reported only the date to his team. He held back the other info and what he planned to do, until he could verify it with his own eyes. He knew his superiors would not approve and if they suspected that Yusuf was speaking about Agent Broadmoor—acting as Malik—he would have been yanked out of the field. But there was too much at stake now: nabbing Farook, uncovering a large terrorist plot, and ensuring Bilal's safety. He was going to try and get him out of this immediately. In fact, he told Bilal to leave straightaway! He gave the boy some money and told him to get as far away from Yusuf as possible.

But the boy didn't.

Early this morning, he got a text from Bilal, who must have gone back—Stan feared it was to offer further help to him. His text said, "Yusuf and men leavin to kill u." Stan grabbed his bug-out bag, got into his Toyota, and sped to

Yusuf's place. He found a naked Bilal dead, throat slit, his phone beside him.

No time for tears. That would be later.

Stan had not been inside the map room before; very few had been. There were two doors, other than the entrance. One was the closet. The other was locked. He picked this lock and entered, flipping on the single bulb. He stood in awe at the main map on the wall. It was of the United States, with Phase One written on top and red circles drawn around Chicago, New York, and DC, two thick circles in the middle of the country, and three other small circles: the city of Jacksonville and two other more rural areas.

Good God, are those targets?

They had strong suspicions that at least one, maybe more high-yield suitcase nukes had made their way into the US, via a "stolen" supply in Russia. The CIA suspected that Russia was complicit in these thefts.

Off the coasts of Oregon and North Carolina were two roughly drawn cigar-shaped objects labeled with Arabic letters. If he read this correctly, it said "Russian." Each cigar had a dashed line running in a concave arc up from each cigar and then down, terminating in a thick red circle. One circle was drawn over the western edge of Kentucky, and the other over Salt Lake City, Utah.

They were submarines!

There were thumbtacks dotting points all around the coasts and the borders of the US. He examined the two in Texas and recognized one of them was right on the edge of Houston and the other, just to the right of this. A thought occurred to him and his eyes flashed to the pin above Panama City, Florida. He stood back and looked again, pulled out his phone and snapped a picture.

At that moment, his whole body trembled.

These were all terrorist cells. All were at border areas so as to easily welcome in new recruits: soldiers for an upcoming war. There were over one hundred thumb-tacks all along the coasts, and based upon the amount of weapons Hameed said they needed, each cell was going to welcome hundreds of soldiers. That meant maybe tens of thousands of jihadists with guns and a desire to kill Americans. First they would launch nukes at our cities and over the country to take out the grid, and then America was going to be invaded. And Stan knew there was nothing they could do to stop it. Their plans were too far along and it was going to happen ... *tomorrow!*

I have to get out, with my kids, now.

Stan dashed out of the room, closing the door with a click. He paused over the lifeless form of the young boy that had helped him, but he did nothing with the body. After jumping into his car, he attempted to text the photo to another agent, but in his haste, he didn't hit "send."

He made two calls, the second to Sara on a separate untraceable phone he carried in his bug-out bag. He was too busy to realize until he was on the highway that Yusuf and his men had returned before he had left and were following him.

Farook had won. He would take down the US, as he'd promised in a video years earlier. And there was nothing Stan could do, or would do, to stop him. But, he wasn't going to waste any more time trying, either. He would be with his kids and they would be together, for however long they had. Together.

A car honked at Stan for his not paying attention and letting his vehicle wander into the other's lane. Reflexively, he waved at the other driver in apology and corrected his path. He glanced once more at his mirror pointed back at him. He barely remembered what he looked like before he went undercover. Before he became this Malik. But, that would change soon enough.

He glanced at the turnoff sign, and then again at the car behind him, and pulled on the wheel, quickly veering off the highway onto the frontage road, which led into a small service station on a T-intersection.

He could feel their binoculars were on him, all his motions being reported back directly to Yusuf.

☾ † ✡ ☯ 🦅

T he person they knew to be Malik, guided his car into the full-service island of pumps. A young worker in a blue striped work shirt dashed out of the building almost instantly and traded words with him. The worker nodded his head mechanically and then proceeded to fill up the car and wash the windows, while Malik ducked inside, ostensibly to use the restroom, a backpack slung over his shoulder, his long black *jubba* fluttering behind him.

Yusuf Habib's red Mazda slowed to a stop behind a row of self-serve pumps at a different island on the other side of the station, but in plain view of the island where Malik's car sat. Yusuf exited his car, his black beard flapping in the warm Texas air, as he watched the station attendant service the Toyota they had been tailing. The other men got out of the car, their weapons shouldered beneath their *jubbas*, hidden but ready. They looked at Yusuf for the word on whether to kill the traitor now or wait for a better opportunity, with fewer people.

Farook's orders were to follow him and kill him where there were the least number of witnesses. Their long awaited plan to take down the infidels would start in only one more day. And his men were needed for the invasion, a few days after this. They needed to remain as innocuous as possible until then, and killing people at a gas station would only damage their cause. They would wait for a better opportunity.

He shook his head "no" to his men, who were unsatisfied with his answer but complied. Yusuf felt their frustration; they all wanted this war to start now. Yusuf put the nozzle back into the pump, pretending to be finished when he hadn't actually used it. He got back into his car and waited. The others followed, and all the doors closed.

☪ † ✡ ☉ 🦅

Two men in a black Suburban pulled into a competing gas station across the street, keeping their distance from both targeted cars. They, too, were trying to figure out their next step. Their man inside, Agent Broadmoor, was supposed to have been turning a new asset and then he had gone off comms. They found him racing out of his apartment, then going to Yusuf's apartment. Now driving his car toward Kansas, with Yusuf and his men were following him. Yusuf's men looked angry, but the agents didn't know why. Something must have happened since Broadmoor went off comms.

"Has Broadmoor made even a squeak on his radio?" said the driver to the other.

"No. In fact, I'm seeing no movement from Broadmoor. Something must have happened. Wait, here he is."

They watched the still undercover Broadmoor dash to his Toyota and slip into it. Immediately, he drove out of the station, onto the frontage road and back onto the highway.

No one noticed he was no longer wearing his backpack.

Yusuf's Mazda pulled out as well, continuing to tail the Toyota, five car lengths behind him. The Suburban followed far behind, staying out of visual distance, relying on the GPS tracking device in Agent Broadmoor's phone, which was speeding along at a healthy seventy-six miles per hour.

☾ † ✡ ☯ ☪🦅

About ten minutes later, a clean-shaven Stanley Broadmoor stepped out of the gas station bathroom and walked through the employee entrance to the garage. There, his cherished Plymouth Fury waited for him. He hoped that his friend, wearing a disguise that made him look like Stan's Malik persona, would be safe. If all went according to plan, his friend would lose both Yusuf and his fellow agents at a seemingly random, but planned, block in traffic in Kansas City, where they would assume he ran and would search for him there.

It was a bold plan Stan had crafted several months earlier in case everything turned to shit, and it certainly had. The world he knew was about to end soon, along with their cherished America. Even if he wanted to, there was nothing he or any of the authorities could do to stop the multiple cells operating throughout the US. The destruction of the US was inevitable. So, it was time.

His kids would be arriving at George Bush Intercontinental Airport in a few hours. He would finally be with his children, for good.

He pulled out of the garage bay, and drove into the lingering sunlight of an expiring day. He hadn't considered that this might be the last sunset he and many of his countrymen would see.

Chapter 22

Frank

July 5th

His old friend adrenaline was back.

After picking the lock, Frank reached behind and Wallace handed him one of the bandana saps as he silently turned the handle and pulled on the door. Only his head breached the space between frame and door.

Just one guard with his back to them: at least this part was going to be easy.

The guard must have heard or sensed something because his head and shoulders perked up, and he started to turn. In his younger days, Frank would have sprung from the room, stealthy and deadly. Now, he knew his knee prevented the stealthiness, but he'd still be deadly. As the guard turned around to face him, Frank brought the arc and the full heft of the weight around to its thudding terminus into the side of the man's head. Frank wouldn't try to slow this man's fall, this time.

Turns out, he didn't have to. Danbury was right there to catch the man as he fell, making that part of their operation silent. Then almost as swiftly, he and one of the other officers dragged the guard inside the room. Danbury returned sporting the guard's AK.

"Hope you don't mind?" Danbury motioned with the weapon and Frank swore he wore a little grin.

Frank smiled too and briskly walked to the end of the hallway, ready to pounce on anyone who came out of one of the doors he passed. The shuffle of footsteps behind him told him that Danbury and crew were on his heels. This might just work.

Just then, without warning, the outside door cracked open.

Frank thrust his arm back, ready to swing, and in sync, Danbury pulled back the charging handle on the AK, his finger on the trigger.

"Whoa, it's just me—" said a man popping in with his hands up in surrender.

"Porter Grimes," announced Frank. "Thank *God* you're safe."

"Major Cartwright, sir. *You're* the stranger they were talking about?" Porter glanced at Danbury. "Sir." Then to the rest of the group he said, "We have to hurry, they're coming here right now to execute everyone."

Several of the group mumbled their worried concerns, but all looked up at this mission's commander, Frank, for his order to leave the building.

"No!" Frank declared as he shot glances to each of the doors along the hallway and then back to the hallway's entrance. "We're going to let them come here and try to execute us."

The group's stunned silence was broken enthusiastically by Wallace, who nodded at him. "Damn smart, sir."

☾ ✝ ✡ ☯ 🦅

C olonel Kadeem and his men walked with precision
to the building's hallway entrance. In a minute, they
would be able put their worries aside and focus on the
mission. It should never have been their job to babysit the
enemy. This was the only puzzling part of their orders:
not to kill the enemy until after they entered the next
phase of their mission, which was still a few days away.
They weren't looking for intelligence; they knew all they
needed to know. Other than a radio operator, they didn't
need any of the Army's men, and certainly not their drone
pilots; they had their own.

The uniforms made sense, although he'd rather be
wearing his own colonel's uniform from the IRG. Certainly it would be nice to be recognized under his real
name and not this dead American's. But they needed to
look like US Army in case anyone like this Cartwright
wandered in, or if the US Army showed up unannounced.
And they did not need the previous occupiers of this base
and these uniforms to still be breathing. At least, that risk
would be mitigated.

They entered the hallway, with Kadeem leading his
five guard-executioners. After the door clicked behind
them, with a slight echo, Kadeem listened to his senses.
They'd kept him alive through two revolutions, and they
were telling him something was wrong. The guard he had
posted in front of the prisoners' door was not there.

"Pay attention," he told the executioners, who raised
their weapons in reply.

Kadeem slowly proceeded forward, his hand on his holstered weapon, his men behind him in lockstep.

Each door they walked past increased Kadeem's tension. When they passed the fourth door, a woman in civilian clothes bumbled out of the last door before the auditorium, giggling. She stopped when she saw the men, wobbling some, like she was inebriated. Her mouth popped open, her intense eyes burned with shock, and her hands were thrown up into the air so quickly, she looked like she might fall over.

"Freeze," yelled Kadeem. The guards aimed their rifles.

The woman appeared to faint, as she fell hard to the floor, just as five men snuck up behind the guards and swung their saps, all connecting at once.

Kadeem knew they'd been had the moment the woman fell, but he couldn't react in time. He'd barely raised his pistol from its holster when the barrel of a rifle punched into his back, almost knocking the wind out of his lungs. "I wouldn't, Colonel," said Cartwright's familiar voice.

Kadeem holstered his sidearm.

"You can get up now, First Lieutenant; good acting, by the way." Frank pushed the rifle barrel harder against the colonel's back, relishing the turnabout. "And why don't you grab the colonel's weapon and watch the door in case someone else attempts to come through."

Wallace rose from the floor with a smile, walked over to Kadeem and pulled out his pistol. "I'll take that, thank you." She slipped by them and listened for others at the door.

"What are you going to do with me?" Kadeem cringed inside at how cowardly he sounded.

"I'm sure you'd like to join Allah in Paradise, but first we need to know a few things."

☪ † ✡ ☉ ☯ 🦅

It always amazed him how a mission's objective changed with the elements.

At first, Frank was going to Ft. Rucker to be chief sales-man for their cause, to plead with the Army to take their intel, so that they would take the fight directly to Farook in Florida. Then he'd be chief salesman for Grimes to convince his son, Porter to come back with him. He had no interest in engaging Farook; that part of the war would be for the younger men and women. Certainly he'd have his hands full protecting their homes in Stowell.

But then the mission changed, when he learned the base had been taken. He would have to rescue Porter and the rest of the troops.

And now his mission had changed again. He'd secured the safety of all the men and women of this base, in-cluding Porter. His new mission was to take it back, as it obviously played a key role in this enemy's war on America. He had the skills to help in this necessary cause. But their mission was greater than this. They needed to also find out why this base was so important: why this base in Alabama? Colonel Kadeem—the man hadn't told them much except his name, yet—would be the one to help them figure this out. But to have the time to do this, they first had to take back the base and kill their enemy.

"We have to get to my truck." Frank pointed to a base map in one of the rooms off the hallway, where all but two of the reservists—who were on watch—had gathered. "So as to not arouse suspicion, we'll have the colonel march me back to the museum, with his five guards following. You five," he pointed to the five men who had reclaimed their own uniforms from the guards. "We'll get the guns and the case of ammo and bring them back here. Finally, we'll arm up and then take the base. Any questions?"

Frank looked first to Danbury, to see if he found any holes in his plan, then to Porter, and then to the rest of the group.

A few moments later they were marching back to the museum. Colonel Kadeem had an empty AK pointed at Frank, who whispered threats to Kadeem if he said anything. The five men pretending to be guards followed quietly, eyes watching all movement around them.

So far so good.

After fumbling with his keys, Frank opened his truck bed. Two of the men pulled the crate from the tailgate and Kadeem chortled to himself, mouthing some Farsi swearword under his breath.

Two of Kadeem's men approached them from the museum as Frank's men were lifting the two crates. One of them asked Kadeem a question, which Frank didn't hear; he looked at Kadeem's face. He knew it before Kadeem's mouth formed the words. Frank grabbed an AK slung over one of the guards and spun around as Kadeem started bellowing his warning. Frank cut both men down and then turned the rifle on Kadeem. He needed him for information, but survival was more important. Kadeem shot him a glance of acceptance for his fate and Frank fired once, ending Kadeem's identity-stealing days.

"Run back to the auditorium," Frank ordered as he scanned for more guards.

Just before they ran behind the corner of the building, he could see dozens of men streaming their way. They were about to become sitting ducks.

☾ † ✡ ☯ 🦅

The battle that followed was the first that Frank had ever lost.

He looked up from the wheel of the convoy truck he had stolen and shot a glance at his side mirror and his pickup following, Porter behind the wheel and Wallace at shotgun. Then he glared at the back of the truck through his rearview mirror, counting the heads. Out of over a hundred, only maybe a dozen had made it. The rest were killed when they were surrounded. He wasn't sure how he and a few made it out alive. But they did.

Danbury and so many others didn't. And it was his fault he couldn't save them.

"Where next?" asked the lieutenant, whose name he had forgotten.

Yes, where? He wondered this too.

They could head to Farook's base, but they were down to maybe a hundred rounds of ammo and four or five AKs and one Berretta pistol. Farook was probably loaded for bear. This would be a suicide mission.

They could head to Stowell, Texas, who could certainly use the help for the coming invasion.

They pulled up to the intersection at I-10: to the east was Farook and certain death; to the west was home and another chance. He put his hands at two o'clock and was pulling down on the wheel when the Hellfire missile hit them from the drone above.

The convoy truck's back erupted. The explosion sent it forward and over, where it came to rest in the middle of I-10. Frank hung upside down, held in his place from his harness. His eyes fluttered for a moment, when he recognized the wetness and the taste of iron.

Before a web of blackness shut out his vision, Frank said a little prayer for the town of Stowell, because he felt guilty for not being able to bring back Porter; then for his country, because he felt guilty he couldn't get enough terrorists; and finally he thought about his godkids. He hoped they made it safely to Florida with his friend Stan.

Then there was nothing.

Chapter 23

Abe

Lexi's palms were pressed hard against her face, teeth clenched, her body folded tight like a cannonball, while she knelt and waited for death.

The gun shots were so close to her, they exploded as loudly as if she were shooting the gun.

But she wasn't hit.

Layered within the ringing in her ears was a voice. It sounded distant, but she knew it was right above her. "Come on," and "over there." She parted her fingers, chancing a glance, and saw a couple of armed men brush by, mostly ignoring them. She released her hands altogether and peered at the man who had been pointing his rifle at them, standing in front of her, offering his hand to her, "It's all right miss, they won't be chasing you anymore."

Lexi looked to her right and saw Travis clutching himself, shaking. She spun around and there was the man whose nose she had broken, lying before the tree line. The man who had knocked her out and wanted to hand her over to his men for things she didn't want to consider. Zach was dead.

She nervously studied the tree line, trying to somehow peek through its shadowy darkness to see if Clyde was still there.

"The others are gone," said the shooter, his hand still held out to her. "Not to worry, our men will make sure that they don't come back."

She looked at the man. His eyes spoke of kindness, his face of hardship. Multiple scars seemed to snake out of a tightly groomed gray-black beard, so many that they appeared to hold his mug together, like seams in a soccer ball. "I'm Sal," he said in a softer tone, thrusting his hand out farther.

Lexi didn't realize she'd been kneeling the whole time, till she rose to accept his hand with hers. She gathered her brother up with her free arm, his body still shuddering with fear.

After several steps she asked, "Is this ... Abe's place?" Hopefully this wasn't some grand mistake after such a long journey.

The man stopped to look directly at her. A welcoming smile grew, making the creases more defined. "It most certainly is." He continued forward, but turned his head at an angle so they could hear. "Do you know Abe?"

"My father was ... a friend of his."

He led them toward a main driveway and several buildings. "Was?"

"He died," Travis said in a froggy voice among his sniffles, looking up to Sal.

"I'm sorry, little man." Sal glanced down to Travis, holding onto his gaze. "That must have been really hard to lose your father." His voice and otherwise ruined face exuded empathy. "What was his name?"

"Stanley Broadmoor, and this is the medal he earned for being brave." Travis said resolutely, pridefully pointing to the lapel of his shirt where he wore the heavy Purple Heart.

Sal stopped so abruptly upon hearing this, Lexi almost ran into him. Facing both of them, he asked, "Stanley Broadmoor was your father?"

"Yes, why?"

"Abe will be happy to hear you both made it. He's been expecting you."

☾ ✝ ✡ ☯ 🦅

"Those shits killed my brotha!" hollered Clyde, spittle flying from his lips. "I want 'em all dead."

"Hang on, boss. Dey gots a lot of firepowah. And dat fence will be hard to get over if der watching," his second in charge offered tentatively, like a cowboy trying to calm a raging bronco.

Clyde pounded the table in his burnt house. "Dammit!"

He dropped his head into his arms and sobbed.

His men stood around him in his blackened home, water still dripping from the ceiling, a dead fish sucked up from the river water they used to extinguish the fire on the kitchen floor.

They waited for their orders, wanting revenge for their boss, but not wanting to wind up dead like Zach and two others who had been killed as a result of that little bitch and her brother.

After a couple of minutes, Clyde raised his head and scowled at his Number Two. "I don't care what you do. You figure out a plan for us to kill every one of those bastards. Now leabmealone."

They all scurried out of his house like field mice, into the sun, and planned their revenge.

☾ ✝ ✡ ☯ 🦅

"I'm Abe. So glad you made it here safe," said the man standing before them.

Lexi and Travis had gotten help from Leo, a skinny young man with a dark complexion and amiable manner. Sal had handed them off to him, and asked that he get them cleaned up and then give them a tour of the grounds until Abe was available.

Lexi wasn't sure what to say. Everyone was so kind and helpful here. And all because of their father's friendship with this mystery man, Abe, who they'd been hoping would provide them safety in this crazy new world where their father was dead and nothing worked.

"I'm Lexi, and this is my brother, Travis." She shook his hand enthusiastically. "Very pleased to meet you."

He took a seat next to them at a picnic table outside in the sunshine. Leo was rewrapping the bandages on her feet.

"Did you know our dad?" Travis asked, watching him carefully. The boy had a bandage above his eyebrow—a deep scratch from their escape through the woods—that stuck out like a pitched tent as he waited for an answer.

She had only seen this face when he was questioning something he didn't fully accept.

"I did. He and I ... well, we've been friends all of our lives. He told me you might be coming here. I'm so sorry to hear what happened."

"How did you know we were coming?" Travis's chin scrunched in, almost making him look comical. *He'll never be a card player when he grows up—if he grows up.*

"He sent a text two days ago and said that you might stop by. I expected to hear from him, and when I didn't, I assumed he might have sent you here if there was trouble."

"You mean like the end of the world?" It was Lexi's turn to be inquisitive, although she regretted that her question came out so snarky.

"Most especially for that reason." Abe rose from the table. "I have a few things I need to attend to. But I'll check in with you later when you've had time to rest and settle in. Please, consider this your home now."

"But, you'll be able to get us to our real home in Arizona, won't you? Daddy said you'd take us there or to our godfather's house in Texas, who would help us get home." Lexi felt herself panic, just a little. She so wanted to be home.

"Yes, of course, that is what I meant. But you make yourself home here, until it is safe. Then, we'll go to Tucson, together." He looked over to Leo, who had just finished her other foot. "I leave you in capable hands." He turned and walked away.

They watched him march over to a small house, maybe no bigger than their garage in Tucson. And like it, this house also had a large antenna tower abutting it, with many antennas on top, jutting out in all directions, and a tangle of wires like vines from large willow trees flowed into the house. Abe spoke briefly to another man coming from the other direction and then closed the door behind him.

A thought lingered in Lexi's mind. It seemed strange to her that Abe, their father's friend, never asked how he died. She'd have wanted to know, if she were him.

Leo laced up Lexi's boot, and then thrust his hands into the air like a rodeo star who'd just finished roping a calf. "Wadda say we go see the grounds now?"

☾ † ✡ ☯ 🦅

"**S**ir." A man rose quickly from the chair, pulling off his headphones, when he saw Abe enter.

"Anything?" Abe asked.

The man grabbed a note pad and flipped to the first two pages of meticulous handwriting. "Mostly chatter from ham radio operators throughout the country. I made some notes here so you can review if you'd like, but nothing relevant to our cause. Oh," he looked back up at his boss, "Sara called twice. She's worried about"—he looked back at his notes—"and I quote, 'about Stan and the kids'." He handed him the pad and walked to the door.

"Thank you." Abe sat in the black swivel chair and waited for the click of the door closing before putting on his headphones.

Abe twirled the dial of the Kenwood transceiver to their frequency and clicked the microphone button, leaning into it.

"Sara, are you there? This is Abe."

He waited, but not for long.

"Abe, so glad you called back. Have you heard from Stan? He left with the kids three days ago. I thought he might be headed your way, even though you two hadn't spoken in years. And I know things are crazy with the nuclear attack and all. Anyway, I'm just worried. Have you heard anything from them?"

Abe looked at the picture of Lexi and Travis sitting on a shelf right above his radio equipment. It was sent to him from Sara recently. Although it showed the two of them just twelve months ago, they both looked older now and more mature.

He clicked on the microphone. "Hello Sara. I'm sorry, but no I haven't heard from Stan or the kids. But I'm sure they're fine."

"I hope you're right. I'm so worried about our brother, and especially our niece and nephew."

Chapter 24

The Broadmoors

41 Years Earlier

The father of three plunged the accelerator of his Mercedes to the floor, whipping the black sedan up to an unsafe speed, desperately trying to navigate their way to the airport and avoid striking one of the many pedestrians clogging this Damascus artery. His children's freedom depended on his speed and precision, and of course a little good fortune granted by Allah would be helpful.

Feisal swerved at the last second, pulling around a large group of men standing in the middle of the street, before straightening his path and shooting down the final stretch to the airport. He glanced into the back seat to make sure this last turn wasn't too jarring to his wife and the kids. She looked up with swollen eyes, clinging to their two-year-old daughter, Saraphene, on her lap. His two boys were book-ended against her, a tangled mass of arms holding each other erect in the seat.

Feisal glanced momentarily to the heavens, once again mentally beckoning Allah to intervene into their fate and get them there safely; although, even that probably wouldn't be enough. They'd have to be very lucky for the private plane he'd hired to make it out of the country, only a few minutes after Syria and Egypt had just invaded Israel. He checked the sky again, this time for Zion's Mirage fighters.

He also knew that once the news spread, the streets would swell like pus in a boil, filling with men, women, and children, cheering their government's fight against the Zionists to their south.

It was worse than he could have imagined.

Feisal tugged heavily on the wheel once again, and brought the speed down to navigate around another large group flowing into this normally busy street.

Feisal didn't care about the politics of his government, and certainly didn't care whether his country attempted to take over Israel. He had nothing against them, never completely believing the propaganda they were fed. He just wanted to keep his family safe. He had wealth, which gave them a comfortable lifestyle. This was the benefit of their connections to their leader, Hafez al-Assad. But he was fearful that they were going to awaken a sleeping giant and lose the war. And with Damascus sure to be in Israel's cross hairs, he wasn't about to take any chances, especially with his kids.

He balled up his fist and pounded the horn as another group swarmed around them, bringing them to a halt. He pounded and touched his gas pedal, inching the car forward, nudging two men in front of the car pumping their fists and holding a banner in Arabic that said "Death to Israel." Both their heads turned and they yelled foulness at his windshield, but they got out of the way, and Feisal urged the sedan back up to 5 miles per hour.

At the airport gate manned by armed guards, Feisal rolled down the window and handed the guard his papers and his children's travel documents.

The guard snatched them and marched over to another guard in the guard shack, who glared at them before drawing a phone to his ear. His lips moved, as he appeared to be talking to someone about their situation. He nodded and then handed the papers back to the first guard, who handed them to Feisal and waved them inside the now open gate.

Feisal raced around the outer edge of the airport fencing to an area only the highest in government were allowed to access. There were several cars in front of him; they were late. But he could see their plane and his closest friend, David Broadmoor, was standing beside it. Within a few minutes, they were at the ramp. It was the moment his wife and he both wanted and dreaded at the same time.

Feisal embraced his friend, thanking him for doing this for his family. He turned to his children. They were tearfully hugging their mother, who was unwilling to let go. When they did, Fiesal hugged his children and made them promise to be good, to live good lives and take care of one another. When he released them for a final time, perhaps the last time as long as he was alive, they walked slowly to David.

"Hello kids, my name is David. You're going to come live with me for a while in America. For fun, I've given each of you American names. You will be called Sara," he said to the two-year-old in his arms. "And you will be called

Abe," he said to the middle child. "And you, the eldest, will be called Stanley."

Chapter 25

Lexi and Travis

July 6th

"Where's the gun?" Lexi whispered to herself, not wanting to wake her brother in the bunk next to hers.

She had just woken after the best sleep she could remember: interrupted only once, she thought by the sound of gun shots. It was just the remnant of a nightmare, actually many nightmares, which seemed to have passed. The light from the single window finally woke her and she had felt like reading more from the Prepper Brothers book her father left her. She promised herself she'd learn all the survival knowledge the book contained within the next few days, so that she'd be better prepared. She dressed and then, picking up the pack, she noticed it felt lighter. Possibly it felt that way because she had rested after lugging the damn thing around on her shoulders for the last two days. Or was she just being paranoid? She checked the front pocket for the gun, and confirmed it was gone.

Scraping around in the dark recesses of her memories, she tried to recall if she had left the bag's front pouch open or had not secured it in a way that would have caused the gun to have been accidentally dumped out. But it was zippered shut now, and all the other items were still in there: her father's wallet, cell phone, note pad and pen.

Someone took it.

Since she'd put it away, before arriving at Abe's place, it had to have been taken by him or one of his people. Maybe it was for her own safety, or theirs; She would ask them about this later.

Lexi undid the top main compartment clasp, stretched the opening and dumped the bag's contents onto the bed. She didn't expect the gun to magically appear there, but maybe she just wanted to be sure before she said something to Abe.

Running her hand through the items—she was becoming more familiar with the bag's contents—she confirmed that the gun definitely wasn't there and nothing else had been taken. An image splashed upon the back wall of her mind.

Was the knife missing too?

She turned the bag so that its front faced her. Besides the lower pouch that held her pistol, there were three other openings: the middle pouch which she'd examine right after, a sleeve on one side that held a water bottle, and finally the sleeve with the knife. She slid out the black Gerber survival knife again, examining its folded blade with ridges—she didn't know what these were used for, but intended to find out. As she slid her thumb along the back of the knife, the blade popped out very quickly and clicked in a fully extended position. After fiddling with it for a minute, she figured out how to unlock the blade and fold it closed and then she tried to pop it open again.

After practicing a few times, she could pop it open instantly. Each time, she held it as if she would use it on someone, wishing someone was there to teach her how. She closed the blade and then slid it down inside her jeans, clipping it over the waistband. It felt cool, and in a way, comforting there, only slightly exposed. Dropping the edge of her shirt over this, she had a hidden lethal weapon. *In this world, even here, a girl couldn't be too careful.*

She folded her legs and then pulled the bag onto her lap and examined the middle zippered pocket. This opened to several purposefully designed sleeves, with various survival items: a black mini-Maglite; a Leatherman folding multitool; a Gerber fire starter on a lanyard; fifty feet of camo-colored paracord—at least that's what the label said; and a little packet with a roll of wire, three carabiners, two pulleys, and several paperclips. She sure wished she could have asked her father how all this stuff would be used. She put everything back and then closed it up. Then she felt something odd about the bottom of the bag.

The very bottom of the bag was covered in a heavy-duty black leatherlike skin, she guessed to protect it against wear and tear. But as she scrunched the bag's bottom inward, she noticed there was something inside, like a magazine. Double-checking the emptied main compartment by feeling first and then searching with the Maglite, she confirmed there was nothing inside. Inspecting the bottom carefully, she then noticed that one edge of the liner flapped open to reveal a zipper.

It's a secret compartment.

A portion unzipped to reveal a small black flexible ledger, with papers tucked into its pages. When she pulled it out and held it up for examination, a seemingly random mess of notes, copied pages, and pictures slid out onto the bed.

Lexi hadn't noticed, but Travis had awakened and was watching her intently.

The loose pages didn't seem to have rhyme or reason: there were fuzzy pictures of men with guns and a fuzzier picture of a man in a car, taken from a great distance; pages in Arabic; and poor copies of emails and letters with thick black lines drawn through whole sentences. Each had hand-written notes and question marks. She recognized her father's handwriting everywhere. The ledger was filled with lots of tight writing in different ink colors, various doodles and side notes. The pages were muted from years of use and smudges made by dirty hands, most likely her father's. She thumbed through the pages, until she reached the last few and read them quietly to herself.

Lots of notes were about her father trying to find a terrorist named Abdul Raheem Farook, who ran several terrorist cells in the United States. She recognized the name, because on all the pictures, by a circle was written "Abdul?" in her father's hand.

Until two days ago, she'd assumed this whole time that her father was a loser who just couldn't handle the heat of his wife dying and didn't want his kids anymore. This loser, for the last decade plus, had been hunting down terrorists? And more specifically this one terrorist, Abdul. Then there was the Purple Heart medal that Travis now proudly wore, awarded to a soldier who was injured in battle. At first she had thought it was someone else's and her father had just held onto it, and she didn't want to sully her brother's rosy view of him. Perhaps it was his medal. Then there was the bug-out bag, the cryptic instructions, the gun. All this evidence pointed to two clear conclusions: Stanley Broadmoor was so much more than she had ever given him credit for, and she had really never known her father.

Mesmerized by her father's notes, a doorway into understanding him in a way she would otherwise not have known, she read more about his pursuit. This Farook character, her father wrote, claimed in some video that he "will conduct the *greatest attack America has ever seen.*"

She was thunderstruck.

She knew then that her father had been right in the middle of tracking down the people responsible for the nuclear attack that killed him and brought down their country. It was Farook who had conducted the nuclear attack.

She shuddered at this. Her mind wondered: why couldn't her father catch him, before it all happened? And why would he take his children, who he hadn't seen in years, on a vacation when all this was happening? Maybe he didn't know the timing. She contemplated all of this.

Her eyes then fell upon a separate note. It was written sideways in a little box.

"I miss my kids! Feel horrible that they've had to live with their aunt and uncle and that I've never told them that it was Farook who killed their mother. That's why I shipped them off, knowing they wouldn't be safe until I found Farook."

From Lexi's lips, the word "Mom" barely escaped, like a whisper.

It wasn't cancer.

She was murdered.

She looked at the last notation, dated July 3rd, three days ago.

I've been caught. They now know that I'm an agent and will kill me. Worse, I realize that I can't stop the attack that will come. So, I'm bugging out with my kids. At least we'll be together.

She closed the book and couldn't hold back her tears any more. So many things she'd thought ... so many assumptions ... all of them wrong. Her father was a hero, who was trying to find their mother's murderer and protect his kids. And when he realized he couldn't stop the attack, he had their aunt and uncle send them to Texas to be with him.

She jumped a little when Travis wrapped his arms around her middle. He was standing beside her and must have been watching her the whole time. She hugged him back. That's what she should have done before when he needed her, but she didn't have anything to give him.

She did now.

"I'm so sorry, Travis." She squeezed him harder and kissed him on his head. "I love you, Travis," her words coming in between sobbing convulsions. "You were right about Daddy. He was a hero. He saved us and tried to save the world. And he..."

She let go, but he was still holding tight to her. A thought burned bright inside—could it be? She leaned over the pile of stuff from the BOB and rifled thru it for the navigation page that went to some place off the coast of Florida. But it was missing. It had their route to this place from another that she thought must have been where they would vacation. But he had said, "So, I'm bugging out with my kids."

This place wasn't a vacation spot; he'd planned for them to live there together. They were going to live there while the world around them ended.

A knock on the door, and both their heads shot up.

Leo, the young man who had cleaned their wounds and led them to their room stepped in with apologies and asked if they were hungry and would they like breakfast.

Lexi was hungrier for the backstory about her family.

Chapter 26

Abby Broadmoor

Eight Years Earlier

They all wore false faces, pretending to be people they weren't.

Abigail Broadmoor's expression was a mask of mock surprise, her arms posed as if she were flailing in an attempt to save herself from falling from the Space Needle. Lexi beside her, attempted no similar theatrics, instead clutching her two-year-old brother's hand, grimacing her distaste at the whole exercise. Travis was simply in pain from his sister's death grip. Both displayed similar scowls for the camera. Stanley snapped their pictures, but he wasn't really there either. Otherwise, he would have demanded smiles from both his children, and he certainly would have appreciated his wife's dramatic performance too. But how could a husband and father play games when he feared for their lives?

It was supposed to have been a simple operation: pretend to be on a family vacation while observing Yusuf Habib meet with another terrorist. He chided himself for accepting their narrative, as if observing the infamous hit man for the number one terrorist on the FBI's Most Wanted list, Abdul Farook, while exposing his family to this threat could be anything simple. Yes, he stupidly bought into it, because of his feverish desire to get Farook.

Their intel said that one of Farook's people was meeting an arms dealer at the Space Needle. The FBI was giddy with excitement over this for several reasons. They were getting closer to Farook; they were getting closer to a large Seattle cell that had remained out of their reach since they realized it existed over a year ago; they might have finally found Shulli "The Bomb-Maker" Salaam, who had been making echoes in the black markets that he possessed Soviet-era nuclear weapons and was making them available for sale. When the Seattle office found out that it might be Yusuf doing the meet for Farook, they asked the only man in the Bureau who had ever seen Yusuf, and that was Agent Stanley Broadmoor.

For Stanley, this was an easy decision; in fact, he jumped at it. That was, until the FBI told him their plan to use his family so that he would blend in plain sight. Because of the narrow confines of the Space Needle, it would be too hard to sneak in agents to observe without being seen. So, this was their plan. And in spite of everything in him telling him to say "No!", he relented and agreed to put his family at risk. It was the biggest mistake he'd ever made and one he would regret up until the day he died in front of his daughter and son, eight years later.

They were too much in the open, playing this game of pretend. Stanley kept his right eye on Yusuf and his left eye at the camera's lens, at his family.

"Honey, how long are we supposed to stand here?" his wife protested loudly.

He ignored her as his focus was on Yusuf—it was definitely him. He could tell by his prominent Lebanese nose. He looked like an evil Sergeant Klinger from the TV show "M*A*S*H."

Stanley was completely focused on reading Yusuf's lips—that was the other reason for his being there. They were too high to mic Yusuf with the parabolic. But if Stanley was close enough, he might overhear or even read Yusuf's lips.

Stanley froze when he saw him say, "The money has been ... We will be waiting for delivery ... at Port of Seattle tomorrow."

"Hello, Stanley? are you even here?" Abby was protesting so loud that all heads turned to see the commotion, even Yusuf's.

Stanley returned his full attention to his wife, but didn't move the camera, "Ah, sorry, hon. I was just trying to get the perfect shot." He snapped the picture and then lowered the camera from his face, offering a large conciliatory grin to his wife.

"That picture left a while ago, with your daughter and son," she said.

They both glared at Lexi and Travis who had long since turned their backs to their father. Lexi was showing her baby brother the Seattle skyline.

Stanley chanced a glance at Yusuf and felt an electric jolt when the realization hit him; he'd been made.

Yusuf was staring directly at him, unyielding when Stanley matched his gaze. The two men were locked into each other for a moment that was much too long for happenstance.

"Come on." Stanley tossed the imperative at her, while snatching his camera bag from the ground and headed for the exit. "Let's go get something to eat." He walked away feigning disinterest, hoping his family would follow close behind, praying that what had just happened really hadn't.

C ✝ ✡ ☯ 🦅

Yusuf pressed and held the 2 on his phone and it speed-dialed the saved number. He held his phone to his ear, while he gazed at the family nibbling on seafood at an outdoor cafe. Except for his phone hand and lips, he remained unmoving in the midday shadows of the Space Needle.

He listened first before answering, straightening his shoulders when he heard the voice on the other end.

"Why are you calling? Are we secure?" demanded the voice.

"Yes, sir. The meet went well and we are on schedule for delivery." Yusuf watched the man pay and usher his family out of the restaurant. Yusuf started moving as well.

"So, why are you calling?"

"I picked up a tail. He may be a Fed, but he's with his family. I wanted your orders before I did anything."

"Do they know about me?"

"Sir, I don't know what they know, only that it was a man who was too interested in me and our business."

"Do what you feel is necessary, but make sure the Feds know not to mess with us. And don't call again, unless it is an emergency." The line disconnected.

Yusuf glanced at the phone to make sure Farook was done. He was pretty hands off, but on something like killing a Fed, he wanted the okay in case it went wrong.

He had just received authorization.

They walked hand-in-hand: the man held the small boy, the teenager between them, weaving through the crowds. Yusuf was very careful. He wanted to be sure that he was correct before he did what he was going to do, which he wasn't yet sure of. They seemed to be a normal family, enjoying a rare Seattle sunny day in August. Yusuf watched them over the corner of his *Seattle Times*, pretending to eat up the city's news. He waited for confirmation that this man was not who he presented himself to be. He knew the look of an agent, the mannerisms that belied their true purpose, and he was watching for that tell-tale sign.

The man let go of his daughter's hand, set his son down and pretended to tie what was a slip-on shoe. Then he looked up. The glance told Yusuf everything. His eyes were careful and practiced. He was an agent. When he stood up, Yusuf jumped, leaving his paper behind.

At a stop light, less than a block from where Stanley had lowered himself to his shoe, they waited for the light to change. The agent had a little bit of a smile etched into his face as the woman, obviously his wife, told him something funny. Yusuf glanced at the kids, a disinterested girl and her younger brother, now holding each other's hands. It wouldn't be them. He looked at the man and woman again, as he worked his way directly behind them, and the agent bellowed with laughter. Yusuf knew the play and struck like lightning. He withdrew an extra-long US-flag stick pin from his lapel, its point withdrawn from a special sheath mounted inside his coat, and stuck the woman before replacing it in an instant. His other hand withdrew a silenced pistol, shielding it with his body then his other hand, he lodged it into the agent's neck.

The agent's laughter trailed off.

Yusuf leaned into the agent's ear and said, "Don't turn around or I will kill your whole family here on the street. You and your agents must back away from this or I will hunt down and kill your kids one at a time."

The throng of people around them pushed them forward, ushered by the green beacon that flashed across the street.

Stanley walked a couple of steps with everyone else and spun around quickly, partially withdrawing his 10mm Glock, but Yusuf was no longer there.

He scanned everywhere, close by and in the distance, but couldn't see him anywhere.

When he looked forward his wife was rubbing her shoulder, having stopped herself, as the crowd worked their way around them.

"What's wrong?" he asked.

"Oh, nothing. I think someone in line accidentally poked me."

The day after the pinprick, the agency broke up the Seattle cell and captured a nuclear weapon that was smuggled into the Port of Seattle, just as Yusuf had said. Stanley was the Bureau hero.

Six weeks later, Abby Broadmoor, mother of two, loving wife to Special Agent Stanley Broadmoor, the man who saved Seattle, was dead. The doctors said it was uranium poisoning; they didn't know how it entered her bloodstream. But Stan knew it was Yusuf who had pricked his wife at that stop light on a warm summer day, all because he allowed his family to be included in an operation. And because Yusuf warned him, saying "I will hunt down and kill your kids one at a time," Stanley wouldn't allow them to be put into harm's way any longer. He officially resigned from the agency; he dumped his kids on his sister Sara's household; and he went deep undercover for an offshoot of the FBI, using a new name, disappearing from sight.

The cover story was that Abby had died of cancer and that Stanley couldn't deal with it and he needed time away from the family. His brother, Abe, knew there was a lot more to this story. He reached out several times to find out how Stanley was faring but Stanley never responded.

Stanley dedicated every waking moment of his life to getting Yusuf and Farook, the man who had given the orders to kill his wife and tear apart his family.

Chapter 27

Lexi

Present Day

L eo led them out the door of their cabin into the bright outdoors, to an open area with several picnic benches. Men clustered around one of the tables, eating and conversing. Another table was crowded with women. All seemed to be enjoying the sunshine and each other.

It felt safe.

When Lexi had arrived here yesterday with Travis, she didn't even really notice the beauty of this place. Willows clung to the bank of the river, delicately swaying in the breeze. Laughter and chatter filled the air.

She had no doubt been too worried about getting away from Clyde and his people or being shot at to have noticed this earlier. The stress of running and hiding and then trying to cope with people dying carried an emotional toll. Perhaps it was that her whole perspective had changed after discovering her father was a good man, someone she could no longer hate. And he had sent them here to this safe place, with people that cared about their well-being.

"Are you coming?" Leo asked softly, a smile on his face, a glint in his eye.

Lexi was fixed in her place, gazing with amazement at open space and the people, as if she had never seen any of this before. But her life was different now. Of course, so were the lives of everyone else in America. In only two days she had gone from being a self-absorbed, angry girl who hated life and everyone around her, to one who appreciated every moment, who appreciated her father, who appreciated her brother. *Maybe I'm not even a bitch anymore.*

"Come on, Lexi. We can sit out here with our breakfast if you'd like."

"Can we?" Travis asked, but he seemed detached, damaged.

"Yes, we can," she answered and flashed a warm smile.

Leo waited for them to catch up and he walked them by two other similar buildings, albeit larger than the cabin they had slept in. They found themselves in front of a large structure with multiple doorways. Out of the second one popped out a man holding a tray of food. He held the door open for them and waited patiently.

"This is our cafeteria," Leo said, beckoning them inside with his arm. A clatter of dishes and the delicious food aromas wafted outside, further drawing them in. Travis led, now dragging Lexi. She was pleased that at least his appetite wasn't affected by his emotional wreckage.

"Thanks, Sye," Leo said as he closed the door behind him.

☾ † ✡ ☯ 🦅

After an egg and cheese breakfast outside (Travis quietly gobbled every morsel), Leo offered to show them the rest of the grounds. He said that Abe purchased this property several years ago and had been preparing for society's downfall ever since. So, he had built this community to be self-sustaining.

Lexi and Travis walked beside Leo, listening to him describe the property and the building's origins, not unlike a guide running through all the stars on a Hollywood tour. They paused at the end of the dock, and stared at the river racing past them to the Gulf of Mexico.

Lexi examined the speed boat bobbing up and down, pulling at its mooring line, wanting to be let go. "Is this the only boat for the whole ... property?"

Leo looked around, not sure of the answer; although he thought there was at least one other boat, he had never been asked this. "Sorry, Lexi, I don't know."

"What's over there?" Travis pointed to some movement past a wall a couple of hundred yards away.

"Let's go take a look." Leo ushered them forward, and then through an open field. "We're actually not supposed to go there, because it's not for everyone to see, but since you're practically family ..." Leo's head swiveled back and forth as if he were a spy about to give away state secrets. They all slunk low and slowly approached the wall which appeared to bound the property. Beyond it was another field and a flurry of activity. Twenty men were moving in unison. At first, Lexi thought they were dancing, but then she realized they were training. Each had a knife, and they were crouched on flexed knees. Then each sprang forward a step, thrust their knives at an imaginary assailant, and twisted. Lexi's stomach protested, threatening to give up the eggs she'd just consumed.

"This is the training yard," Leo whispered. "Only a trusted few are able to train here in hand-to-hand combat."

Lexi did a double-take, her mind reeling. "Trusted Few?" There were twenty of them there. "Combat?" Why were men training for combat? Was it worse out there than even she'd guessed? She studied the leader, a harsh-looking man with a hooked nose. Even though she didn't feel like anyone here wanted to harm her or her brother, she couldn't help but feel a little helpless, like a doe who'd wandered into a hunter's camp.

An alarm sounded and all heads, but one, shot up, eyes skyward.

Feeling like she had just been revealed, Lexi saw that the hooked nose leader of the combat exercises was looking right at them.

She felt a tug on her arm.

"Come on," Leo hollered at them at the top of his lungs to be heard over the screech of the horn, "we need to run; we're under attack."

Chapter 28

Fallujah, Iraq

Twelve Years Earlier

"We're taking heavy enemy fire. We need an extraction," Captain Frank Cartwright yelled over the deafening barrage of gunfire exploding around them.

His team had just cleared a building deep within enemy territory, searching for a Hezbollah terrorist they suspected of many attacks including blowing up the Khobar Towers in Saudi Arabia, which had killed nineteen of their fellow servicemen some years back. The enemy had trapped them on the roof of the building. They knew they were in trouble as they watched dozens of men wearing *keffiyehs* stream up to their building, AKs firing on their position.

"Shit, Captain. Our goose might be cooked on this one," huffed Sergeant Broadmoor, his second in command and his best friend.

"Nah, we've been in worse straits."

The radio blared, "Two Charlie. We have two Humvees approaching your six from the east. They'll be there in three minutes."

"Two Charlie, out."

Frank turned toward the eastern edge of the roof. "Extraction coming to the east in three." He pointed in that direction. "I need this area cleared out on the double."

His team had rushed to him from their positions. Their man assigned the SAW was injured and hung behind the lip of the roof, keeping pressure on his non-life threatening wounds.

"Give me your grenades," Broadmoor hollered. "And I'll need cover fire."

Their three other team members handed him their grenades and took positions along the roof's eastern edge. Broadmoor waited by a pipe that ran along the outside of the building and a couple of feet above the roof line. He held six cylinders carefully, pulling the pins to each, while keeping their handles depressed. "On my mark ... All right, fire."

The three fired their M4s, and Frank fired the SAW in a sweep around the east side of the building, while Broadmoor tossed each grenade, one at a time, trying to hit an imaginary semicircle of protection around that side of the building.

The last one was tossed when the first one exploded; four of the five men were down behind the lip of the roof for cover. Typically the SAW attracted a lot of return fire, which is why usually one of the lower ranked men should have taken over, but Frank continued firing the M249 until it was empty.

After the last explosion, Frank yelled, "Okay, now."

All but Broadmoor slid down the pole. Frank moved closer to the pole, stood up tall and worked his unslung

M4 around each location where he remembered seeing enemy before the blasts.

Broadmoor was close behind when they heard the incoming mortar. Both men leapt, hitting the pole, which unceremoniously unhinged itself from the building, and both men and the pole swung out and rushed for the ground.

Frank remembered the explosion. It was the kind that sounded and felt like it went off inside in your head. His mouth was open, to equalize the pressure, and because of this, most of the Iraqi desert found its way inside. Broadmoor was screaming something and then they hit the ground hard.

Frank felt his leg explode in pain and noticed his consciousness wavering.

Broadmoor was over him, hollering something about a Humvee.

Frank tried to right himself, but couldn't get farther than the sitting position, with his back to all the hollering. He tried to look away from what lay before him, to hear what his friend was yelling, but it demanded his fading attention.

Only a few feet away were the bodies of children, dozens of them. Arms, legs, heads, scattered with other body parts and guns. These boys were some of those forced to fight; their grenades had been tossed at terrorists who turned out to be kids, and they killed them. This enemy put these kids into harm's way, but somehow he felt complicit in their murder. And murder was exactly what had happened here.

As he felt his consciousness slip away, he lost all desire to do this anymore. He couldn't witness another child die.

He lay back down and heard Broadmoor's voice, closer now, calling for Frank, asking if he was all right. But he wasn't, not at all.

Frank's visual periphery was blackening, constricting. It wouldn't be long now.

He reached out, felt Broadmoor's hand, but he lost all strength and then he was out.

☾ † ✡ ☯ 🦅

Present Day

F rank reached out into the darkness and whispered, "Stanley."

He felt a strong hand clasp around his and pull. Comforting words told him, "We've got you, Major."

More force tugged at him from the darkness and he was dragged for a long period, or at least it felt that way. A startling sensation made him jerk: a rough cloth rubbed against his face.

Light.

"Is all of that blood yours, Major?"

Porter was kneeling before him, wiping his face. Frank snatched the towel away from him and continued the task himself as he sat up. The image was complete now.

In front of him was the smoldering carcass of the convoy truck he'd been driving, upside down and its ass-end blown to shit. He turned his torso to see what was behind him and noted that his pickup truck, radio antenna jutting up, was hiding under the thick cover of trees.

Just then, the memories connected and his head shot up and scanned the skies above.

"They're all gone, Major." It was Wallace. He was happy to see she had made it. "After they took out your truck, they came back for us, but we hid under that canopy for a half an hour. When the drone was sure we were gone, we came out to retrieve you. We thought you were dead, like all the rest." Her head was pointed down, supporting what she said.

"Is this all?" Frank asked, glaring at them.

"That's all ..." Porter said, dejected, and then his head sprang up. "But at least you got us out. If it weren't for you, we'd all be dead."

Frank said nothing. With much effort and Porter's help, he rose to his feet. His bad knee hardly responded to his commands anymore.

"Now, do we go after the bastards?" It was Wallace asking the question that already clouded his mind like an angry thunderstorm. He'd made his decision just before the missile hit. Did getting blown up change anything?

When he was blown up in Fallujah, it was their ticket to retirement, his and Stanley's. Even after the promotions, he was done killing people. It was different when they blew up his home. That was revenge. And this plan to share intel with Ft. Rucker ... It didn't matter that they had a Plan B to recruit and take the fight to Farook. He wanted no part of that. He had planned to convince the base of what they needed to do and then leave with Porter. They'd lock 'em up first before he'd relent on this. He'd had enough of war and certainly didn't want it now. They no longer had the manpower to fight Farook. Plus—his mind searched for any excuse it could grasp—he had more people that depended on him and a promise he had made to Grimes, to bring Porter home. It was the path he'd chosen; he'd stick with it.

"We're going to Stowell, Texas. We hope you will come too. We could use your help. But first, we have to take care of our dead."

They were silent as they carried the bodies and piled them alongside each other, stacking rocks on each to complete the makeshift graves. It took several hours. When they were done, they picked through the convoy truck's wreckage, salvaged anything that would be useful, and they drove away from their defeat.

Chapter 29

Clyde

C lyde was no mastermind of strategy and planning, and he knew it. He depended on brute force and fear to win his battles. It was how he had ruled his gang, serving drugs and prostitution to the northern strip of Florida and the southern tip of Alabama along the highway, from Tallahassee in the east to Mobile in the west, right down to the Gulf. It would be how he planned to lord over even more territory now that the bombs had dropped and the police couldn't respond. He had big plans.

But then, this little pixie came along and now his brother was dead, his house burned, his most trusted man Big Mike went traitor on him, and there was a rival gang, right across the river from him, who threatened to take it all? He knew at the root of this black cloud was the pixie and her brother. They were like some bad luck charm which had brought blight to all his plans. Well, that would all change in a matter of minutes.

"Around the next bend, get ready," said Pete, his baseball cap reversed and steady as his hand navigated their boat at a slow and quiet 5 knots. The other three boats were close behind; a total of fifty men and lots of weapons. They would kill everyone, including that pixie and her sniveling brother, and take everything. It all belonged to them. They belonged to him.

"The dock is up ahead."

Clyde signaled two of the three boats to unload along the bank before the dock. Clyde would pass the dock and unload from the north. The final boat would unload at the dock and attack them right at their heart, drawing most of their fire. With most of his forces on the north and south, they should have no problem winning this battle.

He stood tall in his seat as the other men slunk under cover, passing by the dock. He felt like a military general, directing his troops, not unlike a MacArthur or Patton. Perhaps he was pretty good at this strategy thing after all.

They navigated to an opening between some old willows that would provide excellent cover for their boat.

They were all off, checking their weapons, when a horn blasted from the camp. Then gunfire.

"Come on, men, the war has started. Let's take these bastards and make 'em pay for Zach's death with their blood."

$$C \dagger \maltese \odot \text{🦅}$$

"Run, Lexi," Leo called out to her, just behind him. She was clutching and tugging at her brother, whose eyes were wide with fear.

Shots exploded from the dock area. But then many more sounded from the south, from right where they had been standing.

"It sounds like a war," Lexi cried.

She ran hunched over, trying to make herself small and harder for an errant bullet to find. She wasn't sure where they were running to, but knew that Leo was trying to find the safest place for them.

"No!" demanded a man barreling right for them. "Take them to the dormitory with all the women, then grab your weapon." It was Sal, who yelled this as he passed, headed toward the dock and most of the gunfire. The soccer-ball lines crisscrossing his no-longer-gentle face were creased into a gruesome mask of a man intent on killing.

Leo turned right and led them at a run across the circular drive that she had come through yesterday when they first arrived. They were headed to the largest of the buildings, next to the cafeteria. "You'll be safe in there with the other women," he said. "I have to fight with the men."

Lexi could have sworn that his voice trembled as he said this, but maybe that was because they were running and all their voices sounded shaky at this point.

Leo left them at the front door of the large dormitory and then disappeared around the corner.

Lexi entered, immediately seeing the dozen or so women, all cowering in a corner and covered with what looked like black sheets—perhaps their idea of camouflage.

She knew right away she couldn't stay here. She had to go out into the action. As scary as that thought sounded when it entered her mind, she knew it to be true. She needed to see what was happening, and if needed, protect this place from whatever was attacking it.

"Travis"—she leaned over with her face directly in his—"you need to stay here with these women, where it's safe."

He didn't really respond, but his head tilted forward in sort of a semi-nod. He then turned and plopped himself next to the covered women. One of their arms reached out from an undulating pile of black and took him in.

She wished she had her gun right now, but knowing she had her father's survival knife attached to her waistband brought her some measure of confidence. She thought of the image of the men thrusting their knives at an imaginary enemy and twisting. She would do that, if it meant protecting herself or her brother.

She slipped out the door and shut it behind her, walking into the gunfire, all around the camp. It did sound like a war. Surprisingly, she no longer feared it. She would deal with this like everything else that had been thrown at her. She pulled out her knife, snapped it in place, and walked around the corner of the building, mentally preparing herself for the next threat to be tossed at her.

☪ ✝ ✡ ☯ 🦅

Clyde and his men were firing everything they had at this encampment of men and a few women who were running for cover. Yet, in spite of their superior numbers, his men were falling one by one. And even though they were getting shots off, he didn't think they were doing equal damage to the other side.

Every minute or two, they'd try to drive forward, but they kept getting driven back.

In less than ten minutes it was over.

He looked at his rifle, surprised that his Rock River LAR-15 would no longer fire. He should have packed more ammo.

Someone yelled something at him and Clyde looked around. All his men had fallen. Clyde looked forward and saw two men yelling demands from behind their automatic weapons.

Shit!

Clyde let go of his rifle and thrust his hands up. They were defeated.

☾ ✝ ✡ ☯ 🦅

As she slid along the side of one of the camp's buildings, using it for cover, Lexi saw a man half obscured by the building's edge. His bloody left hand was reaching for a knife, like he was about to attack someone she couldn't see. His back was to her. He hadn't heard her. She didn't hesitate, walking toward him with her knife held at the ready to be plunged into his back. She wasn't sure how she decided this—she wished she knew more about human anatomy.

As she methodically stepped, careful to be silent and block out all other noises, she marveled at her calmness. Her heart was pumping like a train engine going up a mountain, but she was resolute. Best of all, she felt no fear.

The man's hand slipped the knife out of its sheath, while she picked up her pace, worried now that she wouldn't get to him before he struck his intended victim.

She was only a couple of feet away: time to strike.

She pulled her knife back and took two quick steps, about to plunge it into him when a loud pop rocked his head back. It exploded, covering her in a mist of red.

Lexi stopped in midstride, elbow back, hand clutching tight to her weapon, shocked that the man she had intended to kill had been killed. But by whom?

A clawlike hand grabbed her neck and pulled at her. "You think because you see men train and fight that you can now fight like one?"

It was the man with the hook nose she had seen earlier in the field, the trainer. He looked like a man-sized hawk whose beak was spitting words at her.

"Your place is with the other women," he spat some more, dragging her around the cafeteria, back toward her cabin. Her eyes then fell upon the picnic area, where this morning men and women had been enjoying their breakfast, like normal people, and she had thought the day looked bright.

Now, five men—she guessed by their dirty outfits they were the enemy—were on their knees with their hands up in the air, while many of the men from the training yard held guns to their heads. A couple more were being pushed in that direction. Beside them were the dead bodies of scores of others. It looked like the war was over.

As Beak Man roughly pulled her along, just before depositing her in her cabin, he said something that jarred her.

"You do look a little like your mother."

Chapter 30

Federal Bureau of Investigation - Washington, DC

Two Days Earlier

All eyes were on John R. Connelly, the Director of the FBI.

The agents and department heads batted around panicked whispers, while their eyes were riveted upward at their boss. A massive bank of screens—only two flickered grimaces from field office heads—covered the wall behind him.

"I've called this emergency meeting because no one has been able to figure out what the hell is going to happen today. As an update, we've raised the threat level to Red. The president and the Joint Chiefs will soon be headed to Camp David with their families. The president will join this meeting in a few minutes. Agent Simpson, please give us an update."

Agent Thomas Simpson, the Executive Assistant Director for Intelligence Branch, hesitated near the platform before pacing to where the director stood. He was, in every practical sense, the very head of all "intelligence" in the FBI, and yet he had nothing to share which they already didn't know. All he could do was encapsulate what his analysts postulated from their suspicions. When he approached the microphone, he cleared his throat.

"In the brief you have, I ended with the facts that we lost comms and then visual with Agent Broadmoor yesterday at thirteen forty-two. As all of you know, Agent Broadmoor was deep undercover, after helping us break up the Seattle terrorist cell and recover a rogue nuclear device. He was getting very close to finding the location of Abdul Raheem Farook. Further, it was Agent Broadmoor that uncovered the target date of July 4th for an upcoming, as of yet unknown, attack on the US."

"Agent O'Mally, sir." O'Mally stood up in the fifth row of the large auditorium. "Do you have any guess on the location?"

Simpson pushed his face into the microphone. "We have no intel leading us to speculate on any specific location. Some of our analysts believe it will be at secondary cities, like San Francisco and Phoenix. Our field offices in each location are beating down every lead."

One of the wall screens, like a big rectangular eye, blinked on. The harried face of Agent Wilber Johnson, the head of the Chicago FBI Field Office, turned to face the group. "Excuse me for interrupting, but I'm told by my agents that we have just busted up a cell at a private home a mile from Wrigley Field. Our Nuclear Specialist says that they've detected radiation that indicates a nuclear device was here. We have virtually shut down the cit—"

"Excuse me," Director Connelly interrupted, "did you say a nuclear device?"

"Yes, I did. Our NS confirmed it, just seconds ago."

Voices erupted all around the room. It sounded like a Beltway restaurant on a Friday night.

"Please, one at a time," the Assistant Director chimed back in.

"How sure are you this was a nuclear device and not just nuclear material?" a nervous agent asked.

"Look, we don't have all—"

Another screen on the back wall flashed on, and a face appeared, already talking. "—just decrypted Agent Broadmoor's phone and you need to see this ..."

The face of Agent Billy Rice from the Houston field office was replaced by a picture of a poorly lit room, with a map on the wall and lots of pins and notations on it.

"... this picture was taken by Agent Broadmoor at Yusuf Habib's apartment. Several of our field agents are on scene now and will be reporting in shortly."

The map was enlarged so that all could see it. Every agent in the room leaned closer.

"What the hell are we looking at, Rice?" barked Director Connelly.

"Sir, it's a map of the US and it shows four target areas: Chicago, New York, Jacksonville, and ... DC."

"We're screwed," a voice broke the hushed silence from the back of the room, no one taking credit for it. Another voice quipped, "Oh my God, the entire government is here today."

"I was just sent an MP4 file," Agent Rice said, also nodding to someone off-screen. "This was just recovered and sent from a laptop in Habib's apartment. You should have this now ..."

"Sir, Executive Assistant Director Thompson, sir," a man said from the first row, tilting his head and touching his ear. "I'm told we should now have the video. It's a recording by Abdul Raheem Farook."

The main screen flickered once and the dark face of a man they had never seen before displayed larger than life. He had a slight smile swimming in a closely cropped black beard with sprinkles of white.

He started in Arabic. "*As-salaam.*" The volume was lowered while an interpreter started speaking, over Farook. "Ahh ... Brothers, our great war against the infidels will begin soon. The first phase will occur on July 4th. As you know, this is known as America's Independence Day. While they are cheering ... no, celebrating, the Great Satan's legs will be cut off at its knees. We will destroy their technology and poison them in nuclear clouds and gas. Then while the infidels struggle to survive, many thousands of our fighters will come and America will bow down to the ... might of Allah."

The video appeared to be unedited, as Farook was interrupted and he turned to a young Indian man in the background. The agents could just barely hear him say in perfect English to the Indian man, "I'll be there in a moment, Leo..."

And then the power went out and the room went black.

Only a few moments later, everyone in that room, along with the Herbert Hoover Building and all of DC, perished at one hundred thousand degrees.

Chapter 31

Abe

L exi sat slumped over, while her disquieted mind played tug-of-war over a cloud of thoughts.

She was no longer disturbed about almost killing that man, or that he'd been slaughtered anyway. She wasn't even too worked up about being covered in the man's gore; her listless hand rose up and brushed against her cheek, pulling some of the blood and brain matter off, and she examined it.

Something else was deeply wrong.

A crucial factoid was misfiled in her head, or her brain was holding it back; maybe an incident from her past that she was repressing, like the women she had read about who were molested, but didn't remember this until years later when an event or image opened up their darkest memories. Thankfully, she was never molested or abused, but she felt some other malevolent secret lurked in the darkest places of her mind, waiting to be pulled out.

Maybe it is there, but it's locked away for a good reason. And here I am, trying to pick the lock.

"Don't be a crybaby," she scolded herself.

Lexi stood up, determined to do something, but not sure what that might be. A small tremor of recognition hit as she realized she was still holding the fully extended survival knife. Shaking her head in disbelief, she folded it and slipped it back into her waistband, before striding over to the cabin's small bathroom.

The next shock of the day was firmly delivered in front of the mirror when some stranger stared back at her. This person covered in a substantial splatter of blood couldn't be her. Could it?

With both faucets opened, she scrubbed at her face and hair. After a while, she felt somewhat satisfied. Her clothes were still soiled, but they were all she had to wear, so they would have to do. She reached over to a stack of clean towels and pulled one off the top, giving her face and head a light tousle. Slinging it around her neck—she was in too much of a hurry to complete the job, desperate to find the answer to her quandary—she marched over to her pack and pulled out her father's journal to look for something. Sitting back on her cot, she thumbed through the pages, unsure what she was looking for, only feeling that it must be there. One of her fingers landed on a page with lots of notes below the name Abdul Raheem Farook, just before several drops of water dripped from her wet hair and tumbled to the paper. The fallen droplets expanded outward, like pebbles making ripples in a pond, blurring the writing at each point of impact.

She glared at the page, looking for her missing clue. It just wasn't there. Realizing some of the words from her father's pen now bled into others because of her dripping, she unfurled the towel from her neck and tossed it over her head, intending to dry her mop completely.

Then it hit.

That one fragment that had been missing; it was the secret she had repressed for so long. And all at once she was horrified because it connected and then she knew everything. It was like she had just taken off dark sunglasses inside and now she could see what was always there, but she had been blind to until this moment.

With her head shrouded in the towel's gloom, not unlike the women must have been in the main dormitory under their black covers, she shuddered. But it wasn't from the darkness: it was from the light of knowledge. Her fingers tugged at the towel's edges so that she was once again eying the page.

Extracting the pen from the pack's front pocket, she clicked out the point, and wrote on the top of the page one word and a question mark. It was rhetorical. Because it was the answer to all the questions that wracked her brain and when she wrote it, she knew it to be correct.

A loud knock at the door went unheard.

The second was louder.

The pen paused below what she had written; with her hand trembling so much, the clutched pen kept marking the book with little black dots. It was as if her mind was taping conclusive periods to its monumental revelation.

Right above this she had written: "ABE?"

The door opened and Lexi turned to face the nightmare she knew to be true. Her eyes swam in puddles, obscuring her vision like a heavy morning mist, but this didn't blur her sight. She could see perfectly clearly now.

He walked through the door, standing tall, with the same welcoming smile that had greeted them yesterday. But that was before ...

He hovered above her for a moment before sitting down in front of her, not saying a word.

It wasn't possible, was it?

She stared at his eyes, which seemed to look right into hers, into the deepest stretches of her mind. She was letting him in, letting him see. She shuddered more at this, but she couldn't look away. She was transfixed by his gaze and what it all meant.

He broke his scrutiny and looked at the open journal in her lap, the big bold letters she had written just above her father's.

The smile grew longer on his face. It was one of recognition.

He knew that she knew.

"It's you, isn't it?" The question leapt from her open lips. "You're the Abdul Raheem Farook that my father was searching for, aren't you?"

He waited for a long pause. Long enough that for a fleeting moment, she thought—no, hoped—she was wrong.

"Yes, I am he," Abe said in a calm and reassuring voice.

"So, why would my father send us to you? Who are you to my father?" She suspected she knew the answers.

"Your father, Stanley, was my brother."

Images of her father popped into her head: the same complexion, hair color, chins, even similar smiles, just like—

"And Sara is my sister. You have the same beautiful eyes."

—her Aunt Sara. "But ..." It was all she could say.

"We all came over from Syria, just before the Zionists bombed our country. We were raised by the Broadmoors, and we all took their American surname. But they were Zion-lovers too and had long forgotten our Muslim ways. Stanley became Americanized and forgot his roots, and he died running away from his calling. He studied the Quran, but his infidel wife pulled him away."

"Is that why ..." Lexi wasn't sure if she had the courage to ask what she needed to ask. "... why you killed our mom?"

His eyes drilled holes in her. For a moment he seemed a little surprised, but then at once resolute, and with the same calm voice he answered, "I don't expect you to understand, at least not yet. But in time, I suspect you will."

A loud thumping at the door caused Lexi to jump and turn to see who it was. Abdul continued to look at her when he addressed the hooked-nosed man coming through the door.

"Yes, Yusuf."

"Everyone is assembled for you outside."

Abdul rose from the cot and walked to the door. "Bring her. This concerns her, and her brother."

"He's waiting for you as well," Yusuf answered

"Good." Abdul turned to Lexi. Her mouth still drooped open; her eyes were blank.

He flashed a grin before walking through the door.

Yusuf didn't ask her. He marched over to Lexi, grabbed her between her clavicle and her neck, and led her out the door.

At first, he didn't squeeze so hard that it hurt, until she slowed, then with a hold like a vise he shot painful tingles down her spine and she matched his pace once again.

There was a crowd of people in front of the wide-opened area leading to the dock. A makeshift platform was set up, which abutted the dock, but was still on land. On it stood Abdul, elevated on a second platform. Before and below him were seven prisoners. Each was bound with rope in such a way that they were sitting cross-legged, their arms tied behind them. They were lined up, a few feet between each one. Standing around the platforms and the prisoners, were thirty or forty others: The men on one side, the women all covered in black on the other. Everyone was quiet.

Travis was standing near the platform, beside Sal, who had his hand on his shoulder. But unlike Yusuf's grip on Lexi, Sal's appeared to be almost comforting. Travis glanced up to Sal, and grinned at him. Sal smiled back.

"Attention everyone," hollered Sal. Then he looked up to Abdul, who was already facing his followers, standing around him.

"*Assalam alaikum*," he bellowed, his strong voice carrying without the aid of a microphone.

"*Wa-alaikum-assalam*." It seemed everyone including Yusuf responded. Only Lexi and the seven hog-tied men remained silent.

"America, or who we know as the Great Satan, has long ago become corrupt. Soon it will be cleansed."

A murmur spread through the crowd. "Praise Allah. Praise Allah. Praise Allah."

"As you know, Allah the Merciful has chosen you to be among his warriors, along with over one hundred groups such as this, comprising thousands of believers. We are all part of a plan that would make Mohammad, peace and blessings of Allah be upon him, proud. Our efforts will bring the caliphate to the whole world, starting here.

"Phase One is complete and with it, America has been brought to its knees. Soon the next phases will start and then we will be joined by many thousands more of our warriors. Together, we will strike at the heart of the infidel. Those who choose to follow Allah's laws will be saved. But, those who do not will perish among the fires where they belong. And when our plan is complete, America will be ours."

The throng of followers cheered and spoke praises to Abdul and to Allah.

When quiet returned, he continued. "The time has come when we can no longer hide in the shadows, pretending, as we have been, to be part of this culture. This culture's sinful ways have permeated this camp and were starting to make us weak. That will stop right now.

"Immediately, we will practice what America will come to learn. We will follow Sharia. All will pray five times per day. And those who do not yet know our laws"—he looked at Lexi, and so did many of the crowd—"will learn the Quran and show respect for Allah's laws."

He paused to make sure all were listening. "Violators will be dealt with just as Mohammad, peace and blessings of Allah be upon him, has prescribed."

Seven men wearing white *throbes*, capped with black *ghutras* emblazoned in white Arabic writing, marched up the platform, each stopping behind one of the seven bound men.

The prisoners rustled, and their eyes grew wide.

Lexi recognized the prisoner on the end. It was Clyde. She lifted her eyes in shock to see that each man was holding in both hands a curved sword

"These men," Abdul continued, "have been found guilty of crimes and their sentence will be carried out immediately." He nodded toward the first man, who without hesitation, swung his scimitar from left to right from behind the first sitting prisoner. A swish and a corresponding spray arced toward Travis, who was splashed with heavy droplets of red. He barely even flinched, like he was in a trance.

The head of the first prisoner rolled off the platform's side and tumbled down the bank into the river. His body, still attempting to pump lifeblood to a brain that wasn't there, remained erect for a couple of seconds before finally slumping over. A small fountain of red spurted twice more as it fell.

Lexi attempted to look away, but Yusuf's claws dug into her head and turned her back to the carnage, just as the second executioner swung—right to left this time—sending gore and a severed head at those followers. A few moved out of its way, but most didn't move, just like Travis.

Lexi's attention may have been forced in that direction, but her eyes stayed on Travis, who remained still, watching every whimpering man die in equally grisly fashion.

She had seen videos of these kind of things on the Internet; snippet after snippet of masked jihadis beheading other Muslims who believed a different version of the same faith, Christians, who of course possessed a different faith, and anyone else who crossed their path:

all murdered in the name of Allah. But, it was supposed to happen in those dark corners of the Middle East. Not *here*, in the United States.

"I love Allah, man. Really, I'll follow him, I really will. Please don't ki—"

It was Clyde, pleading for his miserable life. Lexi couldn't help but be drawn to his words like a spectator to a car crash. She focused on him just as his head was sent forward, the last word traveling with it, "Killllllll," before it bounded into one of the covered women sitting up front. She emitted a small shriek of surprise under her *burka*, but otherwise didn't react.

Lexi looked down too late, catching every bloody moment.

"And Sharia law tells us to submit to all rules imposed on us. If we don't, our punishment will be swift; no matter who breaks them."

Lexi observed Leo marching up to the platform. He looked up to Abdul, waiting for his instructions.

"Leo is a dear servant and like a son to me, but he didn't obey one of our strict rules: he led our guests to a place they shouldn't have seen, yet. And he touched what wasn't his. To his honor, Leo has volunteered to carry out his own punishment."

Abdul smiled at him, while withdrawing his own sword, its blade glittering in the sun. He handed it to Leo.

Leo held up his free left hand and the long saber in his right, so the crowd could see. Lexi wanted to avert her eyes, but she couldn't. She watched in horror as Leo swung the blade, severing his left hand at the wrist.

He was immediately ushered off the stage by men who also attempted to stem the bleeding.

"Monsters," Lexi whispered.

"We are entering a new era, my brothers and sisters. And as your Mahdi, I will lead our caliphate across the whole land. And at my side ..."

Lexi's eyes had remained caste down, head unmoving, as Yusuf's claws were no longer burrowed into her. Now, she looked up because it was quiet. Abdul had paused.

She expelled a long breath as she was stunned to see her brother ascend the platform.

"Travis here was my brother's son. But from this day forward he shall be known as Abdul-Aziz 'servant of the Dear One' and I will raise him as if he were mine. He is already a Muslim, and will continue his studies of the Quran. And one day he will be an Imam like his father."

Travis just stood erect on the platform, gazing forward at no one.

Lexi was hyperventilating, and the world was starting to spin.

This can't be.

Her eyes fell and she was shocked that she was moving toward the platform as well, her legs moving without any help from her. Yusuf's claws practically carried her.

And then she found herself standing next to Abdul, her uncle, the murderer of millions of Americans.

"And Lexi here"—he held up her hand—"will be now known as Suhaimah, which means 'little arrow' ..."

The wood planks of the platform felt like they were moving, undulating under her feet in waves. She looked out at the expectant faces, beaming at her and their leader, who was about to make an announcement concerning her.

She closed her eyes.

"And in less than a month, probably right after we have taken over this country, I will ask Suhaimah to marry me willingly. She will join my other two wives, Samantha and Sarti. But even if she doesn't agree to this, she will become my wife."

Abdul attempted to raise her arm up as the celebratory praises resounded, but her wrist slipped out from his grasp.

Lexi had fainted.

Chapter 32

Travis

Two Years Ago

Travis's path to despair began over waffles.

It was his favorite meal and as a reward for it being his first day of fourth grade, he was able to choose what they would eat that morning. Naturally, it was waffles.

"I get the next batch," Lexi blared at her brother.

Travis ignored her and shoved the entirety of the last of his four waffles into his mouth, his cheeks puffing like a chipmunk's, syrup running down his chin. While attempting to chew, a grin snuck out, revealing his teeth and some of his unchewed food.

"Travis!" Sara admonished. "Smaller bites next time."

"So, why can't we have *bacon* like normal people?" whined Lexi, as she glared at the waffle maker, impatiently waiting her turn.

Sara almost responded to this, but decided against it; they'd been down this road before and Lexi was just being annoying, all because her brother got his wish.

The phone's ringing provided her a diversion.

"Lexi dear, get the phone, would you?"

"Sure, *Auntie*," Lexi replied in a mocking tone, not reaching for the receiver right away. Instead, she continued her waffle-maker ogling, like some predator eyeing a small field mouse it planned to toy with before devouring.

Sara scowled at her on the fourth ring.

Lexi snatched the portable from its cradle without shifting her gaze and stuck it to her ear. "Hello, *Broadmoor* residence; Lexi speaking." Her words were sweet and exaggerated.

Silence.

"Lexi! You know this is the *Smith* Residence," Sara snapped.

"Hello?" Lexi huffed, annoyed.

"Hello, my beautiful niece. May I speak to my sister, please?" the buttery voice asked.

Lexi thrust the portable in her aunt's direction, eyes still on the waffle maker, billowing puffs of steam.

"Who is it?" Sara bellowed.

"I don't know. Someone who says he's your brother," Lexi replied, disinterested.

If Lexi had been paying attention, she'd have noticed that all of the color had immediately drained from Sara's features.

Sara snatched the phone from her and gaped at it for a moment, not wanting to hear what came next, and then finally put it to her ear. "What do you want?" she asked, a barely noticeable tremor in her voice.

"Sara, you're going to burn my waffles," Lexi barked, as she watched in shock as her aunt turned and walked out of the kitchen, leaving her to salvage her own breakfast.

"Is that how you speak to your brother?" His words were smooth, unflappable.

"As far as I'm concerned, you're not family; not any-more." Sara sank into her armchair in the living room, not wanting her niece and nephew to hear them.

"They don't even know I exist, do they?"

"Nor will they! And you'll say nothing: that was our agreement." She found herself having some difficulty breathing.

"The other part of the agreement is why I'm calling. Travis is starting school today."

Sara gulped. "Yes ..." She said tentatively, her voice softer now.

"Except, he'll be attending a different school," the voice said resolutely. "A car is waiting outside to take him right now."

She was feeling dizzy, taking big gulps of air. "And ... and where is that?"

Although she asked, she would rather not know.

"I suppose you'll find out eventually. It's the Madrassa Mahdi."

"Bu-but, what do I tell his school?" Spots swam around her periphery.

"I don't care what you tell his old school. He's going to get a proper Muslim education, even if you aren't willing to provide it for him. *That* was our deal!"

"Wha-what ... if I don't allow him to go?" Her words came out like puffs of air, with very little structure.

"Do *not* cross me. You know who I am. I expect you to honor our agreement. After Stan's wife died and you asked me for financial help because your infidel husband was not able to care for his family, I gave it to you. When your husband was found stealing from his company, I made the problem go away. You'd be best to keep me in your good graces. You understand me ... *sis?*"

She paused for a long time, partly because she didn't want to answer, and partly because she couldn't. "Yes, dammit I understand," she panted the words.

Abdul hung up.

A car horn sounded outside their home.

Sara sat slumped, deflated, and fighting to remain conscious.

It wasn't till the third honk, and Travis shaking his aunt's arm, that she was able to acknowledge it.

She arose and readied him for the car, telling him he was going to a new private school.

She walked him to the limo, Travis firing off questions she didn't answer.

At the driver's side, the window slid down and an arm thrust out a folded piece of paper. A gruff voice announced, "He said to give this to you." The window rolled up once she grabbed it.

"Am I going in this big car, Aunt Sara?" Travis gleamed.

She looked down at his expectant face, almost dropping the note she was handed, still unwilling to answer him and accept this. *Please, not just yet.*

The rear passenger door clicked open beside her and a demanding voice beckoned Travis inside.

She opened the folded page. Inside, scrawled by a hand she guessed to have been the driver's, big letters made Abe's demand obvious.

Remember our deal.

I will get a phone call if his schooling is interrupted by you in any way.

Abe

She watched Travis get into the car, after the voice
called him again.

She knew she was no longer an active participant in this.
Not if she was to hold onto the life she had. She wouldn't
interfere and she would keep her husband safe, and she'd
still watch over Stan's kids.

She observed the car driving away with Travis in its
belly, and retorted to herself, "Besides, how bad could an
American Madrassa be?"

She knew the answer.

☾ ✝ ✡ ☯ ☪

If a visitor, unfamiliar with their methods, were to walk
in, he or she might have to cover their ears because
it would appear that all the kids in Zaahirah's room were
babbling at the top of their voices. But to Zaahirah, the
sonorous notes of the Quran being read out loud, even by
children who didn't speak Arabic, was like music to her
ears.

The kids continued reading the same verse over and over, in unison, at nearly a full yell.

She clapped her hands to interrupt their regimented shouts. "Thank you, children. That was *very* good." She waited for their silence.

"What we are learning about here is how Allah will protect each of us believers until the last day."

Zaahirah was walking around the classroom, watching each of the children to make sure they were paying strict attention.

Flop! Her whip came down hard onto the back of Travis's hands with a crack.

He yelped, no longer gazing out the window. Immediately, he withdrew his hands and grimaced at the bright redness exploding on them. His eyes welled as he looked up at his teacher, unsure what he had done wrong.

"Travis, were you listening to me?"

"Yes-yes. I was, teacher."

"Okay, then tell the class what I was talking about," Zaahirah demanded.

"You were telling us about the last day, and when the Mahdi would kill the unbelievers. And only believers would live." He rubbed his hands, trying not to cry, and pushed away his pain.

Chapter 33

Frank

July 7th

T he incessant drumbeat of cicadas seemed to match the thumping melody in his head.

Finding Abdul's camp was easy enough. But avoiding detection from the drones, which had been searching for them, was a little trickier. Porter had scanned the heavens above and the roads behind them from the truck bed; Wallace had searched for any threats from their flanks and in front of them from the passenger seat; and Frank had driven. They had all ridden in silence, not wanting to discuss the crushing defeat they had just experienced or what lay ahead of them.

They had been headed to Stowell, Texas, but didn't make it more than a mile when Frank stopped them abruptly. Wallace looked at him and Frank at her. And without saying anything, they agreed. Porter, as if on cue, slid open the back window and calmly said, "As my father would have asked if he were here, 'Are we now going to go kick Haji's ass?'"

"Damn straight!" Wallace said, while Frank whipped them around and pointed them back down the highway to what he was sure would be their final act as Americans.

After confirming the access road entrance with the map Frank had taken from the broken-up terrorist base in Texas, they had parked the truck in a thick stand of bushes down the road. This is where Frank's injuries and his fatigue had slowed them down. It was a long couple of hours through the thick Florida brush, but they were finally there, studying their target.

Porter's murmured question, of whether this really was the right place, didn't need an answer as one man after another scurried around the grounds, each wearing traditional Islamic clothes accompanied by the requisite AK automatic rifle. Several times Frank had to blink back the feeling that he was somewhere in the Middle East and not in Florida.

They decided to get a closer look and slowly work their way up to a finger of trees and brush, which almost touched the back of one of the camp's many buildings.

That gave them more sweeping views over much of the complex, where most of the activity seemed to take place.

Almost immediately they saw their problem: Besides the futility in trying to engage even more jihadists with their meager assortment of weapons, they were grossly outnumbered. There were at least two dozen fully armed foreign fighters versus three banged-up US soldiers, one worse off than the others.

Wallace and Porter both glared their unspoken worries at Frank.

"I know, we'll have to set up a diversion, or something," Frank groused, just above a whisper.

"Yah think?" Wallace quipped.

"Even with a large enough diversion"—Porter tapped his pack, an unspoken confirmation that it contained two bricks of C4—"there's just too many of them ..."

He waited for Frank's response. But Frank appeared to have lost interest and was now possessed by something Porter couldn't see. "Major, are you still with us?"

Frank wasn't purposely ignoring them, merely twisting his face and squinting to confirm what he thought he saw. Before he seemed even able to pull his eyes away from the camp, he pulled a picture from his wallet and scrutinized it. Then he resumed the same intense gaze at the same point in the distance, blindly handing the photo to Porter. "Is that the same girl? I mean woman?"

Both Wallace and Porter glanced at the picture and then at the group walking between the river and the buildings, only a short distance away. Behind the group was a pretty young woman with short black hair wearing a sparkling *salwar kameez*. The rest were wearing *chadors*, which looked like *burkas* but did not cover their faces.

"Yeah, it kind of looks like the same person, why?" Porter thought out loud.

"Who is that and why is that important to us, sir?" asked Wallace.

Frank didn't immediately respond, and then finally spun around and sat with his back to the enemy camp, looking deflated. "I'm afraid it's my goddaughter. Which means her brother, my godson Travis, must be here too. It also means"—he exhaled a long breath—"that my best friend, Stanley, their father, didn't survive the trip here."

Frank felt older than he ever had before. Not only were his injuries weighing heavily on him, but so was this unexpected development. Stanley, his friend, was probably dead, as there was no way he'd let his kids out of his sight after waiting so long before collecting them. The texts he'd received from them indicated that they had been on the highway, but if Stanley didn't make it, he'd send the kids to Frank. Stanley dedicated his life to keeping his kids safe. Their being here, obviously captured before they could make it to their place in Florida, confirmed not only Stanley's passing but also Frank's obligation to watch over and protect his best friend's kids if something happened to their only parent; that's what a godfather was supposed to do.

Having experienced so many tough missions and firefights overseas, the last thing Frank expected was that his most difficult and yet most important rescue mission would be here on US soil.

He had to save them.

Before this, when they had agreed to try and strike at Abdul and his camp, they instinctively knew this was going to be a suicide mission, more or less. Yet he'd thought, if they could get a few of the terrorists and maybe slow them down and give America more of a chance, it would be worth the sacrifice. The mission had changed again.

One of them had to make it out with the kids. And they had to do this against a clock that was quickly counting down to some sort of invasion.

How the hell are we gonna do this? Frank mused.

"You know I have to do anything and everything I can to save them?" he exhaled.

"We knew this was a one-way ticket, Major. It's just a little more ... complicated now."

Porter just nodded his affirmation.

Frank turned back around to face their enemy. "You know, I might have an idea..."

☾ ✝ ✡ ☯ 🦅

"Repea—" Abdul frantically twisted the knob up a couple of megahertz, then back down the other way to home in on the signal propelled by minimal wattage, obscured and cutting out between the radio's hissing. "—three or four men, maybe more—*hisssss*—headed to your camp—*hisssss*—stopping you. We killed every—*hisssss*—using the drones, but—*hisssss*—men escaped and are at your location now."

"How long ago was this?" Abdul bellowed at his microphone.

"Yesterday ... been searching all day for them, using drones—*hisssss*—spotted their truck hidden near your property."

"Thank you. The Prophet, peace and blessings of Allah be upon him, would be proud of you." Abdul let go of the microphone button and dropped his headphones onto the table without even attempting to listen to Kadeem's replacement's reply.

He arose from his chair, forcing his mind to go from frantic reserved, before he popped open the door and slipped through. He found Sal immediately and ushered him over.

In his ear, he whispered, "Don't run or look surprised; don't look around. Grab a dozen of your men and do a full sweep of the property. We have a small armed group who has come here to stop us."

"Yes, Sir." Sal nodded and shuffled off, grabbing his men along the way, no doubt relishing the possibility of entering battle once more, and sooner than they had planned.

Abdul watched him go, while he carefully scanned the riverbank, and then the thick brush that surrounded the property. With any luck, he thought, he'd kill these men before they killed any of his own.

☾ ✝ ✡ ☯ ☫

Frank watched like a mud spider ready to strike from its burrow, unseen but deadly.

He tensed his good knee, hidden in the blind of the overgrowth's finger, ready to strike as one jihadist brushed by its tip, unaware he'd just walked by his immediate death. Frank relaxed a little, glad to be the one who remained while the others set up the diversions for his incursion. He longed for his silenced weapons, and did the only thing he could do: wait.

Wallace had trotted quietly but quickly back to the highway, where she would recover their truck and set up their first diversion. She would rig the truck with C4, per Porter's instructions, and guide it to the gate so that it would explode at exactly one hour after her departure. With luck, it would take out a few stunned guards and create a tremendous commotion that would draw to it many others. Wallace would also use her AK to polish off a few more and draw their fire. They would kill a few of the jihadists from the blast, but the blast and gunfire would be more of a diversion than anything else.

Porter would use the remaining brick of C4 on the dock. At the one-hour mark, he'd set one of the two boats aflame, while setting free the second boat as his means of escape. No one would be looking his way because of the gate blast. The fire would then draw many more to it, like moths to a candle flame. When the maximum casualties could be expected—seven minutes by their estimate—the timer would go off and the dock would detonate. And though they planned to kill as many of them as possible, the main purpose for this explosion was to provide further diversion.

With some added luck, these two diversions would give Frank the ability to sneak in and gather Lexi and her brother from the buildings and escape into the woods. Finally, if everything went according to plan, Porter would meet up with Wallace, Frank, and the kids in the other boat downstream and they would all motor away.

That was the plan.

Realistically, there were way too many parts that had to come off perfectly for his plan to succeed and all of them to escape. But maybe for once, they'd have a little luck. They needed some. In the process, if they could kill enough of Abdul's men to hurt their end game, it would be a bonus. They knew they weren't likely going to stop them. Their primary goals were to get Frank's godchildren out and bruise their enemy.

Until they had more sufficient forces, that would have to do.

Frank glumly waited, pushing aside any thoughts of failure. He glanced at his watch for perhaps the twentieth time in the fifty-seven minutes that had passed since Wallace and Porter had left. The first explosion by Wallace should go off any minute. He had long ago seen Porter's signal that he was ready.

The waiting for a plan's execution was always excruciating.

This one was almost unbearable.

The door of the women's dwelling creaked open and Lexi, dressed in a different outfit, along with other women popped out and walked to the south, *in the wrong direction.*

Not only were they walking away from Frank, they were walking toward the dock. If they passed by within fifty feet of the dock when Porter blew it, Lexi and all the other women would likely be killed from the shrapnel alone.

"Shit!" he breathed.

Frank wrung his hands, contemplating his next counter-move, praying the group of women would walk faster. Then his fears grew dire.

Once Lexi and the group of women were exactly opposite the dock, they turned east, and started walking to the dock—headed right for the explosion point. And if they didn't change course soon, there wouldn't be enough time to leave the area before the explosion. Porter had orders, and like a good soldier, Frank expected him to carry them out.

Frank deliberated over his watch once more. As of right now, Wallace was late.

Looking up to the dock, he could see small wisps of smoke taking form on the closest boat. It had started. *Soon a fire would be raging, and then the explosion, and ... Lexi and these women would all be kill—*

A head-banging explosion rocked the ground underneath him, coming from the area where the front gate would be. Most in the camp at first ducked or hit the ground, but then many of the men started running toward the front of the property.

The women split into two groups: one group ran fully onto the dock and the other back toward the building they had come from. Lexi was leading the first group onto the dock.

Shit-shit-shit.

Frank sprang up and raced as fast as his one-and-a-half legs would carry him toward Lexi and the dock. Although he carried his rifle at the ready, he wasn't intending to shoot, not yet. He yelled toward the dock. "Porter, don't blow it!"

The boat was already aflame; Lexi and the others reacted, and halted their run along the dock, deeper over the river. However, they were now standing right where the blast's focal point would be.

Frank shot off two rounds, not at anyone, but in the general direction of where Porter would be, hoping to get his attention and scare the women away from the dock. He yelled again, "Don't blow it!" And then to himself he puffed, "Please, for God's sake, don't blow it."

Several shots sounded in the distance. They were directed at Frank, but he ignored them, steamrolling forward. *Almost there.*

Lexi's wide eyes followed the yelling man with a limp, firing a rifle and running toward them. She ducked down when he fired a few more shots toward them.

Frank realized Lexi was moving to lie flat on the dock rather than scattering, as he had hoped. He bellowed his warning to Porter once more. Finally, from under the dock, Frank saw a thumb stick up out of the water. He wouldn't blow it.

Frank slowed just a bit, and then realized it was now or never: he'd try to grab Lexi. He was only fifty yards away when he felt a powerful blow rock his shoulder, knocking him off balance. Unable to right himself, his momentum tumbled him onto a grassy area, almost striking one of the picnic benches. As he hit ground, his shoulder exploded with pain.

He'd been shot.

He completely failed his godchildren, Porter, Wallace, and his country.

He rolled over onto his back, just as two shadows gathered right over him. One lifted his rifle and aimed it at Frank's head, his finger finding the trigger.

"Wait! Don't shoot him!" yelled a female voice, and the man averted his rifle. The other shadow flipped his rifle around and swung the heavy wood butt at Frank's head, connecting full force.

For the second time in twenty-four hours, Frank was knocked out cold.

☪ † ✡ ☯ 🦅

The term that came to Porter's mind was "FUBAR." As in this mission was FUBAR'd.

He was shocked into inaction, and could only watch everything unfold in front of him. He was a tech and radio guy, listing Basic as his only entry to the plus column of his hand-to-hand combat résumé. He just couldn't think of how or even if he could provide any help with the major down. He was sure that he'd be no help if he were captured, too. So, Porter did the one thing he knew he could do best. Hold his breath.

In high school the breast stroke was his specialty. He was pretty decent at it and won quite a few swim meets, even going to State. But what he really did well was hold his breath. He could swim over one hundred meters in their high school pool, underwater. He figured he needed to clear one fifty to make it to the next bank of trees without being seen. The water was murky, but the current was in his favor. He was pretty sure he could make it.

Under the cover of the dock, he took four long breaths, before holding it and going under.

Because there were no lane markers, nor walls to judge distances, he could only go by his internal count and how long he could hold out before he needed air.

During his high school days, when he came to seventy-five meters, his lungs would expand enough because of the amount of CO_2 building up that he'd have to expel some air. At one hundred, he'd be struggling to stay under and could maybe punch it a few more yards, maybe getting to one-twenty or one-thirty. And although that was in a pool, he didn't have to slow his stroke to turn at the wall and it was never a life or death situation, like now.

It only felt like fifty meters and he was already struggling to stay under, maybe sixty seconds total. He pushed harder, but he had only a few seconds left.

Then something snagged him.

It felt like he was being yanked, and he almost came to a complete stop. He yanked back, but was caught in some growth or unseen debris. He tried to rise out of the water but he couldn't.

His foot was stuck and he was out of air.

Chapter 34

Lexi and Travis

July 8th

L exi's life was over; at least it felt that way.

Her days from here on would consist of walking parts of the camp with the other women (who never spoke to her), reading her Quran (she would be tested on this twice a day), and praying five times per day. Finally, there was the constant reminder of her future as she watched Abdul's other two wives wait for their appointed times to be raped—her words, not theirs. Sarti and Samantha said to each other and the other women that it was their duty and acted as if they were fine with it. But anyone could see it in their eyes; this wasn't the truth. And in days or weeks, this would be what Lexi had to look forward to. Then, it would be her time to be married to her uncle and be raped at his whim. How had this life of hers come to change so drastically in so little time?

Perhaps if she had opened her eyes long ago, she would have seen all the machinery of her life and the lives of those around her working its way in this direction. But she couldn't have noticed anything outside of herself. Her eyes were cast inward for so long, waking every day in the anxious pursuit of living a miserable self-centered existence she called her life.

Had she opened her eyes, she might have recognized that she was a Muslim.

She guessed that's what she must have always been; she was born a Muslim, and her family had come from Islamic roots. Yet they "weren't really practicing their faith," her mother would tell her. And so they rarely followed any Muslim traditions: the only one she could remember was not eating bacon. She still didn't understand that one.

No one had any idea of this in her meager circle of high school and college friends. They acted like, and for all intents and purposes were, a secular family. And after the attack on 9/11, their family kept this part of their lives hidden, at first fearful of repercussions and then later, just forgetting the pillars of Islam. It was fascinating now, but truly scary, to see what Abdul and his followers believed it meant to be a Muslim.

Women had no rights, and as far as she could tell, they were property. They taught that the modesty and purity of their women were paramount, but that felt like just another way to maintain their superiority and control over them. They said they respected and honored their women, when in fact they treated them not much better than the lowly dogs they hated.

Sometime after her mother died, Lexi remembered taking a feigned interest in the events unfolding overseas on their television. But she never felt any connection to the victims, much less the perpetrators who willfully killed women and children in those faraway places, all in the name of Islam. None of that concerned her, as Lexi, in her own way, wore a veil that wouldn't let anything in that might upset the balance of her own sheltered life. It would seem her aunt and uncle and, in a way, her father had enabled her behavior.

If only she'd known.

She certainly had no idea of her father's secret life: that he was fighting a war in the US and who knows where else, against these terrorists. It struck her hard, the understanding of why he had left her and Travis with their aunt and uncle: it was to keep them safe from Abdul, her father's brother.

She didn't hold any of this against Travis. He had little choice, like her. She finally remembered when Travis went to the Madrassa, noticing the change in him right away after he had started fourth grade. For a while, when she paid any attention to him, it was like he was living two lives: his science, which he loved, and this twisted version of Islam, that he was forced to follow. It was no wonder why Lexi and her brother had become so distant from each other and the world around them. And to rub salt into his wounds, she concerned herself with her own skin, all the while Travis was just trying to survive.

And what was further astonishing to her was that first her parents and then her aunt and uncle had kept Abe's existence hidden all this time.

Lexi shook her head and huffed her frustration quietly while pacing behind the women.

And while everyone in her life—her father for his reasons, and her aunt and uncle for theirs—hid Abe from her and Travis, Abdul killed her mother, causing her father to go away, controlled her brother, and plotted his Islam-ic-jihadist master plan to destroy her country.

She decided then and there that even if she died trying she would do her best to escape with Travis. She had no idea how long she had, and suspected it was a lot less than the "month" Abdul had announced, so she probably didn't have much time for planning. She would be ever vigilant, and watch for when that right moment presented itself. Then she would escape, and grab Travis. Finally, if there was any way before she left, she would try to kill her uncle.

Lexi's hand touched the outside of her garments, feeling the curve of her waistband, following it around to the firmness of her survival knife, clipped securely under her clothes, unseen. If anyone had paid attention to her at that moment, they would have caught a dark sneer appear on her face.

"Suhaimah?" called a voice in front of her. Startled, Lexi looked up and found Sarti sternly peering at her. *Wife number one does not care for me at all.*

"Yes?" Lexi answered in an impertinent tone.

"Describe for me Islam's five pillars and how you will be sure to follow them."

Lexi ignored her, her gaze instead being drawn to movement in the distance, by the radio shack. Abdul and Sal were walking to the prisoners' building. Lexi started to wonder again about the crazy man running toward her yesterday, who was shot and then captured. She was still sure that there was something familiar about him. She just couldn't place it.

"Suhaimah?" Sarti bellowed. *She is always angry.*

☾ ✝ ✡ ☯ 🦅

F rank knew his goose was cooked when he was caught. He didn't mind the dying part; he just didn't want to be beheaded.

When he first awoke, he had for just a moment hoped that he'd bleed to death from his shoulder and other wounds. All of him hurt and he was damned tired. But they patched him up well—although he wasn't sure why, as he was destined for an execution later, from what he was told.

Once that flicker of weakness passed and he realized he wasn't dead yet, he knew that as long as he drew breath, there was still a small chance, no matter how slight, he could break out and grab his godkids. He'd be doing this solo now, since he hadn't heard sight or sound of Porter or Wallace. He assumed and hoped that they'd both gotten away. So, even though he was weary from fatigue and his many wounds, he had enough sense to grab what he needed, while they weren't watching.

He was fully aware of the odd and painful predicament they had put him in, but he also understood why. They had placed him, naked, in a jail cell no bigger than a large dog kennel. He was forced, because of the size of his cell and his hands cuffed behind his back, into to a kneeling position. The cell's inward spikes prevented him from resting up against his cage. The floor was carpeted with glass fragments, prevented him from finding a more comfortable position. And they left him in the dark.

Other than the initial glimpse when they placed him here, he could only surmise his surroundings by the pricks around and below him. He'd long ago lost feeling in his legs after the warm pooling of his blood around his knees had started to dry. In spite of this, he had a glint of hope that came from familiarity, and a plan.

Frank knew this routine of torture because he'd been through it once before. While he struggled to remain conscious and focused on his current task, the darkness behind his eyelids was filled with flashes of his other experience.

He knew he would be held here until he broke, and then he would be made to expose his friends, or his connection to Lexi and Travis, or whatever they wanted to get out of him. He wasn't going to wait around for that to happen.

Before leaving Texas, Frank had already made a provision for breaking out of confinement, in the event that he was captured: he had glued two paperclips to his inner thigh. The glue was colored to look like loose skin or something worse, and most men just didn't check there in a strip search.

One of the many things he learned when he joined Special Ops was how to pick locks. He'd gotten quite good at it using just about anything with a point, but he was especially good with paperclips. One of his paperclips was bent like a pick rake and the other like a tension tool. With most locks, the process took a fair amount of time. Sometimes, he just got lucky—*click*—like now, when the locks were pretty easy to pick.

Frank slowly slid his free hand out of his cuffs, carefully bringing both of them around and rubbing the feeling back into his wrists and hands. They were sore, but manageable. The cage didn't even have a lock on it—they must have assumed he wasn't ever going to get that far.

The closure's door was clasped with just a meager button. And now that popped open.

His plan was simple. He'd get out of this cage, unscrew the lightbulb above, and then cry out, begging for help. When they came running, he'd spring to action. If there was only one guard and the torturer, he'd be able to disable them using his skills.

He grabbed the top edge of the cage's open doorway, intending to lift himself out, when he heard a noise outside his room.

They're coming for round two, but I'm not ready yet.

He let go, quickly clicking the cage's door closed.

There were footsteps and voices getting closer.

Frank palmed the two picks and carefully slipped his free hand back into the cuffs, clicking it only once so that it was closed, but still open enough that he could slide his hand out.

The room's door opened, showering him with an almost unexpected splash of light, forcing him to squint.

Abdul Raheem Farook entered through the door, first just a dark form, and then his stern face came into focus. He flipped on the room's single lightbulb, which shot more painful blindness to his eyes. He ignored the new sting.

Farook stood just inside the doorway, with two guards behind him.

"Mr. Cartwright. How are we feeling today?"

Although his voice was smooth, it stuck like a blunt blow to Frank's head, dislodging a long forgotten memory. He knew this Abdul from Iraq. He was *that* Abdul; the one whose Iman forced him to fight a duel to save the lives of his Army unit. The Abdul he remembered was much younger then and looked very different. But that voice was unmistakable.

It was also immediately obvious that Farook understood Frank's reaction, because his next words were in Farsi, "Yes, we meet again, old friend." He continued in English, "Only this time it will not work out as well for you, or your friends. If you're wondering, the woman was killed at the gate and we captured your other man who burned the boat, although I'm not sure what the purpose in that was. Anyway, we will be executing both of you at noon."

Farook seemed to wait, perhaps wanting to see Frank's reaction to the news.

When Frank volunteered nothing, Farook tossed two long items in his direction. They clanged and jingled before coming to rest, directly outside his cage. When he made out what they were, he looked back up at Farook.

"One of those instruments will take your head. It is up to you to choose which one."

Frank glanced first at the scimitar with a curved blade, covered with dried splotches of brown. The other was an old rusty steak knife. He shot a look of understanding and shock back up to Farook.

"Yes, you get it don't you? I will make you a promise. If you tell me some more details about what your mission plan was, I'll make sure that your execution is conducted with the tool meant for this and you will not feel a thing. It's the least I could do for such a worthy adversary.

"However, if you do not answer my questions, we will make you watch your man suffer under the steak knife before we then execute you in the same way. It could take minutes for you to die, very painfully.

"Based on my previous actions, my guess is that you know I mean what I say. So what will it be?"

Farook waited for an answer, but Frank said nothing.

"So be it."

Farook left with one of his guards; the other picked up the knife and scimitar and raced out. Another man walked in with a box of what Frank suspected were his tools of torture.

He was ready.

Chapter 35

Frank

T he first strike of the metal-studded whip to his back brought it all back clearly.

The memory of his first torture was haunting enough but after a body is subjected to enough pain, parts of the brain start to shut down, and memories become foggy. His first Iraqi torturer had brought out virtually the same box of tools as this one and had flogged him with the same device and in the same way.

And so it was here, in a makeshift prison on US soil, that he realized that this torturer was equipped with the same tools and techniques as the Iraqi torturer many years earlier. And like then, he would make it through the flogging until the next part of the torture. And when the torturer attempted to reposition his re-secured hands and start the next round, he would strike. He still had hope.

When he was trained to prepare for torture techniques, the first thing he learned was to just give his captors whatever intel they sought. After all, most systems and personnel were changed the moment you were captured. The key was to live to see another day. Another day alive meant another step toward release or escape. The exception to this would be when your team is not yet able to get out of harm's way, like in this case. Then the best thing to do was to lie. Make up a half-truth that appears to be right, but know that they will probably torture you anyway, and when they do, you will eventually break. Everyone does.

When he was captured on the border of Iraq and Iran, he gave up whatever they asked and they tortured him anyway. Within minutes, he was crying like a baby. He wasn't proud of it, but it happened, and he survived.

This time, he told a lie. And based on what Abdul described, he could craft the lie to better fit what he knew they knew. Also, he suspected that his people were still alive. Wallace probably wasn't killed or Abdul would have said how and he doubted Porter would be caught because he would have swum to safety.

"How many of you are there?" the Dr. Mengele-wannabe demanded. He was a scrawny wisp of a man with gaunt features, his nose so thin it barely held up his thick wired-rimmed glasses.

"Only two of them, plus me. They had escaped the drones in another vehicle and once they had found the camp, they dumped me because they thought I was too old and feeble to be any use to them. I figured they had escaped, but seeing as they were dead or going to be ... good riddance to them. I'm just an innocent—"

Thunk. The metal nuts attached to the torturer's flogging stick struck, bruising more muscle in his back. *I'm way too old for this shit.*

"Why were you attacking the camp?"

"We just wanted to kill as many of you ragheads as we could." That part was true.

The torturer struck again.

"You're Army?"

Frank puffed hard, the last one took his breath away, " Retired... I mean, yes... But, retired. I just found the others and we ..." Frank waited for the next blow. But it didn't come. How many was that? Ten? Fifteen? Dammit, he'd lost count. He was already feeling dizzy.

He watched the man walk around him and felt him unlatch his hands.

It was time.

☪ † ✡ ☯ 🦅

The camp's new loud speakers blared out the call to prayer. "*Allahu akbar*" (Allah is the greatest).

Lexi shot up in her cot, as if she woke from a nightmare.

"*Ash-hadu an-la laha illa Allah*" (I acknowledge there is no deity but God).

But, it was a nightmare—one in which she currently lived. She already knew that this was called the Adhan, or call to prayer, and it would happen every day, five times per day, for as long as she was alive and chose to do nothing to change her situation. It blared so loud that she couldn't even hear herself think. She couldn't imagine what it would be like outside. She'd be deaf inside of a week. At least she didn't have to go into this while they taught her the basics.

The grisly images of what she witnessed yesterday came flooding back to her. So much blood, so much acceptance of murder as part of the enforcement of rules. And women like her had far fewer rights than someone like Leo.

As she waited for the Adhan to be repeated once again, telling believers to line up for the prayer, a thought occurred to her. This might be the time to escape.

She bolted to the door and peered out of the single window that looked out to the main yard and to the Apalachicola. One man after another rushed past her window, quietly hurrying in the same direction, to a building she hadn't been in, near the cafeteria. She suspected that that was what they used for a mosque now.

Leo passed by her window, making her jump. He too was racing to get to the mosque. He held his stump up to his chest, with his only hand. His face looked somewhat paler, and his otherwise expressive eyes were blank as if he were in a trance. In fact, each man looked to be in a trance, like the Eloi who marched to their doom down to the cannibalistic Morlocks' cave in *The Time Machine.*

She remembered the call to prayer the very few times her family went to mosque in Tucson. But the people didn't look like this, and it wasn't so damned loud.

The call blared out again.

Lexi pressed her palms against her ears and decided now was the best time. She could get out before they would notice her, while they were praying. She'd collect Travis, who also wasn't yet allowed to go to prayer. She'd grab her bug-out bag from the locker (she figured that she'd be able to jimmy that pretty easily), and then the lock on her door, and then she'd be gone.

She looked once more at the window and fell backward. Yusuf's face was right there in the single pane, glaring at her.

He threw open the door as she arose. His hand came around and caught her right in the cheek, sending her back down to the floor. "You will mind what you're told, or your time here will be a lot more unpleasant."

She rubbed her face, which felt fiery and hot, and glared hatred at him.

"You were told to read your Quran, not stare out the window. When it is your time, you will go to prayer with the other women. Until then, you stay here as you're told. And do not cast your eyes upon me as you do. You will treat me with respect." He held his hand up and leaned toward her as if he was preparing to strike again.

Lexi cowered back and cast her eyes downward. She so wanted to kill him.

"Good. Now we understand each other." Yusuf left, locking the door behind him.

She looked up and waited to see his shadow pass. Jumping up, she only slightly peeled back the curtain and glanced outside. While she did this, her right hand found her knife, beneath her garment. She flicked it open and backed away from the door.

It was time.

☪ ✝ ✡ ☯ ☾

Frank rarely felt satisfied when it came to killing another man, but this was the exception.

When the wiry torturer attempted to readjust his cuff so that he could better position Frank for the next round, Frank struck. His paperclips were turned so that the tips were coming out of the knuckles of his free clenched fist. Frank surprised the man with several jabs to his neck; one of them caught his carotid and a geyser of blood flowed. In a panic, the man tried to move away, but Frank hung on as the man flailed, trying to stem the flow. Frank quickly positioned himself so that he could hold the man's mouth, muffling his screams, and he wrapped his good leg around him and held on. When the man finally collapsed, the loudspeakers outside thundered with a call to prayer.

Perfect timing.

He found the guard's keys and undid his cuffs—much easier than with the paperclips.

He yanked the man's pants and shirt off him and slipped them on himself. Even though they didn't fit and they reeked of body odor, they were better than going naked—at his age, and with all his injuries, he was bound to scare little children. *Don't want to do that.*

Frank stumbled a little to the back corner of the room. He thought his eyes were playing tricks on him, but after snatching it from the floor, he could not believe his luck. It was the only thing of his they'd saved and the only thing of his that he needed; his knee brace.

After snapping it on, he moved to the torturer's work-table where several tools had been carefully laid out. He selected a big knife and a little one—he imagined this was for filleting skin, intended for him next no doubt—and slowly stepped to the locked door. His body hurt like a son-of-a-bitch, but it was surprisingly functional. And with his friend adrenaline, he might have enough energy to do this.

Finding the correct key from the dead torturer's keyring, he quietly slipped it in the lock, although he didn't have to be too quiet with the call to prayer still blaring. With any luck there would be no guards, but just in case, he was prepared.

He banged on the door and doing his best impression of skinny-torturer-asshole he yelled, "Guard open up, Cartwright has my knife. Hurry!"

He heard a noise by the door and a rumble of keys. At the same time the guard clanged metal keys to door lock, Frank unlocked it from his side and pulled, dragging the unsuspecting guard into him as he drove the large blade into the guard's neck.

Like a sack of potatoes, the guard went down.

Now Frank had a gun.

Chapter 36

Lexis and Travis

L
exi had this.

Her knife easily slipped in between the door frame and the door, in an attempt to unclasp the lock. She didn't need a prepper book for this; she had gotten out of many locked doors at home—lessons self-taught during the multiple detentions imposed upon her by her beleaguered aunt and uncle.

She knew how to open this one.

Like a skilled locksmith. *Click* and the lock came free.

She slowly opened the door, her pack already snugly around her shoulders, and stuck her head out to see if the coast was clear.

Almost as if on cue, a gunshot echoed.

She ducked back.

She considered the sound of the shot for a moment. What she heard was a good mile away, certainly not aimed at her.

Although anxious, she felt steady as she eased her head outside once again, this time looking toward the sound of the gunshot, where she was about to run.

She looked the other way, toward the ad hoc mosque, then to the dock.

Nothing. It was quiet and there didn't appear to be anyone around.

Then another shot: this one from a different direction, followed by another. Then, multiple shots, from every direction.

What the heck was going on?

She looked back at the mosque and shuddered.

There was Yusuf, the hook-nosed man, yelling at men streaming out of the mosque, pointing them in different directions. He seemed as surprised as she about the gunfire.

When he pointed in her direction, he stopped talking and glared at Lexi.

Like a gazelle, she dashed out her door and ran in the other direction, straight for the cabin where she believed she would find Travis: the same one Abdul had originally put both of them in yesterday.

She ran stooped over and hugged each building as gunfire was everywhere, although most of it was concentrated by the front gate.

A quick glance confirmed Yusuf had turned away from her, and was jogging with some of his men to the south, toward the training grounds where she had first seen him with Leo—*Leo lost his own hand for that.*

A rifle's report blasting only feet away startled her. It was one of their men firing at the tree line, in the direction she had been running; it wasn't aimed at her.

There was movement in the trees, just past the clearing. Someone was there.

More gunfire, just behind her, aimed at one of their buildings. She hugged the ground but held her head up to see. Someone from one of their buildings was firing back at their own man.

☪ ✝ ✡ ☯ 🦅

F rank checked his weapon, satisfied that the magazine was full. He pulled back the charging handle and cycled in a round. He was just about to slip out the door, when he heard gunfire. He tried to get a bead on where it was coming from, when more shots rang out, but from a different direction. And then more from other positions.

But none of this was concentrated at him. Maybe it was Wallace and Porter. Regardless, he was done waiting.

Holding the rifle in front of him, he carefully stepped out of the building.

A spray of bullets washed passed his feet and up the wall of the building, just missing him by a few inches.

Slipping back inside, he fired several rounds back at the gunman's direction.

He quickly glanced out the door in the same direction; the same man who had fired upon him was inching forward toward his position. But before he could return fire, shots exploded the doorframe at head level from a different direction.

He stuck his rifle out, keeping the rest of him behind the heavily timbered structure, which appeared to resist the 7.62 round, shot a quick burst in each direction, and then withdrew.

Multiple shots from multiple directions now, all aimed at him.

Dammit! He was pinned down.

☪ ✝ ✡ ☯ 🦅

No time to wait.

The grounds were flooded with Abdul's men, running frantically in every direction, some passing her but paying her almost no attention. They had larger concerns, and so did she.

Ignoring the gunfire, which seemed to be coming from nearly every place around her except the river, Lexi made her final dash in between the building she had been hunkered down against and the cabin that she believed Travis to be in.

The five to ten feet between them was filled with the loudest gunfire and she could see even more commotion in that direction, with Abdul's men firing at green shapes appearing out of the woods.

A bullet ricocheted off the cabin she was running toward and she smiled at her luck: if she had left two seconds earlier, she'd have been hit.

At the door of the cabin, she thumped loudly. "Travis, it's me. Can you open the door?"

A soft voice behind the door said something unrecognizable.

It didn't matter. She knew it was her brother.

She slipped her knife—she had been holding it the whole time—between the door and jamb, popping it open without much effort.

She was a master!

Lexi grabbed his hand from the darkness, glad he was clutching his bag already, and they ran for the northern edge of the property, one hand clutching Travis' arm, the other slipping her knife behind her back, under clothes, but ready to grab it when it was needed.

At first, she thought she might try the trucks, but with all the gunfire by the gate, she didn't think she'd be able to make it out in that direction. So she planned for them to just slip away into the woods. They'd walk to Tucson, if they had to, or find someplace else to live. It didn't matter; she had her brother, now she just wanted their freedom.

She glanced over to her brother. He looked a little dazed, but didn't look very scared. She was proud of him and would tell him so as soon as they were free.

They were coming up to the building with the large antenna, about to dash past, when the door opened, blocking their access. They both froze, as Abdul stepped out of the door directly in front of them.

She let go of Travis and put herself between them, her right hand reaching for the knife.

"Stop!" he demanded. "I don't want you to get hurt. They are attacking us everywhere. Run to the boat at the end of the dock. There are keys in it. No one else will be there. I want to know you two will be safe."

Lexi's hand remained still, her fingertips on the knife's edges just beneath her clothes. It would be easy now, but she didn't pull it out. She gazed for just a moment at this terrorist, this murderer of her mother and her father, and was somewhat dumbfounded. "What?" she said.

"Go! Quickly, I want both of you to escape. Run now!" He yelled.

She grabbed her brother once again and they ran away, headed at a diagonal, right for the dock.

She glanced back and Abdul had already turned away from them and gone back into the building. He wasn't going to chase them.

One of Abdul's men ran past them, but didn't even hesitate; neither did they.

They just ran and ran, until they were there, at the boat at the end of the dock. And no one else was there, just like he'd said.

They jumped on board and she looked down at the ignition, right near the steering wheel, where she assumed the keys would be. It was empty and the keys weren't there.

He had lied.

☪ † ✡ ☯ 🦅

A bdul scooped the volumes of papers from his desk with his palm open and arm extended, pushing the mass into an open valise he held at the edge of the desk. Not caring about their condition, he shoved the documents containing many of their attack plans deep into it and then snapped the clasp shut. In one motion he tossed it at the door and immediately turned his attention to the next item, like he was abruptly going through a mental packing list for a long trip.

Pack the briefcase: Check!

He leaned below his desk and pulled up a box from a shelf hidden in shadows. Laying it on top of the desk, he unlatched it and opened it to reveal a stopwatch sitting on top of a tangle of wires snaking from it to gray clay-like blocks, nested on its bottom.

It was overkill, but he wasn't one to take chances.

He moved the hands to five minutes forward and clicked the button, setting it into motion. Closing the box without latching it again—what was the point?—he pushed it away.

Bomb readied to take out the enemy and hide intelligence: Check!

Clutching his briefcase, he slid out the door, his rifle pointed forward, finger on the trigger.

He had a boat to catch.

☾ † ✡ ☯ 🦅

Frank had found himself back in his cage room, the one he had just escaped from.

This time he had taken a position prone on the floor, rifle aimed up toward the door that had, at least until a minute ago, been receiving all the gunfire. Like a hunter in his blind, he waited for his prey: in this case, the next person to walk through the door.

He knew his enemy's tactics. One of the lowest-ranked men would rush through the door, accepting martyrdom through his bullets, while others followed right behind with overpowering force. Or they would toss in a grenade.

He was prepared for either and waited patiently.

He didn't have to wait long.

A shadow appeared and then stopped by the door, but low, not like someone was about to burst in.

A small mirror slid into view, but only about foot-level in the doorway, and then immediately withdrew before he could lower his weapon and shoot: he was pointed up, around chest level.

An object was tossed through the doorway, in his direction.

Grenade!

Frank spun around and hugged the floor, now inside the cage room, snug against the wall, with his feet crossed and pointed at the doorway. He closed his eyes, covered his ears with his palms and opened his mouth wide.

In an instant, his room exploded in light that he saw through his eyelids.

Frank knew this device very well, as he had used one like it many times. It was a flash grenade, not something he expected terrorists to use: they preferred mostly to blow shit up.

When he heard "Clear!" from the outer room entrance, Frank did two things quickly. He flung himself spread-eagle on the ground, hands splayed out, and he hollered, "Major Frank Cartwright, U.S. Army Retired. I am alone."

"Anyone else in this building, sir?" a reassuring voice asked from the doorway.

"No, I'm it," he replied from the floor.

"Are you able to stand, sir?" the voice asked from above him.

Frank looked up and smiled at the sergeant offering a hand. "Damn straight, Sergeant!"

He held on to the hand, returning the solid grip which turned into a handshake. "Damn, it's great to see you guys. Where did you come from and how the hell did you know?"

"Thank you, Sir. We're from Camp Shelby. My commander received a frantic call from a Lieutenant Grimes from Stowell, Texas, who said his son, a Corporal Grimes, and a Major Cartwright were going to single-handedly take down the head Haji who nuked America. Our commander wanted blood and so we got here as soon as we could, as soon as we could find you."

"Well, thank you, Sergeant. Now, I need to find someone."

"Are there any other prisoners?" the tall Army sergeant asked.

"Not here, but my two godchildren are being held by Abdul and his men. I was just about to try and free them when you and your men showed up."

"Is one of them a young woman, and the other a smaller boy?"

"Yes!" Frank froze, "Where are they?"

"We saw them running to a boat by a dock, followed by another man. One of our men went to—" The sergeant stopped to watch the major snatch up his rifle and charge to the door. "Where are you going, sir?"

"I'm going to get my kids."

Chapter 37

Lexi and Frank

Lexi looked everywhere for the keys, but she couldn't find them.

She could have turned over everything, but there was no use. They were definitely not on the boat. Abdul had lied to her, this was the only thing she was certain of.

She shot a protective glance at Travis who sat on the padded swivel seat beside her, patiently watching her work. He seemed unafraid, or maybe he was just empty. She knew she was, as she searched her mind for their next move.

Maybe we could float away?

She thought if she released their tether to the dock, the current would take them down the river. It was better than remaining here.

Lexi sprang up to undo the rope, just as Abdul stepped on the boat. He brushed past her, sat in the driver's seat and thrust the key—the one she had been searching for—into the ignition. The boat's engine grumbled to life.

Lexi eyed the dock, their only escape, but saw he had already unmoored them. They were starting to drift away, the current grabbing hold of them.

Abdul gunned the engine and the boat lunged forward, sending Lexi tumbling backward onto the deck. Abdul backed off the gas.

"You best sit down if you don't want to go overboard." Abdul gleamed his deceit.

Lexi rose to her knees as Abdul slid the throttle forward again, moving the boat back toward the dock. Her hand found the knife, and she withdrew it, quietly snapping it open. She calculated it was only five feet to Abdul. She eyed him as he studied her and what was beyond her.

Just as she was ready to leap, Abdul brought up the rifle slung around his neck and quickly fired off a round past her.

Hearing it connect, she turned her head to see a man in an Army uniform. He fell into the water, and as quick as he was there, he was gone, like he'd never existed.

She turned back to Abdul again, now more determined.

With eyes fixed on her target, she sprang up as Abdul opened the boat's throttle all the way.

Lexi brought her knife around, intending to connect with his neck, but with the boat's movement not account-ed for in her leap, she connected directly with Abdul's cheek, burying the knife in it.

The boat's motion carried her past him into the floor behind. She turned to stand and saw him rise up, turning to her. His eyes were wide and crazed; she had surprised him with her move. He pulled the knife from his wound and dropped it to the floor. He stood for a moment above her, blood streaming from his face, with a look that swiftly changed from astonishment to anger. He lifted his rifle as if he were going to fire it at her. Lexi was helpless where she was, and he was quick.

They banged into something, maybe another boat, and he stumbled, reaching for the side of the boat in an attempt to buttress his misstep, but he only found air.

Lexi was now the one who was astonished; she watched him tumble over the side and into the water. As he went over, his eyes were no longer wide with surprise or anger: his hand was pressed to his face, so she couldn't see the full expression, but she would have sworn he was smiling just before he slipped into the black water. It looked like he was proud.

Travis was standing over her, offering her his hand.

She lifted herself up and was about to thank him for the helping hand, when she saw what was coming right at them.

"Get dow—" she attempted to yell, but it was too late.

Their boat, at full throttle and the wheel turned slightly, had spun completely around and was now doing 20 knots downstream. They were headed right for a shoreline.

They hit the shore, and then their inertia propelled the boat up and then into ground.

Lexi had tried to pull her body down and take Travis with her, but before she could do it, they were both airborne. She was shocked to find they were traveling over the boat, which crashed into something below them, and they were flying. She felt like they may continue to go upward forever, maybe leaving the atmosphere. Both their bodies spun around, and they saw nothing but cloudless skies, and then trees, and then grass, and then the boat—now much farther away—and then grass again.

Then they hit.

She knew she wasn't dead because her shoulder hurt and she still felt the soreness in her wrists.

Pain was good at this point.

She also felt and heard her heart racing in both her ears. But she heard nothing else. She opened her eyes, unaware she had them closed this whole time and was staring skyward once again. "Travis?" she croaked.

She lifted her head, "Travis?" she said a little louder.

Still no other sounds, not even gunshots.

There was a small rustle in the grass, beyond her feet, and so she pushed up her trunk to get a better look.

It was him.

He looked dazed, and still hadn't answered. "Are you hurt?" She asked again. It almost hurt to talk as she felt her wind had been knocked out of her.

"I ... don't think so," he said in the voice she often heard when he'd first wake up, like he wasn't all there.

They were both going to live.

She lay down for just a second to try and catch her breath. She earned this rest, before they'd have to run away.

A sound was coming toward them.

Lexi lifted her head once again, but couldn't see past the tall grass they were in.

The sound was of someone coming right at them.

She pushed herself up farther and could see it was definitely a man. He wore dirty, ill-fitted clothes, and his rifle was pointed in their direction from only a few feet away. There was no way they could run.

She spun around and threw herself on top of Travis, knowing it was a futile attempt to shield him, but she had to do something. She had nothing to protect them with, no weapons. She smiled at Travis and said, "I love you, brother. I'm so sorry I've been so angry for so long. It wasn't you. It was all me. Please know that."

"Lexi?" questioned the man, from right above them.

"It's okay, Lexi. It's Frank Cartwright. You know, your godfather?"

She lifted her head once more, tears in her eyes. Tears of joy.

Behind the beard and the foggy eyes, she saw it was her godfather: the same man who she'd seen yesterday. He had come to save them.

"Oh my God, it's really you?"

She bounded off of Travis and leapt onto Frank, almost sending him to the ground.

"Ouch! Hang on, I hurt in way too many places to do that. But, I'm damned glad to see you and—"

Her head was buried against his chest, so she didn't really hear too much of what he said, but she heard him stop talking.

"Whoa there, Travis. It's Frank, your godfather. You may not remember me."

Lexi uncoupled herself from him and spun around to find Travis standing holding something at them.

"Now Travis, why don't you put the gun down, son."

Travis was holding Lexi's silver revolver—the one that was missing. *Abdul and his men didn't take it; Travis did.*

"Travis," Lexi cried, "what are you doing?"

She could see he was shaking his head, like he had something stuck in his ear. He backed up and thrust the gun out more and stared at his sister and then at the other man he hadn't recognized.

"My Mahdi said that others would come and try and confuse me ..." He shook his head again. "He said that anyone who doesn't follow our way is an infidel, and it's all right to kill them ..."

"Travis, for God's sake, put the gun down. It's me, Lexi. I may have been a bitch all these years, but that was the old me. I promise you I will be different. We will be different. We'll look after each other. We'll love each other, like we should have. Uncle Abdul screwed with your mind. But it's not your fault. It's not your fault."

Travis lowered his arms, like the gun was too heavy to hold up. His eyes were cast down, his shoulders sank. He looked deflated.

"I love you, brother. I'm so sorry I never said that, but it's true. Come on what do you say?"

Travis looked up, looking like he had accepted what she had said. But then his eyes went wild.

He lifted the gun and fired twice.

Chapter 38

Going Home

T he trip was pretty quiet.

Frank seemed to be able to drive without any problem, even though he had been shot in the shoulder, sustained at least one broken rib and a sprained wrist, most of his back was bruised and angry, and his right knee and all the nerves connected to it were screaming a constant chorus of pain. All could be easily ignored in the celebration of victory. And even though he longed for a bed and probably two days' sleep, he drove.

He glanced over to Lexi, who was staring out the windows, searching for something. She scrutinized each sign, dead car, or worse, dead body—they had seen a few of those. Travis slept in the back seat, his head back, mouth opened, as if he were unconsciously waiting for rain to fall from the heavens. He looked at peace, which was a good thing.

He really thought they had both been shot when Travis fired the revolver at them. Turned out Yusuf was coming up behind them, and the boy took him out, before dropping the gun and running to his sister's embrace. Lexi said they'd been through a lot and that she would tell Frank everything soon enough. When he asked if Travis would be okay, she didn't hesitate to say "Yep."

He guessed they'd all be okay now.

The Army took Farook's base, killing most of the jihadists, while only losing two of their own. A few of Farook's men got away, but Lexi got Faroook. She stabbed the bastard and watched him drown. He couldn't help but feel a sense of pride in his goddaughter.

He was also excited to find that both Wallace and Porter were safe. Each had tall tales about their close calls, but they had made it. Wallace was offered a choice to join the detachment from Camp Shelby or to accompany Porter to Stowell and help the town prepare for the potential invasion. She and Porter left together, while Frank drove Lexi and Travis to Florida and their new home. He decided to take on his godfather duties full time.

Frank looked down the highway that used to bustle with cars, but now they were the only ones moving. Dead cars were everywhere, and so were the bodies. Corpses alongside the road or inside their cars were a more common sight here than in the Middle East.

He wasn't sure where they were going, but Lexi swore that she knew where it was. Based on what she told him, from the map she had committed to memory, the trip shouldn't be too long now.

"STOP!" Lexi hollered and Frank automatically stomped on the truck's brakes, bringing them to a screeching halt.

Frank first examined what was in front of him, sure that he was about to hit an animal—or a person, and just didn't see it, but there was no movement in front of him. He shot a look via the rearview mirror and saw nothing behind them, either. Travis bolted up from the floor, apparently having rolled off the seat, wide-eyed and panicked. Finally, he glared at Lexi, wondering what possessed her to startle all of them so badly. She was breathing heavily, her gaze fixed on something on the side of the road.

Frank quickly turned his gaze in the same direction, but still didn't see anything.

"What do you see?"

She pointed. Her mouth opened, but it was like she couldn't form the words. "It's ... It's our ... my father's car."

All stared at the Plymouth Fury with the busted windshield, gathering dust about fifty feet in front of them.

The truck's door creaked open and Lexi slid outside, feeling drawn to the Plymouth.

Frank turned off the ignition and quickly stepped out and over to her, already in the middle of the eastbound lane. "Lexi, are you sure you want to see this?" he said, standing in front of her. She had told him what happened, and he didn't think his friend, their father, would look very good after a few days in the Florida sunshine and heat.

She just stared past him at the Plymouth, as if it were speaking to her and her alone.

The sound of the crew-cab's rear door opening and closing drew Frank's gaze. Travis, too, seemed to be listening to the silent call of the Plymouth. He started marching toward the car.

"All right." Frank grabbed Lexi's hand, and then offered his other to Travis. "We do this together." Travis took hold and squeezed his godfather's hand.

"Now, your father is not going to look too good. He's probably swollen up because he's been in there four days."

"We know, but we have to see him," Lexi said, still fixed on the car, as they slowly proceeded in the Plymouth's direction. "Besides, there's something I need to do."

Lexi and Travis drew to a stop at the driver's-side back door. They both seemed unable to move forward.

"Would you like me to go first?" Frank asked Lexi and Travis, who were behind him.

Both heads nodded.

Frank had seen plenty of dead, having brought many people to that state of being more times than he cared to count, even if he could. But it was different when it was someone who you cared about. And Stan was his best friend, as well as Lexi and Travis's father. Worse, he couldn't imagine what they were about to experience. So, seeing his friend like this was harder than even he imagined. Stan's skin was almost black and very bloated. His eyes bulged and looked ready to burst. His tongue was the size of a brown balloon filled with water. And of course there was the smell.

"I'm going to be sick," Travis announced and ran away to the back of the car.

"He'll be all right," Lexi told Frank. "I know it's bad because of the smell, but I have to see him."

She trudged forward, Frank letting her by, knowing this was something she had to do.

When she stopped by the driver's side window, her chin and lower lip quivered, and tears streamed down her cheeks.

"I'm so sorry, Daddy, that you couldn't tell us in person what you did for us ... I was so selfish and so wrong ..."

Her head drooped. Her anguish rained down onto the pavement for a solid minute before she looked back up, trying to regain composure. Taking a deep breath, she added, "You saved us, Daddy. We will be safe with Frank. And I will learn from him, and we will protect Travis. I promise you. One day, I will make you proud."

"I know you already have," Frank said to her when she walked back to him, fighting back his own tears.

"Okay, I want to bury him now," she said.

☾ ✝ ✡ ☯ 🦅

"**A**re you nuts?" Frank howled at Lexi.

"That's what I want, and Travis will ride with me."

Frank didn't like it one bit, but one thing he had quickly come to realize about his goddaughter was that when she got a thought in her mind, there was not a damn thing he could do to change it. This was just one more example.

They worked for an hour, trying their best to remove the gore and the smell from the Fury's interior. He soaked a rag with gasoline to clean and mask the stench, figuring that fumes were better than the reek of death. Finally, he had to kick out the windshield, with his one good leg. This actually proved less tricky than he had thought. After two hours, as the sun was setting, it was ready.

Lexi fired up the Plymouth, glad that it started. She couldn't help but smile. Only four days ago, they had left this car for good, and yet she had kept the keychain with the rabbit's foot. She didn't know why at the time. Now she did.

She looked over at Travis, making sure he was properly strapped in and ready. He was grinning at her, looking hilarious in his goggles. Frank had found them in the truck they had taken from Abdul, along with some other equipment.

When she had asked Travis if he wanted to ride in the back, he quickly shook his head "no." She couldn't blame him for not ever wanting to ride there again.

She eased it back into the road as Frank pulled alongside in the truck. When he gave her the thumbs up she yelled out the side window. "See if you can keep up."

"Are you ready, Travis?"

"Mm-hmm," he nodded, trying to keep his mouth closed. His sister had already warned him about the prospect of getting bugs caught in his teeth if he smiled while they drove.

"Here we go!" She stomped on the accelerator.

A flood of air hit them both through the giant opening where the windshield used to be.

Travis and Lexi grinned the whole way to their new home, not caring how many bugs got stuck in their teeth.

Chapter 39

Sunbay Cove, Florida

Lexi insisted it was the right one, pointing to the American eagle doodle on the gate. It was just like the others in her father's notes. Frank at first seemed unconvinced, nodded and then picked open the gate's lock—he promised her that he would make it more secure in the coming days. Finally, they headed down the private road, shrouded in darkness, hoping it would lead to what would become their permanent home.

Neither of them knew what to expect. For this and many other reasons, Frank insisted on leading them through the tangle of tropical overgrowth, with Lexi following right behind him. Frank dragged his rifle onto his lap, then looped the sling around his head, never taking his eyes off the road in front of him. He wasn't expecting anything, but found it was always best to plan for the worst. Hell, Frank only half-knew that Stanley had a place in Florida, but had no idea where it was located until now.

Even though the map Stanley had given Lexi had disappeared and was feared to be in the possession of Abdul's men, she stated emphatically she had memorized it. She had also explained that she figured out the address based on a cypher she found in his notes. Finally she pointed to the eagle doodle. It felt right to Frank as well. *This really must have been Stanley's secret bug-out home*, he thought.

No one could call Stanley's thinking paranoid now. With society collapsing around them, as evidenced by the death and fires everywhere, little to no police assistance (and none likely to come around anytime soon), and thousands of terrorists planning on the destruction of a country he held so dear, he was not taking any chances. Who knows who may have stumbled onto this property or was waiting for them right now? He clicked the selector from *Safe* to *Semi-Auto.*

It was as black as a cave outside. So, Frank's eyes were practically rotating in their sockets, scanning for anything out the ordinary within the limited area illuminated by his headlights. In the spots where the canopy of trees opened up to reveal the sky, the multitude of stars barely cast so much as a glow.

$$\text{☾⋆ ✝ ✡ ☯ 🦅}$$

L exi's eyes were pasted on the truck's taillights, which blinked at her every time he touched his brakes, and that was constant. Each time her heart leapt a beat and she'd touch the revolver snugly resting in her lap. She let her mind wander, reflecting on what they would find, or whom. This house was a mystery to everyone, except her father. She didn't think her mother had even known about this place, because it never arose in conversations. She could only recall two possibly related memories where the subject may have come up: the trip they had taken to Florida for their honeymoon, and only a few weeks before she died, they had giggled over a bottle of wine about how they'd like to retire in Florida. Apparently her father had taken that part to heart.

For these reasons, she suspected he had bought it sometime after her mom had died. A small part of her even wondered if he had kept another secret family here; she had always imagined, back when she thought that her father was a bum, that he had another wife and kids and that was why he had abandoned Lexi and Travis. Then there was the genuine possibility that some bad guy was going to jump out of the void at any minute. And their plodding pace didn't help. She was so nervous she could scream.

Finally, after an intolerably long drive, they could see the form of a house in the murk. Yet, it was impossible to make out much of anything past Frank's giant truck. The driveway they were on ended in a teardrop, allowing them to drive around and pull back out on the same private road. Frank stopped rather abruptly.

Lexi almost ran into him, because her eyes had wandered from his taillights to the house and the drive. She pulled around him and parked so that the house was sideways from them. Frank kept the truck pointed at the front door, perhaps so his lights might help them figure out how to get in.

Lexi turned off her ignition and pulled out the keys—she hoped one of them worked on the door. After quietly latching her driver's-side door, she gazed up at the heavens both marveling at the sheer number of stars and pleading for some light from above—it was a moonless night, when they didn't want it to be.

Then they both saw it.

Only a few feet from her Frank commanded, "Shhhhh." He raised his rifle, getting ready to fire. Lexi already held her revolver, and she pulled the hammer back, pointing it at the house.

"What's wrong?" Travis asked from behind her, clutching her free hand.

Lexi inched down to him, and used the car as cover.

"There's a light on in the house."

☪ † ✡ ☯ 🦅

"**A**utomatic lights," Frank announced to Lexi, after he had done a once-around.

She and Travis had been waiting by the car, covering the door, with instructions to fire her weapon if the front door opened. "It looks empty, like it's been that way for several months. Why don't you try your keys?" Frank suggested.

The sense of relief was overwhelming, along with the sense of fatigue. But when the lock clicked open with the second key on the rabbit's foot chain, they were all filled with excitement. This was their home now.

It had power, and was fully stocked, as Lexi had come to expect of her father—funny how quickly a long-standing opinion of someone could change.

"The electric is powered by solar," Frank announced after doing a complete inspection. Everything else was off-grid as well, including rainwater collection and filtration. The place had a functioning septic system, which

Lexi felt was a blessing. A dock led to an inlet off the Gulf; there was even a boat moored to it.

They settled on bedrooms—with four to pick from, there was ample choices. Frank let Lexi choose first; after all it was her and Travis's home. She chose her father's room.

They washed up and made a quick meal out of a couple MREs, pulled from one of the two pallets full of them in a giant supply room. Frank said there was maybe a year's supply of food there.

Travis couldn't keep his eyes open any longer and so Lexi tucked him in and kissed him goodnight. He somehow managed to save his father's Purple Heart and wore the damned thing to bed. The last thing she would do was try and separate him from it, even if there was the prospect of him getting pricked if he rolled over on it. She was filled with joy when he said, "I love you, Lex." For the first time in her life, that meant something to her.

Frank had asked Lexi to join him on the dock. He had found some beer and had it cooling in the freezer. If she wasn't too tired, he wanted to talk to her about what they were going to do next. The prospect of thinking about a future was not a burden any longer, and with Frank looking after her and Travis, she would not face every day in fear.

She paused in what was now her bedroom with her revolver, unsure whether to take it with her or not. She opted to take it. Although she felt safe because of Frank, she felt safer with the revolver.

Carrying two opened beers, she again marveled at the stars and the amazing smells and sounds coming from the

Gulf. A black silhouette that she guessed was Frank was sitting at the edge of the dock, his legs dangling over its edge, just above the water, staring at the sky.

"Fancy a beer?" she said.

"More than life itself," he said.

She plopped down beside him and they clinked their bottles and toasted to surviving this long adventure.

They were quiet for a long time, their beers almost empty, when he asked, "How's Travis?"

"Oh, he's asleep."

"No, I mean, *how is he?* you know, with the Islamic indoctrination and all? Is he safe, I mean?"

There it was; the safety net had been lowered. Frank was laying the cards on the table. She couldn't see his face to tell if he was really worried or if he was just casually asking. She took his question very seriously, because she had wondered this as well.

"I really believe he's fine now. He's been living a bit of a double life for a couple of years, since our dear Uncle Abdul paid for him to go to a Madrassa. I knew this happened, but didn't want to admit it. Abdul must have had something over Aunt Sara to force her to do this. And right after this happened, Travis changed and became more distant to me. I kind of didn't care then, because I was a self-absorbed bitch. Anyway, I'm sure he's fine now. He gave up the gun and didn't shoot us, that's something right?" She was trying to be funny, but it didn't come out the way she wanted.

He laughed a good belly laugh, and she joined in.

"I know it seems like we can just settle down here and live out our days, but you know, life for everyone else in this country is changing fast."

"Yep," she said somewhat dispassionately. She didn't want to have this conversation, but knew it was going to come eventually. She just had hoped it wouldn't be for a few days. "What do you think we should do?"

"Well, starting tomorrow, you're going to train." He seemed to be waiting for an acknowledgment.

"Train?"

"Yep, I'm going to teach you everything I know about combat and self-defense. That way, if something happens to me, you can take care of yourself and Travis. While this is happening, we'll keep up with what's going on around us. Your father has a pretty good radio setup and I think I can stay in touch with my friends back in Stowell, Texas."

"What do you think will happen with Abdul's planned invasion?"

"Well with any luck, our military will be able to fight back and win. The word will spread, now that they know who's behind this. And knowing this country, and our military, I suspect we've got a good chance."

"I hope so... I think I'm going to bed. I'm awfully tired. And like you said, I have to start training." Lexi started to move to get up but stopped. She leaned over to Frank and wrapped her arms around him. "Thank you so much for saving us. I know how much Daddy would appreciate your being here."

He hugged her back. Although she knew this probably hurt him, he didn't so much as grunt. "That's what a godfather is for." She imagined that he smiled at her, even though she couldn't see it.

She rose up, and something in the distance caught her eye. "Hey look at the skies."

Among the carpet of stars, a lone light coming from the Gulf moved north toward the Pensacola coast.

"I think it's a plane," Frank guessed.

It did look like an airplane. And if it was an airplane, that had to mean civilization and maybe help from other countries, and maybe that meant they would be all right after all. Maybe their military would defeat these terrorists and maybe, one day, things would get back to normal.

Lexi said goodnight and ambled along the dock toward her new home, feeling something she hadn't felt in a long time, and certainly not in the last few days.

She felt hope.

Epilogue

July 9th

They rode in the relative quiet of the boat motor's hum, moving at a constant twenty knots.

With the water of the Apalachicola River like glass tonight, they would reach the coast in less than an hour. There, they would meet up with one of the hundreds of the boats that would dot America's coasts over the coming evenings. Their rendezvous was with one of the freighters from the Gulf.

He was surprised that everything had gone as well as it had. They had suffered some losses for sure, but that was to be expected. Tonight was a night for celebration. Phase Two was about to start, with the help of their Russian partners, and the drone bases they had taken at Ft. Rucker and Creech Air Force Base in Nevada. Soon after, began Phase Three, with the arrival of their troops.

Over the next few days, they would have over twenty thousand soldiers on American soil, ready to fight the infidels. But the infidel's soldiers wouldn't have any fight left in them. Of this he was sure.

Their society would be in chaos, as its populations tried to survive. Their EMPs had exposed the soft underbelly of this animal: easy for them to stick their knives in and eviscerate them.

Their plan was bold, but it was remarkably simple. Phase One was to take down the grid and most electronics. With the Russians' help, they had succeeded. But it probably would have succeeded with far less effort. Perhaps just taking out a couple of the main transformers would have done it. The result would be the same: America without power would be like a world without gravity: there would be nothing to hold American society from flying apart.

The other nukes added the necessary chaos and fear through mass deaths. This also forced its remaining government and military underground, ensuring that as American society devolved, there would be no one to help. Phase Two would weaken the military's remnants, making sure victory would take place in Phase Three.

It was all coming together nicely, though it didn't need to.

With its corruption and perversions, America had fallen asleep, focused on itself long ago. Its citizens' lives always focused on satisfying their own pleasures, rather than heeding the threats that were all around. He and his enablers simply hurried along a process that would have occurred without their help.

Mohammad, peace be upon him, had predicted the end of days. But so did the People of the Book and the followers of Jesu. Now, he would be the one to see it through.

Abdul touched his bandages covering most of his right cheek. And although the wound was painful, he grinned at its presence and accompanying agony in the dark. The doctor told him a healthy scar would remain after it had healed.

It would be a wonderful reminder of this time.

"Mahdi Abdul?" Sal interrupted his thoughts from behind him.

"Yes, my great and noble servant, Saleem." Abdul could feel him touch his robe, and he could picture him bowing.

"I'm sorry that Suhaimah and Abdul-Aziz escaped."

"Not to worry, my friend," Abdul tapped his shirt pocket where he kept the map they had confiscated from the men who had attacked them before they were beheaded. He knew right where both of them would be. And when they were done, he would still collect his son and his new wife.

"I'm sure we'll have no problem locating them."

**To be continued in
ENDURANCE (HIGHWAY Book 2)**

Did you like HIGHWAY?

Help spread the word about this book by posting a quick review on Amazon and Goodreads.

Reviews are vital to indie authors like me. If you liked this book, I would really appreciate your review.

Thank you!

Want to read more about Frank Cartwright?

Learn what happened before *HIGHWAY*, in the USA Today Bestseller, *True Enemy*. Just tell me what email address to send it to and you'll have it for free. This exclusive book is no longer available anywhere else but here.

https://www.mlbanner.com/teshort

Who is ML Banner?

Michael "ML" Banner is an award winning, USA Today Bestselling author of Apocalyptic Thrillers

Michael writes what he loves to read: apocalyptic thrillers, which thrust regular people into extraordinary circumstances, where their actions may determine not only their own fate, but that of the world. His work is traditionally published and self-published. Often his thrillers are set in far-flung places, as Michael uses his experiences from visiting other countries—some multiple times—over the years. The picture was from a transatlantic cruise that became the foreground of his award-winning *MADNESS Series*.

When not writing his next book, you might find Michael (and his wife) traveling abroad or reading a Kindle, with his toes in the water (name of his publishing company), of a beach on the Sea of Cortez (Mexico).

Want more from M.L. Banner?

Receive FREE books & *Apocalyptic Updates* - A monthly publication highlighting discounted books, cool science/discoveries, new releases, reviews, and more

MLBanner.com/free

Connect with M.L. Banner

Keep in contact – I would love to hear from you!
- Email: michael@mlbanner.com

- Facebook: facebook.com/authormlbanner

- Twitter: @ml_banner

Books by M.L. Banner

For a complete list of Michael's current and upcoming books: MLBanner.com/books/

ASHFALL APOCALYPSE

Ashfall Apocalypse (01)
A world-wide apocalypse has just begun.
Leticia's Soliloquy (An Ashfall Apocalypse Short)

Leticia tells her story.
(This short is exclusively available from link at end book #1)

Collapse (02)
As temps plummet, a new foe seeks revenge.
Compton's Epoch (An Ashfall Apocalypse Short)

Compton reveals what makes him tick.
(This short is exclusively available from link at end book #2)

Perdition (03)
Sometimes the best plan is to run. But where?

MADNESS CHRONICLES

MADNESS (01)
A parasitic infection causes mammals to attack.

PARASITIC (02)
The parasitic infection doesn't just affect animals.

SYMPTOMATIC (03)
When your loved one becomes symptomatic, what do you do?

The Final Outbreak (Books 1 - 3)
The end is coming. It's closer than you think. And it's real.

HIGHWAY SERIES

True Enemy (Short)
An unlikely hero finds his true enemy.
(Get this USA Today Bestselling short only on mlbanner .com)

Highway (01)
A terrorist attack forces siblings onto a highway,

and an impossible journey home.

Endurance (02)
Enduring what comes next will take everything they've got, and more.

Resistance (03)
Coming Soon

STONE AGE SERIES

Stone Age (01)
The next big solar event separates family and friends, and begins a new Stone Age.

Desolation (02)
To survive the coming desolation will require new friendships.

Max's Epoch (Stone Age Short)
Max wasn't born a prepper, he was forged into one.
(This short is exclusively available on MLBanner.com)

Hell's Requiem (03)
One man struggles to survive and find his way to a scientific sanctuary.

Time Slip (Stand Alone)
The time slip was his accident; can he use it to save the one he loves?

Cicada (04)

The scientific community of Cicada may be the world's
only hope,
or it may lead to the end of everything.